Lilly's
PROMISE

TERRIE TODD
AUTHOR OF *THE SILVER SUITCASE*

ISBN: 978-1-4866-2311-2
eBook ISBN: 978-1-4866-2312-9

Word Alive Press
119 De Baets Street Winnipeg, MB R2J 3R9
www.wordalivepress.ca

WORD ALIVE
—P R E S S—

Cataloguing in Publication information can be obtained from Library and Archives Canada.

*Dedicated with love and appreciation to the staff and volunteers
at Portage Pregnancy Support Centre who faithfully serve
the women and men of my community, providing
compassionate care during a difficult time.*

"The best thing I can show you to defend life is my life. It has been a great gift."

—Gianna Jessen, born alive during a failed abortion attempt

ACKNOWLEDGEMENTS

Every book is a group project, and I have lots of people to thank.

Kathy Letkeman, besides your expert medical advice and consistent encouragement, you helped pray this book into being and I appreciate you more than you know. Thanks for coming up with Dale's medical emergency and thank you for your commitment to PPSC!

Gloria Harnett, thanks for walking me through the arrival of my paramedics and all they would do.

Bob Tyler, I threw an impossible legal situation your way and you helped me work it through in a way that might almost make sense. I hope readers know that any errors in the law office scene are completely mine.

Dawn Froese, thank you for your advice on how Big Brothers/Big Sisters operates.

Shirley Delaquis of the St. Boniface Registered Nurses' Alumni Association, thank you so much for your guidance in describing what Lilly's world may have looked like during her time in nursing school.

Phil Carpenter, thanks for always being my go-to guy when my story includes anything fire-related. Enjoy your retirement!

Any errors in any of these areas are all mine.

Many thanks to the team at Word Alive Press for all your work on this project and for selecting it as the 2022 Braun Book Awards winner for fiction.

Above all, my thanks are due to my redeemer, Jesus Christ, master storyteller and main character in the greatest story ever told.

PROLOGUE

Lilly Sampson's uncle held tightly to her hand. Men in black suits shoveled dirt into a hole. At the bottom of the hole was a box, and inside the box lay Lilly's mama and baby brother who didn't even have a name yet.

Or so Lilly had been told. Nobody let her see inside the box.

Uncle Henry's hand grew hot and sweaty, but after Lilly pulled hers away to wipe it on her coat, he took it again. She craned her neck to see his face. His hat covered most of his dark hair. His brown eyes looked like her mama's. With his free hand, he wiped away a tear.

On the other side of Uncle Henry stood Aunty Margaret, all in black, arms crossed, purse looped over one arm. The netted veil swooping down over the top of her nose reminded Lilly of the wire she'd seen around Mr. Buford's chicken coop. Aunty Margaret was not crying.

Lilly leaned toward her uncle and whispered, "Uncle Henry?"

Uncle Henry bent over so she could speak directly into his ear.

"I need to go to the bathroom."

He nodded. "We can leave now, sweetheart."

He said something to Aunty Margaret and the three of them turned away from the hole and began walking toward their house. The handful of others who had gathered around the hole left then, too, slowly scattering in various directions.

Uncle Henry picked Lilly up and carried her on one hip.

"You shouldn't carry her," Aunty Margaret said, picking up her pace. "You'll only spoil her."

"She needs a bathroom. We'll get home faster this way." Uncle Henry pulled a hanky from his pocket and blew his nose with one hand as they hurried along.

Lilly patted Uncle Henry's shoulder. "Why were you crying?"

"Because I will miss your mama, Lilly. She was my baby sister. You know that, right?"

How could her grownup mama be anyone's baby sister? Lilly only nodded, as though she understood. "Is my mama and baby brother going to live under the dirt now? In that box?"

"Your mama and baby brother are in heaven with Jesus now, Lilly."

Aunty Margaret let out a snort. "Don't tell her that."

"Why not?"

"I think we all know where Nora is."

"Margaret. That's for God to decide. Think of the girl."

"I am. How will she ever live a different sort of life if she thinks she can behave so foolishly and still have it end well?"

Uncle Henry let out a long sigh. "Perhaps that's what we're here for."

Soon after they arrived at the house, it filled with strangers and food. Lilly had spent the past two nights here, long enough to learn that you didn't drag dirt inside and you didn't make loud noises in this house. Not if you knew what was good for you.

On one of those days, when Aunty Margaret had lost her patience, Uncle Henry had taken Lilly into the backyard and shown her a treehouse.

"Made this for our boys when they were still home." He helped Lilly climb the ladder to the top, keeping his hands close lest she slip. "I guess it will be yours now."

Lilly had climbed to the top and peered down. "Come up, Uncle Henry."

"No, I'm too big. It's just for you."

Now Lilly sat on the living room sofa, her feet just reaching the edge of its cushion. A small plate rested on her lap. She nibbled at the cheese sandwich, then sampled the pickle.

A lady with curly brown hair took the spot beside her and smiled, revealing a gap between her two front teeth. "Hello, Lilly. I'm your Aunt Betty. How are you, dear?"

"Fine, thank you."

"Your mommy taught you good manners, I see." The lady rearranged the items on her own plate as she spoke. "You must miss her."

Lilly nodded. "She's coming to get me. She said she would."

The lady named Aunt Betty pressed her lips together. "Hm. You know this is your home now, right?"

Lilly shrugged. "I guess I can share my new bed with Mama when she comes."

The lady looked around the room, then turned back to Lilly. "My husband Ben is a brother to your mommy and to your Uncle Henry. I'm sorry we didn't get to know you before. You've got cousins, too, but they're not with us today."

Lilly was about to ask what a cousin was when she spotted a boy across the room holding a cookie in each hand. Where had he found those? "Can I have a cookie?"

"Well, I'm sure you can. You should probably eat your sandwich first, though. Poor little tyke. Maybe when summer comes, Henry and Margaret will bring you to our cabin at Clear Lake. We'll have lots of fun together. Won't that be nice?"

Lilly nodded, still eyeing the boy with the cookies. He leaned against the legs of another lady, probably his mama, and stared back.

The lady named Aunt Betty followed Lilly's gaze. "That's Tommy. He lives next door." She raised her voice. "Tommy? Why don't you come say hello to Lilly? She's going to be your new neighbor."

When his mama gave him a nudge from behind and said something in his ear, the boy stepped toward Lilly and held out a cookie. Lilly took it and helped herself to a big bite before the aunty or any other adult could say otherwise.

The boy named Tommy stood staring at Lilly. His mother came over and crouched beside him.

"Hello, Lilly, this is Tommy. We live just next door, so now that you're living here we'll see a lot of each other. You and Tommy are the same age. Your Aunty Margaret tells me you're three, is that right?"

Lilly nodded, still chewing.

"See, Tommy? You're both three. Sweet little thing." Tommy's mother turned to Aunt Betty. "Good to see you again, Betty. Too bad it's under such sad circumstances. Wonderful thing Henry and Margaret are doing."

She took the seat on the other side of Aunt Betty.

"Margaret took some convincing," Aunt Betty said. "I'm not sure she's convinced still."

The two ladies kept talking, but Lilly turned her attention to Tommy.

"Can I see your treehouse?" Crumbs fell from around the boy's mouth when he spoke.

Lilly nodded. Leaving her plate behind, she led Tommy out through the kitchen into the backyard. When they scrambled up the ladder, Lilly's dress caught on one of the wooden planks that served as rungs. She gave it a yank, which set it free but left a gaping hole. The dress had been making her itchy ever since Aunty Margaret had put it on her that morning, so Lilly didn't feel sad about the hole.

Using the wooden weapons left behind by the treehouse's previous owners, Tommy and Lilly played swordfight until his mother called him down.

He backed down through the hole in the floor. "Bye, Lilly. I'll come play again tomorrow. I like your treehouse and your swords."

"Bye."

Lilly watched from the window as Tommy and his mother walked to the house next door, then turned her attention to the street. People were leaving. Some got into cars and drove away. Others left on foot. One woman walked across the street and entered a tall green house on the other side, an empty cake pan in her hands.

"Lilly?" Aunty Margaret called from the back door. "Come inside now. It's going to cool off soon. Be dark before we know it."

Lilly obeyed, but when she reached the back step Aunty Margaret let out a gasp. "Look at your dress!" She seized Lilly's elbow and yanked her inside. "Look what you've done. I should throttle you. Didn't your mother teach you anything?"

Aunty Margaret unlaced and pulled the shoes off Lilly's feet, then turned her around roughly and began undoing the buttons down the back of the dress. "Now I'll have to fix this. If I can ever get it clean. Oh Lord, what did I do to deserve this?" She pulled the dress down around Lilly's ankles. "Step out."

Lilly did, embarrassed to be standing in the middle of the kitchen in only her underwear. Even more so when she heard Uncle Henry's voice.

"What's all the fuss?" He stood in the doorway between the kitchen and living room.

"Look at this, just look at this!" Aunty Margaret shook the dress in Uncle Henry's face. "Did your sister know nothing about raising children? We can't afford to be clothing this child if this is how little she's going to appreciate anything."

"Margaret, calm down. She's a baby."

"She's three! Old enough to know better."

"Anyway, didn't you make that dress out of leftover fabric? It cost us nothing."

"It cost *you* nothing! I spent hours on it, trying to make her respectable for…for a very unrespectable woman, that's what for. Why do I bother?" She turned to Lilly. "Go upstairs and put on your nightgown."

Lilly ran to the stairs and started up, then slowed as soon as she was out of sight. The argument in the kitchen continued. She strained to hear Uncle Henry's soft voice.

"Margaret. It's just a dress. What is this really about?"

"This is never going to work."

The squeak of the kitchen pump and the splashing of water drowned out whatever Uncle Henry said next, but Aunty Margaret's voice was loud and clear.

"She's *your* kin, not mine. I don't see why Ben and Betty couldn't take her."

"They've got their hands full with their own. Besides, I thought you always wanted a little girl."

"I did. But not this way."

"Well, at this stage of our lives, this is the only way it's going to happen. She'll grow on you, you'll see. She needs a mother."

"Don't you let her call me *mother*!"

"That's not what I meant. She needs two parents. Now, for the first time, she'll finally have that."

"That's the other thing. How do we know she's not the spawn of the devil himself?"

"Margaret. Please. Whoever her father is, the child is innocent. This is our duty. Our Christian duty. And I know you're a good Christian woman."

Lilly reached the top of the stairs and heard no more. She put on her nightgown and climbed into the bed where her new doll, Patty, sat waiting. The previous day, a nice lady had appeared at the front door with a man Aunty Margaret had called Reverend. She'd brought flowers for Aunty Margaret and the doll for Lilly.

"This is Patty." The lady had held the doll out toward Lilly with a smile. "She's a little ragged because she was well loved. I know my little girl would be happy for you to have her."

Lilly had felt too shy to ask where the lady's little girl was and why she'd be happy to give away her doll. Besides, she wanted the doll.

Now she snuggled Patty close and whispered in her ear. "When Mama's done living under the dirt, she'll come and get us. You'll like her. She doesn't yell or get cross."

Maybe tomorrow Mama would be done living under the dirt.

CHAPTER ONE

Diana

EDMONTON, ALBERTA, CANADA
2019

It's happening again.

I'm in the perfect dress. Its dazzling white satin accentuates the tan I worked on half the summer. The atmosphere intoxicates those gathered with the scent of exotic flowers, the glow of flickering candlelight, and the glorious strains of a string quartet. Libby, in her periwinkle dress, charms the crowd and drops cherry blossoms just like she rehearsed. I'm floating along on Dad's arm as he walks me down the aisle between four hundred smiling guests.

Ryan stands at the front, a bit pale but handsome in his black tux. I focus on him, my jaws already aching from smiling so much.

When we reach the front, Dad kisses me gently on the cheek and whispers, "Love you, Princess." He hands me off to Ryan and takes a seat beside Mum, who dabs her eyes.

Ryan and I face each other. Pastor Ralph does his bit. We say our vows. 'Til death do us part. We exchange rings, and I take a second to admire the rose gold band on my manicured hand.

My sister moves to the piano and begins to play "The Day Before You," which Ryan and I chose together. Becky's pulling it off like a professional. As she sings, we move to the registration table to sign the documents to make it official. The final step. I sign first, then return the pen to the pastor, who hands it to Ryan.

Ryan takes the pen.

That's the point where I always wake up with a hammering headache. As though my brain cannot process what happens next.

Another night ruined. Throwing off the covers, I sit up and run a hand through my hair. No point trying to sleep. The dream always puts me in a mood. It's been ten years since my wedding day. Surely by now I should be over it, but the stupid dream keeps coming and I can never predict when.

My sister Becky says I keep myself too busy and distracted, trying to forget, when a few good therapy sessions might be all I need. Then she proceeds to the guilt trip.

"You're always too busy to come visit us, Diana," she nags whenever we talk. "How can *you* be the busy one when *I'm* the one raising three kids?"

She doesn't mean it to sting. And I give her no reason to think it might. Besides, I love my niece and nephews almost as much as I love my freedom.

I shake off the dream for what feels like the thousandth time and yank on my bathrobe. Mouse materializes from wherever she was prowling and rubs up against my leg. Her glossy grey fur shimmers in the dim light. I shuffle to the kitchen and pour a little milk in her bowl.

"I shouldn't be spoiling you like this."

The cat merely meows her approval and laps the milk while I pour room temperature tea from earlier in the evening into my favorite "You Are My Sunshine" mug. Another gift from Dad. I stick it in the microwave and punch some buttons. Three o'clock. My alarm will go off in two hours.

I take the tea to the table where my laptop sits open and pull up my email. Mouse finishes her milk and hops onto my lap, curling up and purring in seconds. How does she do that? No recurring, disturbing dreams for cats, I guess.

I stare at the new emails awaiting my attention. The first is from the DNA Ancestry thing I did weeks ago. That's my sister's fault, too. Becky sent me one of those DNA kits. That must be what pops up when you ask Alexa what to get a single woman for her thirty-fifth birthday. Becky seems to think I already have everything else. A lot she knows. I could use any number of things, from theater tickets to a new garden hose. Free oil changes. A spa day. Better yet, a donation to Compassion to send some little girl in a developing country to school.

The DNA kit sat unopened and forgotten in my desk drawer for a couple of years. Then one day while decluttering, I found it again and sent my saliva sample in the prepaid package to their state-of-the-art lab and forgot about it for the second time.

Until now. I open the results.

The cousins and second cousins showing up on Mum's side are exactly what I expect, a bunch of Italian names. Dad's side, however, confuses me. He never had siblings, so I have no first cousins on his side. But in the second-to-third-cousin range, several people are listed with a confidence rating of "extremely high." Except their last names don't add up. I recognize his mother's maiden name, Sampson. But our name is DeWitt. It doesn't show up anywhere, not even once. On the other hand, the name Tidsbury shows up too frequently to be a coincidence. I don't know anyone by that name.

Must be a mistake.

I want to call Dad, but it's too early, even with the one-hour time difference. And even if he is up, Dad's hearing loss makes a normal phone conversation frustrating. I generally find myself yelling and repeating until I'm exhausted. For a retired doctor, Dad is surprisingly resistant to wearing his hearing aids and to technology in general. At seventy-seven, he still says he'd rather write a good old-fashioned letter, but Becky did finally manage to teach him to use email.

I fire one off to him.

> Dad, are we related to anybody named Tidsbury? What can you tell me about the accuracy of these DNA kits? Our name isn't even showing up on mine.

I hit *send*. Dad will probably tell me I'm wasting my time on useless, unscientific nonsense. Then he'll launch into his regular rant about how he doesn't understand why "that handsome firefighter" and I aren't more than just friends. He means Shane. "You'd be perfect for each other," he tells me every time we talk, even though they haven't even met.

And he wonders why I don't visit more.

Neither Dad nor Becky understand how I can be content as a single woman with a best friend who happens to be male.

I scroll to the next email. It's from Big Brothers/Big Sisters, reminding me that Carly and I are due for our annual review, where we'll sit down with our worker and discuss how things are going and whether we want to continue with the mentorship program.

I enter the meeting in my calendar and close my email. Carly's gorgeous face smiles at me from my desktop screen, her shiny black hair hanging nearly to her waist. My fifteen-year-old "little sis" is smart and funny and intensely insecure.

I loved her instantly when they matched us almost five years ago. I don't think I could handle it if she wanted to end our relationship.

I close my laptop. I should crawl back into bed, but now Mouse is fast asleep, and I hate to disturb her. I rest my head on my arms across the tabletop, thinking of Carly. Her single mom and two younger brothers share a small apartment close to my job at city hall, so it's been convenient to do things with her. I pray I haven't given her any reason to stop being my little sister.

• • •

I awake, confused, to the beeping of the alarm clock. The sleeve of my bathrobe is damp with drool. I stumble to the bedroom and turn off the alarm. Mouse is stretched across my pillow. She lifts her head and gives me a look that says, *shouldn't you be getting ready for work?* before curling up again and closing her golden eyes. Rotten cat.

• • •

I'm just nicely settled in at my desk when my phone pings. It's an email from Dad. I wait until my coffee break to read it, completely expecting a scolding for wasting time and money on the silly DNA thing—even if the money was Becky's. Instead, my father is full of surprises.

> Dear Diana,
>
> Your letter intrigues me. DNA… deoxyribonucleic acid, the carrier of genetic information. Fascinating stuff. I believe your results are accurate, but it's a very long story. I only learned it shortly before my mother passed away. I wish you could have known her. I'm not sure why I never attempted to tell you girls everything your grandmother shared with me, but guess what? I've decided to write a book! My memoirs. Oh, I doubt I'll ever publish it or anything, but it would be good for you and Becky to know my whole story. As they say, those who refuse to learn from history are doomed to repeat it. I'd hate that for you.
>
> Here's the thing. After hunting and pecking out the first chapter on this computer, I've concluded I'd do better writing it out in long hand. I really need help. Someone who can not only type it up but make corrections as they go. Would you consider this, Princess? Take a look at what I've done so far and let me know if you think it's worth pursuing.

In fairness, I can't tell my story without first telling my mother's. For you see, Diana, neither you nor I would be here at all if my mother had succeeded with her plan back in 1941. And to understand that plan, we really need to go all the way back to Mother's childhood in the 1920s and a secret far too heavy for any eight-year-old child to carry.

Let me know if you want to tackle this project with me.

Lovingly,
Dad

CHAPTER TWO

Lilly

Lilly Sampson pulled from her pocket one of the three wooden matches she'd pilfered from Aunty Margaret's metal match holder beside the kitchen stove—the one with the rose painted on it, the one she wasn't supposed to touch. Her hands shook as she watched Tommy, his lips pressed together, pull a rag from one pocket and a small Aspirin bottle from the other. When he took the lid off the bottle, the unmistakable odor of gasoline fumes wafted up. He doused the rag with gas. Lilly held the match out to him, but he shook his head.

"You do it," Tommy whispered. He pointed a finger upward, indicating his plan: the pane of the shed's small window was missing, leaving an open space with a jagged glass edge. She would light the rag and he would toss it through the hole into the shed.

Then they'd run for it.

Fingers shaking, Lilly struck the match against the rough boards of the shed's wall. Her weeks of practice proved themselves as the tip burst into flame, lighting up the night. Tommy held the gas-soaked rag to the flame and it woofed into a blaze. He tossed it through the window, pulling his hand back quickly with an oath. Had he burned himself?

Before Lilly could examine his hand, Tommy was gone, taking off in the opposite direction from where they'd come. Lilly dropped the still-burning match and followed.

They looped around, crossing the road further down and doubling back through a vacant lot until a grove of trees hid them. Tommy reached her treehouse first and scrambled up, Lilly on his heels. They scurried on all fours to the window and peeked out. Sure enough, smoke rose from the shed across the street. Lilly squeezed her eyes shut as a crackling sound began, followed by the bark of a neighborhood dog, then another. Tommy startled her by grasping her hand. She held on, glancing at his face. His gaze was fixed on the shed. Flames leaped through its upper corners, lapping at the roof until one side collapsed inward. Sparks rose, floating to the sky.

Something vile rose in Lilly's throat and she pressed her free hand to her chest. "What if no one calls the fire department? I should go wake up Uncle Henry and Aunty Margaret."

Tommy shook his head. "The fire will put itself out once the shed's burned up."

Lilly couldn't even blink as the three remaining walls of the shed came down all at once, taking the roof with them. The flames soared higher still. Surely the fire truck would come clanging down the street any moment. She stretched her neck out the window and peered in the direction of the fire hall.

Tommy pulled her back in. "Don't let anyone see you!"

But there was no one to see her. Why had the blaze not captured anyone's attention? Tommy gasped, pointing. The fire had jumped from the Tidsburys' shed to their house. Flames danced from one corner of the shingles.

Lilly sucked in her breath. "William's bedroom is on the top floor. We have to do something."

Tommy didn't argue, but he grabbed Lilly's arm just above her elbow and looked her in the eyes. "You go sneak back into your house and pretend like you just woke up. I'll do the same and we can both wake the grownups. No matter what happens, we can't tell anyone. Ever. You got it?"

"No matter what? Even if—"

"No matter what."

Lilly nodded. As she headed toward the ladder, Tommy pulled her back to the window. "Look!"

"Fire!" Mr. Tidsbury ran into the street in his pajamas, a bucket in his hand. "Fire!" Surely the whole neighborhood could hear his cries. "*Fire!*"

Lilly sat glued to her spot beside Tommy. He didn't so much as shift positions or twitch. Mr. Tidsbury ran toward Lilly's house and pounded on the door, shouting for help. Then he ran back toward his own house, now engulfed in flames. Mrs. Tidsbury stood in the yard in her bathrobe, surrounded by four of her five children—none of them William. They all stared up at the top-floor windows, crying and hollering.

Where was William?

Suddenly, the entire neighborhood seemed to burst out of their homes and converge on the fire with buckets of water, brooms, shovels, whatever they could grab. Everyone was shouting orders or screaming. Finally, the whistle at the fire hall pierced the night as the crowd struggled to extinguish the flames. The fire truck wailed down their street, four men hanging off its sides. When it stopped, three men unrolled hoses and began dousing the home with water. One of the men ran into the burning house.

Lilly bit her lip until she tasted blood. *God, please let William be all right. What we did was bad. You probably won't hear my prayer. But William shouldn't have to pay.*

It wasn't supposed to go like this. The fire truck was supposed to come earlier, put out the fire. By tomorrow, Mr. Tidsbury was supposed to be joking about how fate spared him the effort of tearing down his old shed, how he and William would have the new one up in record time thanks to the fire.

Lilly sucked in a deep breath when the firefighter came back out, carrying William in his arms. Was he alive? Surely he was injured if he needed to be carried. In the chaos, Lilly could make out only the odd word or phrase here and there. *Ambulance. No time for that. I'll take him! C'mon, go go go!*

Through all this, the fire roared and crackled, drowning out nearly everything else. The fireman laid William in the back seat of a car. His mother climbed in the passenger side and the driver took off. They disappeared around the corner at the end of her street.

Lilly turned her attention back to the fire. "What if it spreads to our houses? What if we burn down the whole town?"

"Shh! That's not gonna happen." Tommy spoke the words slowly, as though he willed them to be true. "But we should get back to our beds. Our parents are going to be checking to see if we're all right."

But it was too late. Aunty Margaret was heading back toward her own house from across the street, her pink bathrobe flapping around her bare ankles. Surely, she would make a beeline for Lilly's room and then suspect the truth when she didn't find her there.

"I have to go!" Lilly spat the words out, turning once again toward the tree-house ladder.

"Wait!" Tommy caught hold of her sweater. "If they ask, the siren woke us both up. Right?"

Lilly stared at him. Tommy was right. No one could ever know they'd deliberately set the fire.

What if William dies? Hot tears sprung to her eyes and she blinked them away. She nodded but didn't trust herself to speak. *Why, oh why, had they done it?*

Tommy's eyes were still on hers, ablaze with a fire of their own. "Say that when you woke up, the commotion was already going on, your aunt and uncle were gone, and you climbed up into the treehouse to watch. I'll say the same. Just in case anyone noticed us up here."

"Okay." Lilly stifled a sob and hurried down the ladder. Her aunt and uncle called her name from the front door.

"I'm here! I'm fine."

From the corner of her eye, Lilly saw Tommy dash for his own back door. Her stomach churning, she ran into Uncle Henry's embrace and hoped she would never see Thomas DeWitt again as long as she lived.

CHAPTER THREE

Diana

I finish reading the first installment of Dad's book. He's not a bad writer, but his opening chapter doesn't get me any closer to answers. I let out a frustrated huff and give him a call.

"Hello, Princess."

"Hey, Dad. Glad you got your call display figured out. Does it give my actual name, or does it just say 'Princess'?"

The nickname, according to Becky, has a story behind it. She remembers being cuddled up beside Mom to watch the royal wedding of Prince Charles and Lady Diana on TV, live at three o'clock in the morning or some silly thing. Mom went into labor with me the next morning and named me Diana Elizabeth. Dad's "little princess" label lost its charm somewhere between the royal divorce and Princess Diana's death.

"Pardon? Can you speak up, Princess?"

Here we go. I raise my volume. "Never mind. I got your first chapter, Dad."

"What did you think?" Dad is yelling, prompting me to raise my voice more.

"Well, it's good, but it reveals nothing about the glitch in my ancestry report."

"You sure about that? Thomas and Lilly DeWitt became your grandparents."

"I know that much. Obviously those little pyromaniacs grew up and got married. So where does this Tidsbury family fit in?"

"We'll get to that in a few chapters."

"A few chapters? Dad. Can't you just tell me?"

"Tell you what?"

I sigh. "For starters, why did Lilly live with her aunt and uncle? What happened to her parents?"

"I'm thinking of putting that in the next chapter."

"Dad. Listen, I'll help you with your book. I'll do all the typing and editing you want. I'll even help you figure out how to publish it if you want. But I just need this one little detail solved. It's bugging me."

"Why?"

It's a good question. I don't have a good answer. For some reason, Carly comes to mind. She doesn't know who her father is and my heart aches for her over that. It's not fair. I don't know. Maybe I've connected the two things in my head.

"It would just be helpful for me to know, Dad."

"Can you speak up, Princess?"

Grrr. "Write the next chapter, Dad. I gotta go."

We say our goodbyes and my impatience floods me with guilt. I refuse to dwell on it.

After work, I go to pick up Carly for our weekly outing.

Her mother answers the door. "Hey, Diana."

Tonya is a thirty-three-year-old version of Carly. Same gorgeous brown eyes and long black hair. Tonya's younger than I am, so I always feel more like Carly's aunt than a big sister.

"Hi, Tonya. Is Carly ready to go?"

"She's got an English test tomorrow. Any chance you could help her study a bit? English is not my strongest subject."

"Glad to. As long as you handle the math."

Carly comes around the corner, her hair swinging as she loops one arm through a backpack. "Hi."

"Hey, Carly."

We pick up chips and Slurpees before heading to the park where we find a bench. Carly opens her textbook and for the next hour I help her diagram sentences and match parts of speech with definitions.

"You know this stuff better than you thought. You'll do fine." I'm bent on improving Carly's confidence. "Let's pack up the books and do something fun."

We throw a Frisbee around for a while, then Carly asks if we can just walk around the park's circular path.

"Sure."

We've done this often. Each time, Carly shares another glimpse into her life and helps me remember what it was like to be a teenager.

A few minutes in, she gives me one of her shy, sideways glances that indicates she has something important to say.

"What's new in your life?" I frequently need to prime the pump.

"I've got a boyfriend."

"Really?"

For the next forty minutes, I hear about Josh. Josh's sweet personality, funny jokes, fantastic looks, sports prowess, and cool style sense. He is too good to be true, especially for a sixteen-year-old boy. I keep my opinions to myself and listen.

When I drop her off at home, I have one question before she climbs out of my car. "Your mom knows about Josh, right?"

"Yeah, of course." She hops out and slings her backpack over one shoulder. "See you next week!"

I drive off with a silent prayer. *Lord, I sure hope she's telling the truth. Show me how to do my part, whatever that might be, to help Carly navigate this exciting new development.*

• • •

Shane texts Friday afternoon and informs me that it's his turn to pick the movie we'll see tonight.

I don't mind the action movies he usually selects, even if they aren't my first choice. He gladly sits through the real-life dramas I like. Whatever we see, we make a point of spending at least thirty minutes discussing them afterward, usually over ice cream—or just coffee, if we've consumed too much popcorn at the theater. That's something Dad taught me, too: "If you're going to give your time to a movie or play, do yourself a favor and take time to discuss it. Every story has a message."

That night Shane picks the latest *Terminator* movie, starring Linda Hamilton and Arnold Schwarzenegger, followed by our favorite hangout for coffee— Linda's Diner. We argue, as usual, about the characters' deepest fears and darkest moments until the waitress hovers around our table, hinting that it's time to evacuate the premises.

In the parking lot, I boil down the first chapter of Dad's memoir for Shane, since he is already aware of my DNA quest.

"Makes my blood run cold," Shane says.

"What does?"

Shane is usually pretty laid back and I can't imagine why Lilly's story would anger him.

"I've seen too much destruction by arson," he explains. "Loss of property. Burn patients. Precious memories gone forever."

I should have known.

"Damages in the millions, all because a couple of little pyromaniacs got hold of matches or a lighter. I'd like to wring their scrawny necks if we could ever catch 'em. Where are the parents?"

Shane talks tough, but his passion has led him to get involved as a big brother. He's mentored three different boys over the years, investing in their lives and really making a difference for kids with no positive male role models. He's the one who got me started as a big sister. We both find it heartbreaking to see how little encouragement some kids receive, but at the same time it's heartening to discover how little it takes to make an impact.

"I'll be sure to tell Dad of your concern," I say, with no attempt to stifle my amusement.

He rewards me with a sheepish grin.

We climb into our cars and return to our respective homes. Me to my little bungalow with Mouse, and Shane to his apartment with his guitar.

• • •

In my next email to Dad, I joke with him about Shane's response.

> I do hope Lilly's fire-setting story has a happy ending or Shane might have to come out there and track somebody down to see justice served.

Dad's next email tells me more:

> Dear Diana,
>
> Sorry to leave you hanging with your grandmother's story. I got another chapter written, this time by hand. Becky showed me how to scan the pages and attach them to an email, so I hope I'm doing this right. I'm feeling very technologically advanced, but I'm wondering if this works like mail where I have to pay more if there's more in the envelope. Is my interweb bill going to go up if I send too much?

Anyway, back to my mother's story. I wish I could make your firefighter happy and say her dangerous prank had a happy ending. Then again, who's to say how things might have gone if their plan had unfolded the way Lilly and Tommy expected?

As I click on the attached PDF and wait for Dad's scrawl to appear on my screen, I try to remember where his previous chapter had left off. Oh yes… poor William Tidsbury was being taken to the hospital.

CHAPTER FOUR

Lilly

L illy stared at the remains of the Tidsbury home from her bedroom window, thinking about William while Aunty Margaret brushed and braided her hair. She'd learned not to cry out every time her aunt yanked too hard, wincing instead.

William Tidsbury had been admitted to a hospital in Winnipeg with his legs and feet burned. He was a smart kid. Quiet. Hated it whenever anyone tried to call him Billy or Willy or anything other than William. Preferred books over baseball, which meant he wasn't exactly popular. Maybe a little goofy-looking, the way his ears stuck out and pushed his straight brown hair in odd angles, but Lilly thought he was nice.

He was no Tommy, though. One of the games she and Tommy had played since first grade was private detective, tracking William's movements from their vantage point in the treehouse, pretending he was a foreign spy. Unfortunately, William's activities seemed to be limited to sitting in his tire swing reading a book or helping his mother in the garden. Tommy and Lilly would eventually find a new game.

"Will William's parents build a new house over there?"

"I'm sure building another house is the least of their concerns right now." Aunty Margaret pulled Lilly's two braids together at the bottom.

"Will they come back? Where are they, anyway?"

"I heard that Mr. Tidsbury and the other children are boarding with Mrs. Collins so he can be near his work. And Mrs. Tidsbury is staying in the city to be with William as much as possible. He's going to need a lot of surgery and therapy."

"What's therapy?"

"He'll need help learning how to walk again. Right now, they're just hoping they can save both his feet."

What did that mean? Lilly chewed her lip. "Will he be able to come back to school in September?"

"I really don't know." Aunty Margaret finished and turned Lilly around to face her. "Even if he's well enough, who knows if they'll stay in Summervale? I hope they do. But they really need our prayers. Especially William. Burns are terribly painful."

Lilly went to the treehouse without a word. She knelt in the semi-darkness, certain God would not hear her prayers but desperate to help somehow.

"God, I'm sorry. If I could go back, I wouldn't do it. I didn't know anyone was going to get hurt. Please don't make William pay for my sin. Please make him better. I promise, I'll never start another fire. Please just make him well. And please help his family get a new house."

Preferably not across the street. How could she bear to see them every day? On the other hand, the glaring hole and empty yard across the street was a constant reminder of what she had done.

On Sundays at church, the pastor always gave an update on William's condition and reminded the congregation to pray for him. Lilly's hopes rose when the latest update revealed William had taken his first steps. Then her heart sank.

"Although we're overjoyed that he's walking," the pastor read from Mrs. Tidsbury's letter, "please continue to pray. He will surely be left with a permanent limp and is still in much pain. Pray that he won't get discouraged and give up trying to improve."

The pastor cleared his throat before continuing. "Please also tell the congregation that the fire department completed their investigation, and they believe an accelerant of some type was used. We did keep a gas can in the shed, but it was removed the day before. Everything was removed in preparation for tearing down the shed as we'd planned. They now suspect that we deliberately set fire to the shed and things got out of hand. We know this isn't true. If anyone can give us any information, if anyone saw anything, please come forward."

Lilly stared down at her shoes. She couldn't bear to make eye contact with anyone, least of all Tommy.

When the preacher then launched into a fire and brimstone sermon, she was certain he must be glaring straight at her. Surely she was bound for hell. How many good deeds would it take to outnumber this evil one?

The adults of the church had held meetings and mobilized help for the Tidsbury family in the form of clothing and cash. One family offered storage space for donated furniture and other household goods to be kept until such time as the Tidsburys were ready to use them. Posters were up at the grocery store, post office, and probably other places Lilly hadn't visited. The posters listed clothing sizes for the five children and encouraged people to give what they could. Lilly wanted to give William her overalls, but Aunty Margaret said they were too small and too worn.

If she happened to see Tommy anywhere, Lilly avoided him. She spent hours alone in the treehouse, distracting herself with storybooks or her long-neglected doll, Patty.

Relief arrived when it was time for their week at Uncle Ben's cabin at Clear Lake. For seven entire days, Lilly swam, hiked, fished, and read comic books with her cousins. Too busy to think about William or Tommy or the fire, it was easy to keep her secret. Only late at night, after her cousins fell asleep, did she dwell on it.

One such evening as she lay staring at the ceiling, adult conversation drifted in from the next room. When she heard her name, Lilly leaned toward the door, straining to hear.

"Does Lilly ever ask about Nora?" It was Aunt Betty. Who was Nora?

"Never." Aunt Margaret's voice was harsher than Betty's. "I thought she would have asked about her mother by now, but she doesn't seem the least bit curious."

A conversation she'd had with Tommy when they were still preschoolers came to Lilly's mind. It had happened the day she taught him how to pull out the kitchen drawers and use them like a ladder to reach Aunty Margaret's cookie jar when no one was looking.

"Why do you call your mum 'Aunty Margaret'?" he had asked around a mouthful of oatmeal cookie.

Lilly had shrugged. "I dunno."

"Don't you have a mum?"

"Course I do." Lilly had pocketed the pilfered cookies and pushed the drawers back into place.

His brown eyes squinted at her. "Where is she then, your mum?"

"She lives at the graveyard with my baby brother. Under the dirt."

It had been enough to satisfy Tommy at the time. Lilly had pieced together more in the intervening years. Her mama had been Uncle Henry and Uncle Ben's baby sister. When Mama had died, Uncle Henry and Aunty Margaret took Lilly to raise as their own, even though their children—all boys—were nearly grown.

Aunty Margaret spoke again. "Do you think I should bring it up? See what she remembers?"

"I w—wouldn't." Uncle Ben's voice was easy to discern from Uncle Henry's because of his stammer. "No point opening a can of w—worms if she doesn't w—want to know."

"She seems happy enough, don't you think, Margaret?" Uncle Henry had never given Lilly reason to be unhappy.

Aunty Margaret was another matter. "What does happy have to do with anything? She should be grateful she's not being raised by your sister."

"Margaret." Uncle Henry's tone sounded like a warning.

"What? You were the one who insisted on taking her in."

"Don't say disrespectful things about the departed."

"Well, it's true and you know it. I'm not one to judge, but my biggest fear is she'll grow up just like Nora. Those immoral ways can be inherited, you know."

Aunt Betty chimed in. "She seems very well-adjusted and contented to me. I agree with Ben. If she ever has questions, she'll ask. Until then, I wouldn't worry about it."

The conversation turned to other topics and Lilly tuned them out. Had she heard her mother's name before? *Nora.* What had happened to her mother and brother? Did she have a father? Where was he? And how had it been decided that Uncle Henry and Aunty Margaret would be the ones to take her? Surely even Uncle Henry wouldn't want her now if he knew what she'd done.

• • •

The day the family returned home to Summervale, Lilly sat in her treehouse staring across the street at the Tidsburys' barren lot. Nothing had changed. How was William? Would he be at school when it started in a week?

She jumped when someone scrambled up the ladder. Tommy's head poked up through the hole and Lilly stared at him, speechless.

"You're back," Tommy said. His blonde curls were longer than normal.

Lilly narrowed her eyes. "Have you been coming up to my treehouse the whole time I was gone?"

"No. I saw your family get home. I was watching from my bedroom window. We need to talk." He climbed the rest of the way into the treehouse.

"I don't want to be your friend anymore, Tommy." She turned to continue gazing over at the Tidsbury property.

"I know you don't. But listen. I heard my parents talking. Wondering why they never see you with me anymore."

"Really?" She refused to look at him. "What did you tell them?"

Tommy shrugged. "Nothing. They weren't really askin' me. Dad told Mum maybe I was growing up. Getting too old to play with girls."

That sounded reasonable. Let them think it. "So why are you here now?"

"Because of what Mum said next. She thought it seemed kinda funny that we were thick as thieves—that's how she put it, thick as thieves—until that fire at the Tidsburys'. And then all of a sudden, it ended."

Lilly took this in. She'd thought none of the adults would notice. "Did she ask you about it?"

"The day after the fire, Dad asked me if I knew anything about it. But Mum said, 'He slept right through it, Fred.' And that was the end of it. I thought."

Lilly stared out the treehouse window again, avoiding the yard across the street. Aunty Margaret's hollyhocks towered up against the back of the house, their brilliant pink and coral blossoms showing off. Bees buzzed around them. If only she could become one of those tiny bees. No care in the world except gathering pollen and doing what you were created to do. No secrets to be ashamed of.

"We need to start playing together again." Tommy moved to the window and stood beside her. "So no one suspects."

Lilly let out a long sigh. Though she'd never admit it to Tommy, she had missed him. The secret they shared tugged like a string, connecting them no matter how far apart they stayed or how silent they remained.

"Okay. But I thought we weren't going to talk about it ever again."

"We're not. Not after today." Tommy reached into a pocket and pulled out a handful of jacks. From his other, a small rubber ball. He sat cross-legged on the floor. "From now on, everything is back to normal. C'mon, let's play."

He tossed the jacks and bounced the ball once before she joined him on the floor. Maybe they'd never talk about it again. But would she ever stop thinking about it?

• • •

On their first morning back to school in September, Tommy and Lilly walked together as usual but with few words. Was he thinking the same thoughts she was? Would William be in school? The most recent update from church had made it sound like he would.

In their new classroom, the familiar scents of chalk and freshly polished floors greeted them. Their teacher had already assigned seats in alphabetical order. Several students between DeWitt and Sampson provided a buffer between Tommy and Lilly.

She found the desk with her name right behind Norma Sadney's. She placed her supplies in the desk, then checked to see who'd be sitting behind her. Her heart sank. The teacher's carefully inked letters spelled out *William Tidsbury*.

Lilly had no sooner taken her seat than all eyes turned toward the door. The buzz of conversation in the room stopped, words cut short in mid-sentence. Here came William, walking with the aid of two crutches on his forearms and braces on both legs. His school satchel had been replaced with a rucksack so he could carry it across his shoulders. He made his way slowly into the room and headed down the row toward Lilly. She dared not look at Tommy. She couldn't force herself to meet William's eye either, as much as she might want to.

Striding into the room with a brisk pace and a powerful voice, a middle-aged woman in a navy-blue dress addressed the class from beside the teacher's desk. "Good morning, everyone. My name is Mrs. Forrester and I'm new this year. I'll be teaching Grades Four through Six." She picked up chalk and wrote her name on the board in a beautiful script. "I'd like to especially welcome Marlene Dayholos, whose family is new to town." She waved a hand toward a girl with black braids seated in front of Tommy. "Marlene, can you say hello and tell us what grade you're in?"

The girl stood. "Hello. I'm in Grade Five."

"Class, will you welcome Marlene please?"

"Welcome Marlene," the class chimed in unison as she took her seat.

"I'd also like to give a special 'welcome back' to William Tidsbury, who I understand had a pretty tough summer. William? Can you raise your hand?"

All the kids in front of Lilly turned around, but she stayed focused on the teacher.

"We're so glad you're well enough to start the year with us, William. Would you like to tell the class a little about your experience? Can I call you Billy?"

William cleared his throat. "Well… our house burned down. I got burned some, too."

"Did you want to share anything about all that?" the teacher coaxed, a toothy smile on her face. "No? Not today? All right then. That's fine. Maybe another day when you're up to it, you can give a full report on your adventures at the hospital and so on. Class, this is the same Billy you've always known. He might not be able to run as fast right now, but let's all do our best to make him glad to be back in school, shall we?"

Lilly raised her hand.

"Yes? What's your name?"

"Lilly Sampson, ma'am."

"What did you want to say, Lilly?"

Lilly took a deep breath. "His name is *William*. Not Billy."

• • •

At recess, the girls gathered around the big oak tree on the schoolyard to discuss their summer adventures. Lilly sat on the grass, half-listening to the conversation. Her gaze kept straying to where the boys played tag, calling out taunts as they dashed away from whomever was *It*. William leaned against the side of the school, watching the other boys. Seeing him alone was nothing new. Seeing him without a book was. When the teacher came out to ring the bell, William immediately headed for the door.

He was still the last one inside.

• • •

By the end of the week, Lilly couldn't stand it. At recess, she didn't bother following the girls to their usual spot but went straight to William. "Hello."

"Hi, Lilly."

She glanced toward the girls, but so far none of them were paying any attention to her or William.

"Thanks for standing up for me." William leaned against the wall. "With the teacher, I mean. She hasn't called me Billy again."

Lilly nodded. "How come you're not reading? You can still read, right?"

"Of course I can still read. Fire didn't hurt my eyes." William looked around the playground. "It's just hard to hold a book is all."

Lilly looked at his hands, thrust through the rings of his crutches and gripping the handles. "Can't you put your crutches down? Lean them up against the wall?"

"I might lose my balance and fall."

"Then just sit on the ground."

William let out a long, loud sigh. "I would need help getting up again."

"Oh."

William's feet were covered in thick socks while the braces held his legs rigid. Lilly forced herself to stop staring at his legs. The clear blue September sky and the joyful sounds of the other students should have filled her heart with gladness, but the gloom felt relentless.

"Do they still hurt?" she asked.

William nodded.

"They're getting better though, right? You won't need those braces forever?"

"Yeah. Doc says I just need to keep at it. Keep practicing."

Lilly bit her lip. "Want me to go get a book? I could read it to you. Or… just hold it for you. Turn the pages."

William shrugged. "Nah. Taking books outside is against the rules."

"Well, maybe she'd make a… what do you call it? An exception."

"I don't want to be an exception. Besides, I'm supposed to be doing stuff on my own. If you read to me, it will only slow me down."

A big rubber ball hit the side of the building right beside William's head, making them both jump. Lilly ran after the bouncing ball and picked it up with both hands. When she turned around to figure out who'd thrown it, William had crumpled to the ground.

"William!" She ran toward him, letting the ball drop.

"Just lost my balance, I'm all right."

A Grade Six boy named Martin picked up the ball. Tucking it under one arm, he stood watching William and laughed.

"What'sa matter, Crip? Did da widdle baby faw down?" Martin pressed the ball against his own chest with both hands, then faked hurling it straight at William, who tried to dodge. The bigger boy held onto the ball, pulling it back with a laugh as he turned to jog back.

Like a match bursting into flame, a streak of red came from out of nowhere and tackled Martin from the side. Both boys landed on the ground. The ball went flying. They wrestled in the dirt, fists and feet flailing.

"Leave William alone!" the attacker hollered.

The teacher threw open a window and stuck her head out. "Stop it immediately!"

Martin ran back to his buddies, swiping at a bloody nose, while the boy in red sat panting on the ground.

It was Tommy DeWitt.

CHAPTER FIVE

Diana

I am loving Dad's chapters. But at this rate, he might never get to his own birth. Will I ever learn my grandmother's whole story?

At lunchtime, I call my sister.

"Dad is driving me nuts, Becky. I ask one simple question and instead of answering he starts doling out Grandma Lilly's story in bits and pieces when he clearly knows the whole thing already. Can you try to drag it out of him?"

"Why?"

Water splashes at her end of the phone. Washing dishes? Bathing kids?

"What do you mean, *why*? Don't you want to know?"

Becky chuckles. "Of course. But what's the rush? We'll get it eventually."

"His handwriting is horrible."

She just laughs at me again. "He's writing a book, Di. Do you realize what a treasure this is going to be when it's done? I think it's marvelous. Gives him something to do, too. You have no idea how restless he's been since he retired. Well, since Mom passed, really."

I sigh. "I guess."

"Be patient. Hey, listen. If you're in such a hurry, why don't you come home for a few days? Maybe you can pester more out of him."

Does she deliberately try to irritate me every time she refers to Manitoba as "home" when I've been gone for eight years? I let it slide this time.

"You could have access to Dad twenty-four-seven. Get him talking. Solve the mystery and return to Edmonton satisfied."

"Yeah. I suppose. But I've only got one vacation day left this year." I used my three weeks in one fell swoop by joining my church's mission trip to Mexico last January, allowing a few days on each side of the trip for preparation and recovery. Best decision I ever made, except now it means I have to work every week until next year.

"A long weekend then? Tack on your one vacation day and you could have a solid three days with Dad, provided you fly."

I don't know how to tell my sister I used up any travel dollars in my budget on the mission trip, too. She seems to think that as a single career woman, I have unlimited resources.

"Maybe," I say.

"Or… what about Dad flying out there? He can afford it. I can help him book tickets and see that he gets on the right flight. You can meet him at the airport and take him back again. I bet he'd love to see where you live and work. And he could meet your Shane."

"He's not *my* Shane." I roll my eyes even though she can't see me.

"Whatever."

"Do you think he'd do it? Would he be okay with flying?" Dad has made only a few flights in his life, when he was much younger. He still calls flight attendants "stewardesses" and then finds himself at a loss when they aren't female.

"Well, you know Dad. Takes his time with everything. I'll see him tomorrow. I'll gently plant the seed and then, if you invite him, maybe he'll warm up to the idea."

• • •

I like the prospect of Dad coming to Edmonton. If he comes for a long weekend, I won't need to miss any work. Maybe I can keep him focused long enough to tell me the rest of his mother's story. Who knows? Maybe I *will* introduce him to Shane. I can picture the two of them hitting it off.

I put the suggestion in my next email and receive a surprisingly swift reply.

Dear Diana,

My heart is warmed by your invitation, but I'm afraid I'm much too old to be jetting off across the country. Your sister tells me I'm being silly, that flying is easy but… I don't know. I'm not as adventurous as I used to be. It must feel odd to see your once capable and professional father so short on confidence, but you'll understand one day. I wish I'd had more compassion for my parents as they aged. When Mother told me her life story, she did so with a sense of urgency that I didn't comprehend. I didn't know we'd lose her so soon after. Now I suspect she had a hunch and was desperate to get her story out.

Maybe it's best I didn't know she was ill. Nothing like helplessly standing by to make you feel useless. Especially when you're supposed to be a healer and have the answers.

Thanks for the invitation, but I believe I'll stay right here. I need my own bed and routines. You'll understand that one day, too.

I sort of understand it already, but I'm not about to admit it. Becky accuses me of being set in my ways, too afraid to try new adventures. She usually says those things in reference to my love life—or lack thereof. But her insinuation did prompt me to say yes to the mission trip and to being a big sister, so I clearly proved her wrong. Why can't she see it? Maybe because in her narrow world a woman isn't complete until she snags a man. Well, I snagged one once. My hook might as well have been tangled in seaweed.

I keep reading.

Instead of me coming to you, why don't you make a trip home? That way, you can see all of us. I know Becky's household is noisy and chaotic, but if you don't mind my sofa, you could stay here with me. It's nice and quiet, although Ralph and Pansy next door tell me I play my music too loud. As if Tchaikovsky could ever be too loud.

You and I could have a swell time! We could stay up late, chatting and eating popcorn, although those darn kernels get caught in my dentures these days. I do better with cheese and crackers. You could tell me about your life in Edmonton and I could tell you the rest of my mother's story in person. It's a doozy.

Love,
Dad

Dad will take a little more convincing, but I suspected as much.

• • •

On our next movie night, Shane and I spend more time discussing Dad's latest chapter than the movie. I whine to him about how Dad is feeding it to me one crumb at a time.

Shane stirs his coffee thoughtfully. "At least we know William survived."

"Yeah. I'd just like to know how we ended up related to him."

His eyes narrow. "You said Lilly and Tommy ended up married?"

"Right."

"A pair of firebugs."

"They were eight years old, Shane. I'm sure they learned their lesson. Look how they stuck up for William."

"It's a mental illness, you know."

"What is? Being a firebug?"

Shane nods. "It's called pyromania."

"I know what it's called, but isn't it more of a... compulsion?"

"That's what compulsions are. Mental illness. Kleptomania falls in there, too."

"Which one is that? Compulsive stealing? Shoplifting?" I bite into my rhubarb muffin.

"Right. Of course, they didn't call it mental illness back then. Or even compulsion. It was just misbehavior."

I speak around a mouthful. "Sin?"

"It can be hereditary, you know." Shane seems to be watching me a little too closely.

"You think I might be a firebug too?"

He lets out a noncommittal hum. "You tell me."

"Don't be ridiculous. I don't even burn real candles in my house."

"Thanks to me."

"Well, that's true."

Like any good firefighter, Shane spotted the candle on my kitchen table within seconds of his first visit to my house—even though he'd only been dropping off a donation for our fundraiser. He'd given me a royal lecture, then had the nerve to confiscate my candle. The next time we saw each other, he handed me a gift bag with three battery-powered candles inside, complete with spare batteries.

I love him for it. The candles simulate all the ambiance without burning up, and I never need to worry about leaving them unattended.

"I converted you, didn't I?" He grins from behind his coffee mug.

"Speaking of conversion… you never did answer me about visiting my church."

Shane attends the smallish church he grew up in but has been expressing a need for something different lately. His church is mostly made up of little gray-haired women who constantly try to set him up with their granddaughters. I love teasing him about it, but somehow he doesn't seem in the mood today. "You know we have a great single adults group."

"So you've said. Like, a thousand times."

"What are you afraid of?" I know he'd love our singles group.

"Sounds like a matchmaking scheme. Same reason I didn't go to Bible college back in the day. Everybody called it 'bridal college.'"

I roll my eyes. "I assure you, it's not. In fact, you insult me. I've been part of the group for at least six years and no one has asked me for a date. Nor have I tried to initiate anything."

"Because it's mostly women. Am I right?"

I think about it a minute. "Yeah. I guess it is. So? Once everyone knows you're not interested, they'll leave you alone. Besides, maybe you actually *would* find someone. Ever think of that?"

"Oh please. Not you, too."

We drop what is obviously a sensitive topic.

• • •

On Saturday, I take Carly roller-skating. She's never tried it, and I haven't been on roller-skates since I was her age. We have a blast, but after two hours of her energy I'm glad to be driving her home.

"How are things with you and Josh?" She hasn't mentioned him all day.

"We broke up on Monday."

"Oh." I keep my eyes on the road. "You don't seem very bothered by it."

"That's because we got back together on Wednesday."

"Oh."

"Yeah. It's all good."

"You should introduce me sometime." I pull to a stop in front of her building.

"Yeah, I will. Okay, goodbye."

How do parents do this? I'm exhausted and not that keen on being a voice of caution. I make up my mind that I'll call Carly's mom as soon as I get home and have a little chat, just to make sure she knows about this boyfriend.

When I get home, my inbox holds another lengthy email from Dad, with an attachment. I change into my pajamas and brush my teeth, then settle in for a good read with my favorite throw blanket draped over my lap and my favorite cat curled up beside me.

> Dear Diana,
>
> Surprise! You and Becky have talked me into it. "Life's too short to be such a big chicken," she said. Cheeky thing. She found something called a seat sale, although I don't want to buy the seat. I only need to rent it for the length of the plane ride, ha ha. Nonstop, Winnipeg to Edmonton, so I don't have to worry about rushing to another gate and getting myself lost or missing a connection. You mentioned the Canada Day long weekend would work well for you, so that's what we picked. I sure hope that's okay. Becky wanted to call, but I wanted to tell you myself. Get your sofa ready! I'm already packing.

I can hardly believe it. Dad is actually coming. The dates will be perfect, too. I immediately begin to plan stuff we can do. I'll give him my bedroom and take the sofa, of course. I'll give him a tour of city hall, my office, take him to church, introduce him to my friends. Will he be up for a drive to Jasper? I'd love to show him the breathtaking Rockies and take a delicious picnic along. He's always wanted to see Jasper—every bit as beautiful as Banff but far less touristy. We can talk the whole way there and back.

His email details his flight numbers and times. Then he gets back to Lilly's story, which seems to be turning into Lilly and Tommy's story.

> From my last chapter, you know that my dear mother had a great deal of loss and carried around a pretty horrific secret for one so young—not to mention a load of guilt. Rightly so, I suppose. But she was not alone. Lilly and Tommy kept up their friendship through their growing-up years. While my mother also continued to befriend William and stand up for him on the playground and such, Tommy kept his distance from William.
>
> "It's not that Tommy was an awful person," Mother told me when we discussed it. "He just couldn't face seeing the results of what we had done, while I kept looking for ways to make amends."
>
> Somewhere during these years, Mother discovered more about what had happened to her parents. Her mother, younger than her

closest sibling by several years, was known as a woman with a mind of her own. She married young, against her parents' wishes, only to be deserted by the fella later. When Lilly was three, her mother died in childbirth—along with the baby. Mother and infant were buried together.

Meanwhile, Mother's Uncle Henry and Aunt Margaret had always wanted a girl. By this time, though, their four boys were nearly all grown and it took a lot of work on Henry's part to convince Margaret. She was not what you'd call a warm woman. Mother went by the name Sampson until she married. She told me that whenever she asked relatives what her father's last name was, they always told her the same thing: "Your mother was a Sampson and so are you." But I do wonder if her sketchy origins, along with Aunty Margaret's rejection, caused some insecurity that led to foolish choices.

Anyway, I finished another chapter, based on what Mother told me about how her friendship with Tommy blossomed into romance. If you can accurately call it that.

I open Dad's attachment and begin to read, ignoring the nagging thought that I'm forgetting to do something.

CHAPTER SIX

Lilly

1937–1938

Lilly finished her morning oatmeal with her Chemistry notes spread out over the kitchen table. The headline on the front of Uncle Henry's newspaper caught her eye: FAKE RADIO WAR STIRS TERROR THROUGH U.S. AND CANADA. She skimmed the article. An American movie producer named Orson Welles had aired a dramatization about creatures from Mars invading Earth. Listeners had panicked, thinking it was real.

"How silly."

"What is?" Aunty Margaret added hot water to her dishpan.

"People thinking aliens have invaded just because of a silly radio show."

"Oh, yes. I read that, too. Glad we missed that one. Can't believe people fell for it." Her aunt wiped a dish and placed it on the shelf. "I certainly wouldn't."

Uncle Henry chimed in. "Don't be too quick to judge. It's easy to say after the truth comes out."

Aunty Margaret released a *humph* and Lilly turned back to her Chemistry.

Uncle Henry stood while he tossed the paper onto the table. He leaned over to kiss Aunty Margaret on the cheek. "Want a ride to school, Lil?"

"No thanks. Tommy will be waiting for me."

"So are you two an item now?" Uncle Henry grabbed his hat from the stand near the door and stood with his hand on the knob.

Aunty Margaret let out a snort. "Haven't those two been an *item* since they were practically babies?"

"You know what I mean. He's taking you to the Halloween dance, right?"

Lilly bristled. "Yes, but we're just friends."

"*Best* friends, I'd say." Aunty Margaret was clearly fishing for information.

"What's wrong with that?" Lilly refused to look at either of them.

Uncle Henry opened the door. "Ooooh. Methinks she dost protest too much." The door was closed with Uncle Henry on the other side by the time Lilly's pencil hit its mark.

Aunty Margaret picked it up off the floor. "You broke it."

"Blame him, not me."

"Lilly." Aunty Margaret laid the pencil beside Lilly's textbook. "Pencils don't grow on trees." She took a seat, forcing Lilly to meet her gaze.

"They sort of do, though."

"Apologize."

Lilly focused on the textbook in front of her. "I'm sorry."

"And you should not be spending so much time with Thomas DeWitt. Or any boy. People will think you're just like..." Her voice faded as she refolded the newspaper.

"Just like what?"

Aunty Margaret stared at her for several seconds. "Nothing. If you know what's good for you, you'll take my advice and spend more time with the girls."

"Tommy and I hardly see each other anymore, with him working at the hardware store and me at the grocery store. Besides, I've got goals. You know that. No time for boyfriends and all that."

Aunty Margaret frowned. "That's another thing. This business of being a nurse. I'm not sure it's for you."

"Not just any nurse. I'm going to work in a specialty area, with burn victims. It'll require... so much more. Psychology and... and compassion. Toughness and... and well, you can't have a queasy stomach, that's for sure."

Aunty Margaret let out a long slow sigh. "Do you realize how much money your uncle is prepared to gamble on this?"

Lilly nodded without hesitation. "Definitely."

Aunty Margaret paused but didn't leave her chair. "Does this stem from what happened to William? Seeing him suffer?"

Lilly swallowed. "Maybe. I don't know."

If her aunt knew the whole truth, she'd know that Lilly's aspirations had everything to do with William. Even though it was too late to help him, maybe she could help others with similar injuries. And maybe, just maybe, God would have mercy on her.

• • •

Lilly's friendship with Tommy had deepened through high school even though they'd kept their promise to never discuss their childish misdeed, even with each other.

While William remained a friend to them both, he lived in his own world of books and solitude despite regaining enough strength to walk without braces or crutches. He would limp through the graduation line at the end of this year alongside his classmates, probably earning top marks and delivering the Valedictorian speech.

Although Tommy had stood up for William more than once, Lilly had never seen the two boys talk or spend any time together.

Tommy had ambitions of his own. One Saturday afternoon in January after knocking on the Sampsons' door, he burst into the kitchen without waiting for a response.

"I did it, Lil."

He didn't need to explain. Tommy had been studying for the volunteer firefighters test for weeks. Fire Chief Carpenter had taken Tommy and another boy to the city that morning to complete their testing.

Now Tommy's eyes were lit up like an inferno and Lilly ran to give him a big hug.

"Congratulations!"

She thought her heart might stop when he picked her right up and swung her in a full circle.

"Top score!" Tommy's face beamed. "And I want to take my girl out for dinner to celebrate."

Lilly liked the sound of being "his girl." When they walked into the Polynesian-themed restaurant arm-in-arm that evening, dressed in their finest, it was exactly who she wanted to be. Tommy's girl. The thread that had tied their hearts together through the years had strengthened into a cord. No one knew her like Tommy did. How could they?

Tommy was the youngest man on the list of volunteer firemen, but also the most dedicated. Even when not called to a fire, he spent most of his free time at the fire hall and was willing to clean equipment, mop floors, whatever he could to be there and keep learning.

"I'll be chief one day, Lil. The youngest ever, I bet," he announced one warm evening in April as they walked home from the movie theater hand in hand.

Meanwhile, Lilly studied hard to earn the best test scores she could.

• • •

In mid-May, Uncle Henry drove Lilly to St. Boniface Hospital for her nursing school interview. As they drove up to the building she'd seen only in photos, her heart soared at the idea of returning here as a student in the fall.

Before he dropped her off, Uncle Henry reached over and took her hand. "You'll do well, Lilly."

Lilly looked into his kind eyes. "I wish Aunty Margaret thought so."

"Don't worry about her. She doesn't mean it."

But Lilly knew better. Aunty Margaret hadn't wanted her in the first place, and the only reason she'd agreed to this plan was the hope of getting Lilly out of the house—the sooner, the better.

She dashed into the building and found the right room. A nun looked up from a solid wooden desk.

"Lilly Sampson?"

Lilly stood in the doorway. "Yes, ma'am."

"Have a seat. I'm Sister Marie-Therese."

"How do you do?" Lilly sat on the edge of a chair and clasped her hands to hide the trembling.

Sister Marie-Therese sat poised behind her desk with forms in one hand, a fountain pen in the other. "I've been perusing your application, Lilly. You've answered question seven in a very interesting way."

Lilly raised her eyebrows. Was remembering the questions an important part of the interview process?

The nun continued. "The question is, 'What do you hope to accomplish as a nurse?' Do you remember your answer?"

Lilly nodded. "Yes, ma'am. I hope to eventually work with burn victims."

"That's a precise ambition. Any particular reason why?"

Lilly swallowed. "I… grew up with a boy who was seriously injured in a house fire… across the street from my home."

"I see."

Lilly cleared her throat and brushed imaginary lint from her skirt. "He's going to be our class valedictorian."

"Good for him. Working with burn victims is a noble goal, Lilly. Are you aware of the extreme demands of that particular specialty?"

Lilly had done some reading on it. Burn patients suffered intense physical pain, but often their emotional wounds ran far deeper as they struggled with loss of limbs or disfigurement. Some lost their own sense of identity.

"I know it will be hard. I have much to learn."

The sister nodded. "A teachable spirit. Compassion. I like that. Would you say you feel called to this work?"

Lilly shifted her gaze back and forth between the only two items on the sister's desk: a telephone and a lamp. Should she lie and say that she definitely felt "called," whatever that meant? Was it required for admittance?

"I... truthfully don't know, Sister. I'm not sure I know what being called would feel like. I just know it's what I want to do. What I *think* I want to do."

Finally, she met the woman's eyes and saw only compassion there.

"I appreciate your honesty." The nun shuffled the pages, skimming to the end. "Well, Lilly, I see no reason why you wouldn't be a wonderful asset to our school. Your marks are top-notch, you're healthy and motivated. Your scholarship will cover your first year." She slid a page across the desk toward Lilly and handed her a pen. "I just need you to read over this page and sign it, indicating you understand the rules and regulations and that you intend to abide by them. If you have a question about any of them, now's the time to ask."

She sat back in her chair, waiting.

Lilly had read the list when she'd received the application package, but she went through it again:

1. Tuition shall be $100 for the year and includes books and uniforms.

2. Shifts will be from 7:00 a.m. to 7:00 p.m., seven days a week, with one half-day off on a rotating schedule. On half-days off, students are required to attend morning and evening classes.

3. Each 12-hour shift includes a 2-hour break during which students are expected to rest on one of the cots provided in the basement sleeping room. No conversation or noise is allowed in the break room.

4. All students are required to live in residence.

5. Any and all outings must be approved by the Director. No dating is allowed without express permission by the Director and must include a prior interview with the boy. Any dates granted will take place under strict supervision, on campus.

6. Lights out is 10:00 p.m. every night.

7. Reasons for automatic dismissal include, but are not limited to:
   —Academic failure during probationary period
   —Marriage
   —Pregnancy

8. Other reasons for dismissal or suspension include, but are not limited to: disobedience, misconduct, insubordination, or neglect of duty. Each incident will be considered on a case-by-case basis at the discretion of the Director, whose decision is final.

9. No vacation will be granted until the student has successfully completed her 3-month probationary period.

10. Smoking is not allowed.

11. When not in uniform, students must wear skirts or dresses. Slacks are not allowed.

12. Results of all course examinations are sent home to the student's parents, who are then required to sign and return forms to the nursing school.

13. A monthly weight record shall be kept of all students. Failure to maintain weight may result in denial of privileges.

As Lilly raised the pen to sign the document, the sister interrupted her. "No questions?"

Lilly shook her head. "No, ma'am."

"Very well then."

Lilly signed her name and date on the lines indicated, then slid the paper back across the desk to the smiling nun.

"Congratulations, Lilly." The sister rose and held out a hand. Lilly stood and shook hands with her. "Welcome to St. Boniface School of Nursing. We look forward to having you join us in the fall."

Lilly turned to leave but paused before opening the door. "Sister?"

"Yes?"

"Is it possible to get my textbooks early?"

The nun smiled broadly. "Oh, I do love a keen student!" She came around her desk and pulled the door open, waving Lilly through. "Let's go see Sister Marie-Claire and see what she can do about that, shall we?"

• • •

Lilly perused books all the way home while Uncle Henry drove in silence, grinning whenever Lilly shared an interesting bit from one of the textbooks. After sharing the good news with Aunty Margaret, Lilly piled the books in her room and announced that she was headed to the hardware store to tell Tommy.

"Invite him over for supper." Uncle Henry's smiling face confirmed his support of the relationship. "Then we can all celebrate together. That all right with you, Margaret?"

"I suppose."

• • •

After the supper dishes were done and put away, Lilly and Tommy walked to the park on the edge of town. They found a comfy bench where they could watch the sunset over the little lake. Pairs of Canada geese waddled around importantly, their nests hidden from view and known only to them.

"Happy?" Tommy placed an arm around Lilly's shoulder.

"Mmhmm." She nestled into him. "So happy."

"You deserve this, Lilly. I'm so proud of you." With his other hand, he covered both of hers.

Without warning, hot tears began to sting Lilly's eyes. When she tried to blink them away, more followed, landing on the back of Tommy's hand.

"Hey." He lowered his head to peer into her eyes. "What's the matter? We're supposed to be celebrating, not crying."

Lilly tried to smile, but a huge sob escaped instead.

"Hey now." Tommy pulled a handkerchief from his pocket and handed it to her. "What's this about?"

Lilly wanted to say she didn't know. That maybe it was just nerves about going off to nursing school. But she knew better. The tears were from remorse, but how could she tell Tommy when they'd agreed not to discuss it ever again?

"Please don't say I deserve this. I don't, Tommy. Don't you see? I don't deserve this… or you… or all the support… any of it. I don't!"

"Of course you deserve it. You worked hard for those good grades. I don't know anybody who's been as dedicated as you—"

"But all the good grades in the world can't make up for—"

"Shh." Tommy pulled her into a tight embrace, and she continued sobbing into his shoulder. He stroked her hair. "It's okay. Shh. It'll be okay."

His shirt muffled her voice, but she didn't want to pull away. "I don't think it will. How can it?"

"We were just kids, Lilly. Just stupid kids who made a dumb mistake. We're good people. William is fine. You're going to be a wonderful nurse. You're going to help hundreds, maybe thousands. I'm going to be the best fireman ever. We're good, Lilly." He tightened his grip on her. Was he trying to convince himself as much as her? "We're good."

CHAPTER SEVEN

Diana

"Dad was an absolute trooper." I call Becky as soon as I have Dad safely in my car, headed home from the airport.

"Oh good. I really wanted this to go well so he'll travel more often. Now get off the phone. You shouldn't be driving and calling."

"It's hands-free, you goof."

"I don't care. It's still distracting."

I check my mirrors. "Becky. If you were sitting in the passenger seat, we'd be talking a mile a minute."

"Yes, and that would be distracting, too."

"Good grief. You're turning into Mother."

"Thank you. And thanks for calling. You and Dad have a great time. I'm hanging up now."

Click.

"Bye."

Whoa. She really meant she was hanging up. Didn't even say goodbye.

I turn to Dad. "You doing okay?"

He fiddles with his hearing aids. "Oh yeah, sure. You drive in the city like an old pro."

"Well, it's been home for eight years, Dad." I smile.

"Has it really been that long?"

"Hard to believe, I know."

Dad grows quiet, taking in the view. I point out my church. "We'll go on Sunday morning if you like. We can choose between a nine or eleven o'clock service."

"Princess, I just want to experience your life. Do what you do. Meet your friends. That Shane fella."

"You will."

"And that little sister." His eyes twinkle at me from under bushy grey eyebrows. "I pray for her, you know."

"You do? Aw, Dad, that's so sweet."

"Carly, right?"

I turn onto my street. "Yes. I invited her along on our picnic tomorrow."

"Maybe I could even see your office where you work."

"City hall will be closed for the long weekend, including Monday. I suppose we could pop in before we head to the airport on Tuesday." I pull into my driveway. "Or I could show you around when it's empty."

"They trust you with a key?" He ducks. As though I'd swat my seventy-seven-year-old dad.

"They do. But If I'm going to take you there, I'd like to show you off to my co-workers."

"Well, we can play it by ear. Maybe not my ears, though. They don't work so good." He chuckles at his own joke. "So this is your place."

I lead Dad inside and introduce him to Mouse, who rewards him with a purr as he strokes her silky grey fur. After showing him around my little house and yard, we eat a bite of lunch and Dad declares it naptime. He tries to protest against taking my room but then gives in when I explain that I already moved my clothes and everything I'll need for the weekend from my room.

He's snoring in minutes.

I text Shane. *Hey. Dad made it. Want to come have dinner with us?*

His response is immediate. *You bet. Bring a salad?*

I send him a thumbs-up and spend the afternoon cooking. Mom's lasagna recipe is always worth the effort, and Dad may not have tasted it since her passing. Becky isn't known for her culinary skills. I even make a loaf of garlic bread from scratch, heating up the entire house in the process. When Dad gets up, he helps me put a fan in front of the screen door and figure out which windows to open and close to get cooler air flowing through the house.

Shane shows up right on time with a Caesar salad in hand. "It smells fantastic in here."

"I know!" I'm probably beaming a little too much. "Sorry for the heat. Hopefully it'll be worth it. We'll eat out on the deck."

Dad walks into the kitchen from where he'd been setting out plates on the patio table.

"Shane, this is my dad—Dr. Dale DeWitt." I speak a little louder than necessary, hoping Shane will take the hint and do the same. "Dad, this is Shane."

"Pleased to meet you, young man." Dad gives Shane a hearty handshake. "Diana tells me you're the fire chief. How does someone so young get to be a fire chief?"

Shane chuckles. "Not so young anymore, Dr. DeWitt."

"Oh, call me Dale."

"Shane's being modest," I jump in. "He's the youngest fire chief this city has had, and one of the youngest in the country."

"Good for you. My father was a firefighter."

"Yes, Diana told me."

Dad pats Shane's shoulder as the two of them walk out to the patio. "Bet you've seen a lot of tough stuff over the years."

"That I have. You, too."

"Oh sure. I try to dwell on the success stories."

Shane nods. "That's what I tell my team."

I follow with the lasagna and we all take seats. "Would you like to say grace, Dad?"

"Love to." Dad automatically reaches out his hands to hold both of ours like we always did growing up. He closes his eyes and waits.

I take Dad's hand and give Shane an apologetic grin. He grins back, taking Dad's other hand and reaching out to hold mine.

Whew.

I take his hand and listen to my father pray.

"Lord, thank you for bringing me safely here, for this wonderful day. Forgive me for not coming sooner. Thanks for this chance to spend time with my beautiful princess and thank you for the wonderful meal she's prepared. Please bless it to our bodies' use. Amen."

My face feels like it must be every shade of red under the sun as I glance at Shane and see his ear-to-ear grin directed straight at me.

"Let's dig in," I say, managing to distract the men with food.

They both eat with gusto, Dad praising my efforts to the point of embarrassment and Shane complaining that he won't be able to move.

As if. Shane is the fittest forty-year-old I know. He never misses a workout at the gym and spends his days off hiking or kayaking. In the winter, he plays on a recreational hockey team *and* a basketball team. Sports is the one thing we don't share, and he rarely lets me live it down.

I clear the dishes, and when I return with brimming mugs of coffee the conversation has turned to professional interests. I sit quietly as the two men talk easily about their experiences.

When Dad goes inside to use the washroom, Shane watches him walk away before turning to me. "I'm impressed."

"With Dad?"

"Yeah. He's kept himself abreast of the latest methods to treat burn victims, plastic surgery, and all that."

I nod and take a sip of my coffee. "He reads a lot."

"I can tell. Is he equally interested in every specialty?"

"I'm not sure I know what you mean."

"I mean, could he carry on a conversation with anyone else just as well? About other areas of medicine?"

I hate to confess that I don't really know. "Not sure. He's a pretty smart guy."

"I like him."

I smile. "I like him, too."

When Dad returns, I begin to prod.

"Dad, I've been sharing your book with Shane. He was particularly interested in the fire story."

Dad nods. "I can understand that. Nasty business, that."

Shane leans in. "Did Lilly and Tommy ever confess?"

"Yeah, did William ever find out it was them?" I chime in. "Was restitution made?"

Dad holds up his coffee mug. "If we're going to be here long enough for me to answer all those questions, I'm gonna need a refill."

We move into the living room. Ten minutes later, settled in with a fresh cup of coffee, Dad is ready to start reading aloud the pages he scrawled on his flight. Mouse curls up beside him.

"Did I ever tell you what a smart student my mother was...?"

CHAPTER EIGHT

Lilly

1938

Graduation day finally arrived, a warm Thursday afternoon. From her vantage point on the gymnasium stage, Lilly had a clear view of her aunt and uncle's faces. Next to them sat Tommy's parents, beaming at their son and at Lilly.

She tried to still her shaking hands. She'd be delivering the salutatorian's address in a few moments. She and Tommy had written it together, the way they did most things these days. If only it was Tommy giving the speech, but rules were rules; she'd earned the second-top marks. Tommy might be more comfortable with public speaking, but he'd ranked somewhere in the middle of the class.

As predicted, William was the class valedictorian of 1938, meaning Lilly's speech would precede his. At least she wouldn't have to follow what was sure to be a highly polished and moving masterpiece.

When her name was called, she walked to the lectern and unfurled the rolled-up paper she'd been twisting in her hands. After reading the first paragraph covering all the usual thanks to parents, teachers, and fellow students, she finally glanced up at the assembled crowd. Her heart racing, she quickly looked down at her notes and kept reading.

"Many of you know that I was raised by my Uncle Henry and Aunt Margaret. Today I want to publicly thank them for giving me a home and caring for me as their own. I want to acknowledge their sacrifice and commitment. I hope to make them proud."

Then, all too aware of William's presence behind her, Lilly delivered the carefully constructed words that left her feeling like the biggest hypocrite in the world.

"We live in an age when we can no longer take kindness and goodness for granted. Read any newspaper and you'll see. Conflict abounds. War and rumors of war threaten our planet. Dark and destructive forces appear to be gaining ground. But each of us can make a difference. By being light in this world, by brightening our own little corner, each of us—working together—can accomplish far more good than evil.

"For myself, I believe my way to bring light to the world will be through the field of nursing. Specifically, I hope to serve those who suffer from burn wounds. I'm pleased to have been accepted into the St. Boniface School of Nursing for this fall. I know that Summervale High School, our community, the family in which I've been placed, have all prepared me for this work. I believe it is my calling and I want to encourage my classmates—indeed, all of you—to find your own and pursue it with all that is in you.

"I'd like to end with a quote from Florence Nightingale, who overcame everything life threw at her, including her parents' disapproval and the horrible conditions of war hospitals. She said, 'I attribute my success to this: I never gave or took any excuse.' May we all follow her example, by owning up to our mistakes and misdeeds, by continuing to move forward at any cost, and by always giving and expecting our personal best."

Lilly glanced up once more before returning to her seat as the crowd applauded.

Next, the principal called William up. Lilly swallowed hard as she watched him limp to the lectern and grip both sides with his hands. He carried no notes. He seemed to study the clock at the back of the room for a moment. Then he took a deep breath, followed by a scan of the crowd from left to right. A few people cleared their throats as though willing him to start. Lilly's heart pumped as emphatically as it had for her own speech until she worried the grads beside her could hear it.

Finally, William began. "My life changed on June 30, 1928. Ten years ago today. Most of you know the story, so I'll recap as briefly as possible for those who don't. I was eight years old, asleep in my bedroom, when our home caught on fire. I was the last rescued. I suffered severe burns to both my feet and legs, as well as damage to my lungs. We lost our home."

Lilly wished she could disappear, just slide into a crack on the floor. She didn't dare try to catch Tommy's eye. He was undoubtedly gritting his teeth, staring at the back of William's head, willing him to change the subject. She focused on her hands, forcing them to stay folded on her lap. She bit her lip and squeezed her eyes shut lest they give her away. Whatever she did, she would not look at William or scan the crowd for his family. But try as she might, she could not stop herself from listening intently as he continued.

"In the months following, I underwent many surgeries and skin grafts. I confess, there were days I was in so much pain I prayed to die. But today I can truthfully say I'm thankful I lived. I'm not glad this happened to me—I wouldn't wish it on anyone. But because of my suffering, I've learned something in my eighteen years that for many takes a lifetime. Suffering produces endurance. Endurance leads to character. I know that I am a stronger person today than I would have been had this not happened to me.

"Of course, I can only say that because of the support I received from so many. I wish to thank my parents first and foremost, for all they did for me. The doctors, nurses, therapists—too many to name. Thank you to this school and community—to my classmates, for your acceptance and encouragement."

Lilly bit her lip, recalling the classmates who had been mean to William. He'd been nicknamed Gimpy, and not just behind his back. Did he truly feel grateful or was he as big a hypocrite as she, saying words that were expected, that would paint him in a positive light?

"I'd especially like to thank Miss Connor, our school librarian. I'll never forget the day I returned to school after the fire, still on crutches, still in pain. I'd always loved books, so walking into the library felt like sanctuary to me. A selection of books had been laid out on a table for students to peruse. Miss Connor stepped toward me with six or seven other books in her hands.

"'William,' she said. 'I chose these for you. I think you'd like them. Tell me which three you want to start with and I'll put them in your bookbag for you so you can carry them easily.'

"At that point, our new teacher intervened. 'Those are far beyond Grade Four level,' she said.

"Miss Connor turned to the teacher and said, 'Why don't we let William decide what level he enjoys?'

"That day, Miss Connor became a hero to me. Books became more precious than ever. My lifeline. Miss Connor encouraged my love of reading and my thirst for knowledge. Her example motivated me to enter the field of library studies at university in the fall. I hope to continue to inspire young people and nourish a love of reading in future students like Miss Connor did for me. In many ways, she gave me my life back, or at least my reason to keep going."

William wrapped up his message with a Mark Twain quote: "The man who does not read good books is no better than the man who can't." He returned to his seat to a standing ovation. Clearly, the whole community admired him.

When the ceremonies ended and the class tossed their mortarboards into the air, the hugs and farewells began among her classmates.

Eventually, Lilly found herself face-to-face with William. She shook his hand. "Great speech, William. I'm glad you lived."

"Thanks. Me too." He leaned in and they exchanged an awkward hug before she continued down the line.

When she reached Tommy, he grasped her hand. "C'mon. Let's get out of here."

"Already?" Lilly scanned the crowded room.

"Hey, we've got our diplomas. A beautiful day. What more do we need? I want to spend it with my girl."

Lilly smiled and followed him out. "Party starts in an hour. We have to at least make an appearance."

"Why?"

"Tommy! It's our class. Our grad day will never come again. We can't just ditch everyone."

Something was eating Tommy, that much was clear.

"I don't see why." He wrapped one arm around her. "Let's go to the park."

"Don't be silly. We at least need to return our grad gowns." Lilly pulled him back toward the school and the crowd.

He tugged free from her, removed his gown, and tossed it to her. "Here. You can return mine. I'll pick you up at your house in an hour."

"Tommy, what's going on?" Lilly stood there, Tommy's rumpled black gown filling her arms. "Did William's speech get to you?"

Tommy stared at her. Finally, he turned to leave. "I'll see you later."

Lilly swallowed the lump forming in her throat and squeezed her eyes closed to stop the tears. She returned both gowns and found her aunt and uncle. Uncle Henry gathered her into a hug and told her he was proud. She returned his embrace, then turned to Aunty Margaret. Her aunt was already climbing into the car. Lilly got in the back seat and rode home in silence.

Twenty minutes later, Tommy arrived at the front door and walked Lilly back to his house where they got into his father's car. They waved to his parents and headed to the grad party hosted on a farm west of town, the home of one of their classmates. A bonfire was already burning as they pulled onto the yard.

"Should have known," Tommy muttered as he parked the car. "Sorry, Lil."

Lilly didn't need to ask what he meant. The sound of crackling flames had created anxiety in her for the last ten years. While Tommy had deliberately subjected himself to the smell of smoke, it had only brought back vivid and painful memories to Lilly.

"It'll be okay," she tried to reassure him. "If William can stand it, so can I."

Tommy let out a snort. "It's not the fire. It's William I can't stand being around."

Lilly closed her eyes a moment. "Listen, the dancing's about to start."

The barn doors stood wide open and the tuning of guitar, accordion, banjo, and fiddle reached their ears. The Prairie Dogs, three brothers and a cousin in their twenties, played for all the local dances.

Tommy looked her in the eyes. "William won't be dancing."

"I thought we agreed we'd never talk about this again. Now come on." Lilly threw open her car door and stomped toward the barn.

Immediately the smell of the bonfire assaulted her.

Push through it. Just keep pushing through it and eventually it will hold no power.

She walked past the fire and into the barn where she pulled Tommy into a clumsy swing dance and laughed as convincingly as she knew how.

By the third song, she'd danced with two other boys.

When she returned to Tommy, the smell of liquor escaped from him. Her eyes grew wide. "Where'd you get it?"

"C'mon." Tommy took her elbow and led her out of the barn and around the corner. He pulled a bottle from inside his jacket and handed it to her. "Here. Trust me, a few sips and the smoke won't bother you anymore."

• • •

Tommy and Lilly were the first to leave the party, though they didn't return to their own homes until nearly morning. In her quest to forget, Lilly clung to the only person who understood what she was feeling and experiencing. Tommy did the same.

Cling to one another they did. Far too much.

CHAPTER NINE

Diana

Just as Dad finishes reading his latest chapter, Shane's cellphone chirps.

"Sorry, guys, I need to check this. We're short-staffed tonight." He stands as he reads the text. "Gotta go. Sorry. Nice meeting you, Dr. DeWitt."

I follow him through the house. "Want your salad bowl?"

"I can get it another time."

"You just want me to wash it for you."

"You know it." He climbs into his car and rolls down the window. "Thanks for the great dinner."

"Hey, you off tomorrow? Why don't you join our little road trip to Jasper?"

Shane starts the engine and begins backing out of my driveway. "Sure, I can do that. I can help drive." He roars away with a grin.

The turkey. He knows I never let anyone drive my car.

Dad retires to my bedroom and I spend the rest of the evening typing up the chapter he just finished reading aloud, fixing mistakes as I go along. Dad must have been tired or distracted when he wrote this one. He spelled nearly every instance of the word *was* s-a-w, and he's mixed up his *there*s, *their*s, and *they're*s.

When I finish and turn out the lights, I realize a lamp is still on in the bedroom. I tap gently on the door.

"Dad? You still up?"

When there is no reply, I push the door open a crack. Dad has obviously removed his hearing aids and doesn't even notice me. He sits on the edge of the bed, writing furiously on a yellow pad.

I pull the door closed, anticipating the next chapter of Lilly's story, and hope he isn't overdoing it.

• • •

In the morning, I fill Mouse's food and water dishes to the brim. Dad and I load a cooler and other essentials into the trunk of my red Honda, then stop to pick up Carly first and then Shane. The two men take the back seat and Carly sits with me. I soon realize we should have done it the other way around. The old guy and the teenager both fall asleep despite the scenery that grows more outstanding with every passing kilometer.

Shane leans forward in his seat and speaks into my ear. "You two must have stayed up pretty late last night."

I catch his reflection in my rearview mirror. "Too late, probably. We're an hour behind Manitoba, so it feels even later for Dad. How was your night?"

Shane focuses out his window. "House fire. Somebody's backyard fire pit is too close to his house. My guys had it out by the time I got there, but I fined the homeowner bigtime for breaking the by-law."

"Damages?"

"Some. He'll need to replace siding and insulation on one side of his house, and I doubt his insurance will cover any of it, given the situation. Wiring is likely messed up, too. Hope he's learned his lesson before someone gets hurt."

Shane is big on people learning their lessons.

I just nod. Carly wakes up and the three of us play Road Bingo for a while, getting distracted on nearly every letter as we discuss the latest happenings at work or school or our favorite songs or events in the news. "What letter are we on?" and "Whose turn is it?" become the catchphrases of the day, punctuated with laughter that we try to stifle so as not to wake Dad.

The closer we get to the national park, the more wildlife we see. Shane spots an owl, a coyote, and half a dozen elk. Carly points out a moose in the distance.

Our bingo game is abandoned somewhere around the letter "O" when we encounter a black bear standing in the middle of the road. I hit the brake.

We stop and wait. Oncoming cars stop, too, until two lines of five or six cars face each other while the animal refuses to budge. Dad wakes up and identifies the bear as a female. Carly pulls out her phone and takes pictures through the windshield. Finally, a cub emerges from the trees to our left and catches up with its mother.

"Pull over." Shane starts opening his door before I'm safely parked on the shoulder and begins videoing the bears with his phone as soon as he's out.

How can a guy so keen on fire safety live so recklessly?

"Careful," Dad cautions.

But the animals carry on into the forest on the other side.

"Want to stretch your legs as long as we're stopped, Dad?" I open my own door and get out. So does Carly.

Stretching and yawning, Dad joins us.

"Have a good nap?" I yawn myself.

"You bet. Sounds like you could use one, though. I'm good to go now. Want me to drive awhile?"

Having Dad drive my car is the last thing I want, but how do I say so without hurting his feelings? Especially when he's right. I am clearly tired.

Carly holds up both palms. "Don't look at me. I plan to sleep the rest of the way. Also, I don't have a driver's license."

Shane comes to my rescue. "I can drive if you like."

Is that a devious grin below those mischievous eyes? The two men have me in a corner.

The car keys are still in my hand. To tease Shane, I hold them out as though offering them to Dad.

"Tell you what, Dad." I veer the keys toward Shane at the last second. "Why don't you sit up front while Shane drives and you two can chat while I snooze in the back?"

"Even better." Dad pats Shane's arm.

We carry on down the road with the new seating arrangement and Carly is asleep in minutes. I close my eyes, but my discomfort level with someone else in control of my vehicle won't let me sleep. The front seat conversation doesn't help.

"So, Shane, tell me about yourself. Did you grow up around here?"

"Always lived in Edmonton. You?"

"Oh, I started out in a little town in Manitoba. Got my education in Winnipeg and practiced there all my life. Married a nurse. She gave it up when the girls came along. What did your parents do?"

Shane clears his throat. "Dad was a carpenter and contractor. Retired now. He's remarried and moved to B.C. with his new wife."

"Did your mother pass away?"

Oh Dad. Don't go there. I should have warned him. I open one eye and see Shane fiddling with the air conditioning.

Finally, he answers. "We've lost touch. She and Dad divorced when I was eight."

"Oh." Dad nods his head slowly. "That's hard on a kid." He barely waits another breath before asking, "Suppose that's why you and my daughter are just friends? Too hard to commit?"

Dad, puh-lease! I want to stop him, but I've already been feigning sleep too long. Besides, if I'm honest, I want to hear the answer as much as Dad does. Maybe more.

Shane appears to take it in stride with a chuckle. "Could be."

"You don't have a girlfriend?"

Dad!

"No."

I really want to peek again but can't risk it.

"Don't you think you could see Diana as something more? She's a wonderful gal."

Good grief, Dad, really? No wonder I haven't invited you out here before.

"She is. She had great parenting, I bet."

Dad chuckles. "Her mother gets the credit."

"Did you always know you wanted to be a doctor?"

Whew. Shane is changing the subject. Darn.

"Not always, no."

"Can I ask you something?"

"Sure, ask away."

"Did you have much experience with mental illness? With patients, I mean."

"Oh sure, a little. Back in the day, they didn't have so many terms for it. People would suffer 'nervous breakdowns' and the like." Dad clears his throat. "In most cases, I referred people to a psychologist or psychiatrist. Some of them used electric shock treatments. Sometimes it helped, other times not. I saw a lot of changes in that field over the course of my career."

Shane lets the subject drop. Dad must take the hint because he quits asking awkward questions. Unless I miss it. I do manage to doze a little.

In Jasper, we enjoy a picnic of submarine sandwiches, carrot sticks, and grapes. We spend two hours hiking and enjoying the sights, with frequent breaks for cookies and trail mix. Carly takes selfies and posts them.

I love watching Dad revel in the beauty. I swallow a lump in my throat when he stands gazing at the mountain view, reciting from memory in a clear voice:

"I will lift up mine eyes unto the hills, from whence cometh my help. My help cometh from the Lord, which made heaven and earth."[1] He turns to Shane and me. "Psalm 121. Thanks for bringing me here. It's too wonderful for words."

I expect Dad to be worn out enough to sleep all the way home, but he surprises me. Shane asks him what made him decide to go into medicine.

"Oh, I'll give my mother credit for that," he says. "Honey, did I tell you she studied to be a nurse?"

"Well, you told us she was accepted into nursing school, but that's as far as we got. How did that go?"

Dad reaches into his backpack and pulls out the yellow pad he was writing on last night. "We'll probably end up dividing all this into two chapters, Princess." He leans toward Carly. "Could I prevail upon you to read this with your nice, clear, youthful voice?"

I guess Carly can't resist those charming blue eyes of Dad's.

"Sure, I'd love to." She takes the pages and stares at them. "This is in cursive."

I let out a guffaw.

"Seriously, I can't read cursive." Carly tries to decipher Dad's scrawl. "Is that... 'one'? No. 'Only'?" She shakes her head. "I really want to read this, but we'll be here all year. It's like a secret language."

Still laughing, I catch her reflection in the rearview mirror. "Don't feel too bad, Carly. Dad's penmanship isn't exactly calligraphy."

"Not sure I could read calligraphy either."

"Want me to have a go?" Shane reaches for the pages, but Dad snaps them away from Carly.

"Never mind," Dad says. "I can read it fine. You'll listen, right, Carly?"

"For sure I will."

Dad's voice is surprisingly clear as he catches us up on his latest installment.

CHAPTER TEN

Lilly

1938

After their indiscretion on grad night, Tommy and Lilly agreed it wouldn't happen again. Not the alcohol and not the sex. They kept their word about both until one night in late July. Alcohol wasn't a factor that time.

The following morning, Lilly visited the cemetery. She knelt by her mother's modest grave marker, feeling little connection to the names engraved on it.

Nora Sampson
June 16, 1902–August 5, 1923

Even in death, her mother's married name was not acknowledged. Were her parents even legally married? Below her mother's name was engraved "Baby Boy Sampson," with only one date.

Lilly did the math. She'd been three years old in August of 1923. She closed her eyes and tried to draw on her memory. Surely some image of her mother remained locked inside somewhere, but no matter how hard she tried, she came up with nothing. Nothing except for the one family photograph hanging in the hallway. The entire Sampson family had posed for a group portrait when Nora was around ten years old. Lilly pushed the image from her mind and let the quiet surroundings settle her… a gentle summer breeze stirring the trees along one side of the cemetery, birdsong pleasing her ears and the sun warming her face.

She'd visited this spot only a handful of times, all since the age of thirteen. Was it a deep-rooted longing for her mother that drew her or was it simply a place to discover her own thoughts and sort out her feelings before taking them anywhere else? A place to voice secrets that couldn't be shared elsewhere? She inhaled deeply before she began to speak in little more than a whisper.

"Hello, Mama. Sorry I don't come more often. I suppose it doesn't matter all that much to you. Can you even hear me? See me? Are you with God? I don't remember you at all. Maybe if you were here with us, I wouldn't even like you all that much. Maybe you wouldn't be the one I could confide in, but I like to think you would be. More likely... *you* wouldn't like *me* all that much. Not if you knew the stuff I've done. Especially now."

Lilly's shame prevented her from looking directly at the grave or the marker. She lifted her gaze toward the treetops, where two squirrels chased each other as though they hadn't a care in the world.

"You can be glad you're not here to see what a mess your daughter is making of her life. I keep making one stupid mistake after another. I know Tommy and I should not be doing what we're doing. We have to stop. He agrees, but we still do it. Why don't I have any self-control? It's as though there is some kind of tight cord binding me to him and I never feel close enough. So we get as close as two people can possibly get and then we only feel miserable afterward. At least I do.

"I'm relieved to be going off to school soon. I may not see Tommy for months. I'll miss him, but the forced separation will do us good. And the busyness."

• • •

One gorgeous August day, Lilly sat in her treehouse with *Physiology and Anatomy*, the last book from a stack of five, on her lap. Nursing school was starting in one week, and she'd be saying goodbye to everything and everyone familiar. Her treehouse had stood the test of time in sturdiness, though it felt far too small now.

Lilly sat on a pillow with another behind her back, perched beside the window where she could see Aunt Margaret's garden and the back door of Tommy's house. Long legs extended in front of her, her feet nearly reached the opposite wall.

She and Tommy had both kept busy, she at the grocery store and reading her textbooks, he at the hardware store and fire hall. He'd helped put out a few grass fires, usually set by people burning garbage on dry, windy days. Each time, he'd tell Lilly the story in meticulous detail until she tired of hearing it. Did he need to convince himself he was saving lives and homes? Redeeming himself? After reviewing each step of what happened, he'd talk about ways it could have gone better, how they could have acted more quickly or extinguished the fire faster. He always had an improvement plan for next time.

The night before Lilly was to leave for Winnipeg, Tommy planned a special farewell date. He told her to dress in her finest, which happened to be her graduation dress. She took time to sweep her hair up with combs and paint her nails red.

Uncle Henry whistled when she came out of her room. "Wow! That boy better be taking you somewhere fancy."

Tommy arrived with his usual shave-and-a-haircut knock before opening the door and sticking his head inside. "Howdy, all. Ready, Lil? You look great, by the way."

"Thank you. Yes, I'm ready." Lilly grabbed her purse from the bench by the front door and linked her arm in Tommy's. "You look very dashing yourself."

Uncle Henry walked over and placed his callused hand on the doorframe. "Don't stay out too late now. Big day tomorrow."

"I'll have her back in good time, Mr. Sampson."

• • •

But when Lilly tiptoed to her bedroom well past midnight, she knew her aunt and uncle would have no idea what time she'd come in. Even from the bottom of the stairs, she could hear them snoring softly. They trusted her and Tommy completely and would have gone to bed at their usual time.

They trusted too easily. Lilly and Tommy had blown it again.

• • •

By seven the next morning, the Sampson family was on their way to Winnipeg in Uncle Henry's car.

"Too bad Thomas has to work today." Uncle Henry smiled at Lilly. "You know he would have been welcome to ride along. Shucks, I would have welcomed the male company."

Lilly only grinned.

Aunty Margaret raised an eyebrow in Lilly's direction. "I'm surprised he wasn't over to say goodbye this morning."

"We decided to say our goodbyes last night. Thought it would be easier that way."

Lilly turned to look out the window. The full truth was, she and Tommy had agreed they wouldn't try to see each other this morning as a sort of penance for what they'd done. Now she regretted it, wishing he'd at least have waved from his window. Instead she'd ridden away from their neighborhood with an empty heart.

"You two will miss each other, but you'll be so busy," Aunty Margaret said. "You'll probably fall into bed exhausted every night and the time will go so fast."

"It'll be harder for Thomas." Uncle Henry nodded as he drove.

Lilly looked up at her uncle's reflection in the rear-view mirror. "What makes you say that?"

"Well, you have a whole new exciting adventure waiting for you. Lots to do and learn. New friends to make." Uncle Henry pulled out onto the highway headed for the city. "While nothing is really changing for Thomas except that *you* won't be around."

Lilly nodded. "I suppose. This is what he wants, though."

Aunty Margaret turned around and studied Lilly's face. "You don't seem very excited."

Lilly took a deep breath and let out a sigh. "Just nervous, I guess."

She could—and would—write to Tommy as much as time allowed. But she had to let go of the shame and regret and start fresh. Her long-held dream was finally coming true. She'd force herself to engage fully in every moment, to be grateful and give this opportunity all the effort it deserved.

"You're going to do just great." Uncle Henry's reassuring voice warmed Lilly's heart and added to her guilt at the same time. "I have no doubt that in three years we'll be attending your graduation and you'll be at the top of your class, with every hospital and clinic in Manitoba offering you a job."

Lilly laughed. Her heart's desire was still to work with burn victims, but she knew a lot could change in three years. She focused on fields ripe for harvest as they drove down the highway. Gradually, houses became closer together until they were surrounded by the city. Uncle Henry steered the car over the bridge spanning the Red River. Lilly could feel her heart racing as they continued south on Tache Avenue, past the magnificent St. Boniface Cathedral. She stared up at the gorgeous architecture, wondering if there would be time to visit while she was here and whether they welcomed non-Catholics.

Suddenly, the hospital loomed before them and Uncle Henry pulled up to the main doors. He turned off the engine and reached out to touch Aunty Margaret's arm when he saw she was reaching for the door handle. "This might be our last chance to say a prayer with Lilly."

Aunty Margaret nodded.

Uncle Henry turned in his seat. "How you holdin' up back there, Lil?"

"I'm fine." Could he hear her heart thumping?

"I'll pray." Uncle Henry reached back and held Lilly's hand in one of his while he grasped Aunty Margaret's with the other. "Lord, this is a big day for our Lilly. Thank you for calling her into this noble profession. I pray that you will fill her with good health, with peace, with the knowledge of your presence and your hand on her life. Help her to sleep well at night so she has all the energy she needs for her studies. Help her to learn well. Give her strength, dear God. Bless her. In Jesus's name, Amen."

"Amen." Was Aunty Margaret actually wiping away a tear?

Lilly whispered an amen of her own. "Thank you," she murmured.

The three of them piled out, and Uncle Henry and Aunty Margaret helped her carry her two suitcases inside where a nun was directing traffic. "Welcome here, I'm Sister Marie-Irene. Orientation is through those doors. You'll receive your room assignment and the day's schedule inside. Please say your goodbyes here."

Lilly turned to accept a warm hug from her uncle, a stiff one from her aunt. At least it was something. "Thanks for everything."

"Be sure to write." Aunty Margaret swiped another tear from her face.

"If they don't keep you too busy," Uncle Henry added, blinking hard. "C'mon, Margaret, let's get out of everyone's way."

The pair fought their way back through the doors they'd entered. Lilly picked up both suitcases and headed into a big room filled with luggage and at least two dozen girls who all appeared to be around her age.

• • •

By ten o'clock that night, Lilly and her new classmates had received a tour of the hospital, their classroom, the kitchen, and the dorm. She'd smiled to hear the cathedral bells ring at six. She'd eaten her supper with gusto, been introduced to eight or ten girls whose names she could hardly keep straight. Her assigned room was just big enough for a single bed, small dresser, and desk. Her head spun with everything they'd been told in orientation. More books had been added to her pile. The rules had been reviewed once again, with many more than Lilly remembered from her interview meeting. Words like *physiology* and *bacteriology* swam in her head, along with the wall plaque she'd stopped to read in the students' common area:

I pledge myself to a life of personal purity and womanly dignity and to the maintenance of the high standard of my profession. I pledge unswerving loyalty to the best traditions of my Alma Mater, and I promise never to take or administer harmful drugs or to become a guilty party to any criminal attempt upon human life.

I pledge perfect fidelity and conscientious obedience to the directions and instructions of the physicians or surgeons under whom I am serving and I will devote myself conscientiously, painstakingly, and wholeheartedly to the care of the patients whose very lives are committed to my care.

Lastly, I pledge myself to keep sacred and inviolable whatever matters of an intimate nature may come to my knowledge in the home where I am called to serve.

Lilly read the pledge over twice. She'd be expected to recite it aloud on graduation day. Could she truly promise such excellence, given her track record?

CHAPTER ELEVEN

AUTUMN 1938

September blurred into October and then November. Lilly loved her classes, loved working on the wards and practicing what she was learning. But the pace was killing her. How did the other girls find time to socialize and create disturbances, playing practical jokes on one another or planning popcorn parties in their common area? She'd spent every spare moment studying and barely found time to write home—one week to Tommy, the next to her aunt and uncle.

In Tommy's last letter, he'd complained about the infrequency of her letters. One Sunday night before lights out, she scribbled out an extra letter for him.

Dearest Tommy,

I'm sorry I can't write more often. I'll try to do better, but I can't make any promises. This is much harder than I expected. The other girls all seem to be making friends and keeping up, but I don't know how they manage. By the time I finish my shift each day, it's all I can do to get my required reading done before lights out. Once or twice,

I've fallen into bed with my clothes on. The other girls are friendly, especially a tall blonde named Sheila. I don't think she ever sleeps. She's tried a few times to include me in dorm shenanigans, but I think she may have given up on me.

In early November, the girls lined up for their monthly weigh-in. After Lilly stepped off the scale, Sister Marie-Therese invited her into her office. Lilly took a seat, expecting the woman to sit across the desk. Instead the sister stood leaning on her desk only inches away.

"How is everything going for you, Lilly?"

"Fine, Sister. Is… there a problem?" She'd scored high on all her tests so far. Were there issues with her practical work?

"I sure hope not. Your performance has been superior. I've just noticed a few things. You're usually alone when I see you in the hallways or at meals. Have you made friends?"

Was making friends a requirement? Lilly squirmed. "Well… I think I'm getting along fine with everyone. The girls all seem very nice. I guess I prefer to spend my time studying."

"Are you happy?"

"Sure."

The nun studied her face as though looking for hidden clues. "Anything you want to tell me?"

Lilly shrugged. What was the nun expecting of her? "I really enjoy my shifts and the classes. I'm learning so much!"

"You seem tired."

Lilly took a deep breath and let it out slowly. Was it that obvious? "It's challenging, but I'm sure my energy will pick up once I'm used to the routine."

Sister Marie-Therese looked at the chart she held in her hand. "You've gained weight."

Lilly laughed softly. "My compliments to the cook."

The nun did not smile in return. "You actually eat very little."

Lilly swallowed hard. Were they really being watched that closely? She *had* been eating lightly. "Maybe I need to eat more. Maybe that will help get me through the day with more energy."

"Maybe. I'd like you to see Dr. Watson for a complete physical, just in case. In the meantime, I need to ask: are your monthlies regular since you arrived?"

Lilly's face grew warm. "Um…" She had not had a period since school started. She'd been too busy to even notice. "No, I… I guess they haven't."

This time it was the nun's turn to take a deep breath. "In that case, I have to ask: Lilly, is there any chance you could be pregnant?"

Lilly stared at the rosary clipped to the nun's habit. Pregnant? What should she say? Pregnancy was grounds for immediate dismissal. What if she were? How could she return home to Aunty Margaret and Uncle Henry, after all they'd sacrificed?

Better to lie. Slowly, she shook her head.

"Is that a no?"

Lilly tried to nod, but she felt tears trying to escape. She squeezed her eyes shut tightly and opened them again. The room blurred.

"If… a student told you it was *possible*… would she be dismissed? Even if she *wasn't* pregnant?"

The nun stared at Lilly so long and so hard, she regretted asking the question.

Finally, Sister Marie-Therese cleared her throat. "Not necessarily. There is certainly room for grace, provided her misdeeds stayed in the past, especially if she showed the kind of promise on the ward that you have. But we are not a reform school."

With that, she walked around her desk and picked up the phone.

Lilly focused on the view beyond the window. Light snow was dusting the ground. *Oh God, if you care at all for my future, please don't let it be true. I'll do anything. I'll become a nun. I'll be the best nurse and the best nun that ever walked the earth, just please don't let me be pregnant.*

Sister Marie-Therese hung up the phone and handed Lilly a note. "You're to report to Dr. Watson's office at two o'clock, then come back to see me tomorrow at the same time."

• • •

By the end of the following day, Lilly was on a train headed home to Summervale. Her suitcases jiggled in the overhead baggage compartment. Her textbooks had been left behind. She was never to darken the doors of St. Boniface School of Nursing again. Her dream was over, and her heart was numb.

• • •

At the Summervale train station, no one awaited her because no one knew she was coming. She left her bags with the stationmaster and walked to the cemetery, clutching her coat around her against the cold November breeze. Not a tear had fallen since Sister Marie-Therese had delivered her grave confirmation that Lilly was pregnant and must pack her bags immediately. Now the wind stung her eyes, making them water. Priming the pump. By the time she reached her mother's grave, a torrent of tears had escaped, and she fell in a heap in front of the cold, hard headstone.

"I'm in trouble, Mama." She paused for a deep breath. "I'm going to have a baby."

This time, no tweeting birds joined the sound of her voice.

"How could I have let this happen? It's not like I don't know better. I never should have been alone with Tommy, never should have shared that bottle the first time. It clouded my judgment. I should have stopped him right from the first sip. The first touch. Why was I so stupid?"

Lilly felt only disgust for herself. Disappointment.

"What will Aunty Margaret and Uncle Henry say? I'm so embarrassed, Mama. And what about Tommy? I don't know what to do."

Would Tommy offer to marry her? He'd been working hard Monday through Friday at the hardware store, Saturdays at the fire hall. As a volunteer fireman, he did not receive any compensation until called out for a fire—but those were few and far between. He'd be at the store now. Should she go straight over there and tell him?

"What's going to happen to me, Mama?" Would she die in childbirth like her mother had? What if the baby survived and she did not? "I don't want someone else raising my child. Sorry, but that's the truth. I'll never be good enough for Aunty Margaret, especially now."

Lilly had heard about other girls who'd become pregnant and were sent away for half a year. They would return to school with sad faces, academically behind their classmates, out of the social loop. Whispered rumors followed them everywhere. At least she was out of high school. Maybe it wouldn't be so bad for her.

"Just tell me what to do, Mama. Or God. Somebody? Just tell me the next step to take." Lilly closed her eyes again, allowing the tears to make their way down her face. She lost track of how long she sat there, listening for something she wasn't sure she'd ever hear. Then, with surprising clarity, like the most distinct thought she'd ever had, came the words: *Tell Tommy.*

• • •

"Are you sure?" Tommy's brown eyes begged Lilly to admit she was joking, even if her words were anything but funny.

Lilly nodded. She'd gone to the hardware store, arriving just as Tommy was getting off work. After his initial shock at seeing her, he'd carried her suitcases to the park where they now sat.

"You already told your aunt and uncle?" Tommy ran a hand through his hair.

"No. I… I wanted you to be the first to know."

"I gotta let this sink in." Tommy gazed into the distance for what felt like an eternity to Lilly, then turned and stared at her. "I'm sorry, Lil."

Lilly shrugged. "It takes two."

"I know, but… you're the one who has to give up school. And… and… how *are* you? Are you feeling all right?"

She nodded. "Been tired and a bit sick in the mornings but it always goes away, so… the doctor said I'm in good health."

"When—?"

"Late May." May seemed a long time away.

Tommy picked up a multicolored rock and shifted it from hand to hand. "Do you think your aunt and uncle will be mad?"

Lilly let out a sigh. "Disappointed, for sure." Unable to look directly in his face, Lilly stared at Tommy's hands. His knuckles were turning white as he gripped the rock.

"What about school? Your nursing plans?"

Lilly pressed her lips together, then drew in a deep breath. "This isn't necessarily the end of that forever. School will just… have to wait, I guess. Indefinitely. I can't think about that right now."

"Let's get married."

He said it so abruptly, Lilly thought she'd heard him wrong at first. Her face must have reflected her confusion.

"I'm serious, Lil. It's only right. For once, let's take our wrongs and make them right. I'll get another job so we can afford a place of our own." Tommy stood and began pacing in front of the bench. "We'll get married as soon as possible. Take some time to, you know, get used to each other. And then we'll welcome a little baby. We'll be good parents, too. We will!"

Lilly gave him a half-hearted smile. He was being sweet, but was it what he really wanted?

"Unless you don't want to. But Lilly, I'll support you, whatever you decide." He sat beside her and leaned in. "You know that, right? I'm not going to run off."

This brought tears to Lilly's eyes. "Like my father?"

"I'd never do that, Lil. We've been together through thick and thin already. We shouldn'ta done what we did, I know that. But it's done now. I want to make it right."

"I've been going back and forth about it all afternoon. What about adoption? I mean, I was adopted, and... well... I could have done worse."

"Could you go back to school after?"

"Not to St. Boniface. But—I dunno, maybe somewhere."

"Yeah." Tommy turned the rock over in his hands. "But wouldn't we always wonder? You know... where he is, who's raising him? What does he look like?"

"Or her."

"Yeah. Or her."

Lilly wiped away the tear that had reached her jawline. "That would be hard. Uncle Henry would be even more disappointed, I think, if we gave it up. He loves babies."

Tommy let out a big sigh. "Maybe this is our chance to redeem ourselves. For everything."

Lilly wasn't sure that was how things worked, but if it would relieve their load of guilt even a little, it would be worth it.

"I can't imagine giving a baby away for someone else to raise." She certainly couldn't imagine raising one alone, either. Or the stares and comments sure to come her way before and after the baby arrived. She could, however, imagine herself married to Tommy. "We're already bound to one another, Tommy. Aren't we?"

"Yes." He nodded slowly. "So... are you saying that's what you want to do? Get married?"

A bubble of something unfamiliar stirred inside her. Was it joy? "Well, if you call that a marriage proposal, it might just be the sorriest one I ever heard."

"Oh, that's what you're needing, is it?" Tommy tossed the rock to the ground and reached into his left pocket. "Well, darlin'. If I'd known I was going to get engaged to be married today, I'da dressed up proper and gotcha a ring." His phony accent made Lilly laugh.

The contents of his pocket lay in his hand and he studied them: a nickel and two pennies, a screw, a few inches of string, and a key to the hardware store. His other pocket yielded only a handkerchief. Stuffing everything else back into his pockets, Tommy held the string in his hand and got down on one knee in front of Lilly. She stifled a giggle.

"Lillian Grace Sampson, I would be grateful if you would do me the honor of becoming my wife and allowing me to tie this string around your finger. Will you marry me?"

Lilly could think of nothing she'd rather do. It felt wonderful to be asked. To feel wanted, cared for. Tommy wouldn't let her down.

"Yes!" With a huge smile, she threw her arms around him and pulled him to his feet. She held out her ring finger and let him tie the string around it. "So... where do we go?"

Tommy held her hand in both of his. "What do you mean?"

"To get married. We're just going to run off and get married, right? Tell everyone when we get back, so they can't try to stop us?"

The confusion on Tommy's face made him look like a little boy again. He shook his head. "That's not a good plan, Lil. I can't do that to you. You deserve a wedding."

"But—"

"No buts. Who's going to try to stop us?"

"I don't know. Your parents? Mine?"

"They won't once they hear the whole story. And if someone tries, we'll figure out a way to make it happen without them. I want you to have a wedding, Lilly. A proper one, with a minister and everything. Flowers and... candles... and a real ring. I'll get you one tomorrow."

Lilly smiled. She was going to be a bride. A wife. Maybe not a nurse like she'd planned, but perhaps even that someday. Meanwhile, she was going to be a mother. *A mother.* What could be better?

• • •

That evening, Tommy's parents joined him and Lilly in the Sampsons' living room. Aunty Margaret had recovered from her initial shock at Lilly's return and accepted Lilly's lie that she'd been granted a weekend pass. She served tea, a bewildered look still on her face. The two men appeared uncomfortable.

Once everyone was seated, Uncle Henry cleared his throat and looked at Tommy. "Well, young man, you're the one who called this meeting. Wanna fill the rest of us in or do we need to guess?"

"No, sir, I'll get right to it. As you know, Lilly and I have been friends for as long as we can remember."

"A little more than friends these last few years, I'd say." Aunty Margaret looked at Tommy over the top of her glasses.

"Right. And, well... I've asked Lilly to marry me and she said yes. We want you all to be the first to know."

The room grew silent. It seemed interminable, although it was probably only a few seconds before someone spoke. Tommy's mother went first.

"Oh my!" She clapped her hands together in front of her. "Well... I can't say I'm too surprised. I figured you two were destined to be together. But... so soon?"

"You'll have a long engagement, of course," Aunty Margaret added. "Get married after nursing school?"

Tommy shook his head, but his father chimed in next. "Long engagements are never a good idea. I appreciate that you two want to be together, believe me. But what's your rush? You have your whole lives—"

"Now, Fred. Have you forgotten how young we were when—"

"No, I have not forgotten." Fred DeWitt turned to his wife. "But times have changed. These kids have careers to look forward to. Lilly has three years until graduation, am I right?"

"I agree with Fred," Uncle Henry said. "Long engagements only make it harder to resist temptation."

"Henry!" Aunty Margaret's face turned a vivid shade of red.

Lilly imagined her own must be every color of the rainbow. She focused on her feet.

"I'm just saying..." Uncle Henry examined his knuckles. "Well, we were young once, too. I think we all know how hard it can be to wait for... for, um... the privileges that go with marriage and the... um..."

"It's too late for that." Lilly blurted it out before she could rethink it. "I'm having a baby. Next May."

She continued to stare at her shoes as perspiration trickled down her sides. Aunty Margaret's clock ticked on the mantel. Was anybody going to say anything? Had they not heard? Had she even said it aloud or only imagined it?

Tommy came to her rescue. "It's true." He cleared his throat. "Lilly was asked to leave school as soon as the doctor confirmed it. I want to do right by her. And the baby. We want to get married as soon as possible."

"Oh." Mrs. DeWitt raised a hand to her mouth. "Oh, Thomas." She didn't say, *How could you?* But Lilly could hear it in her tone.

"That's different then," her husband said. "It's disappointing, son, but… I'm glad you want to do the right thing. I'm sure the Sampsons agree."

Neither her aunt nor her uncle had made a peep. Lilly couldn't bring herself to look at them.

Finally, Aunty Margaret spoke with a tremor in her voice. "You… you got *kicked out*? What about your scholarship?"

Lilly's voice was barely above a whisper. "I'm so sorry."

Tommy leaned toward them, his hands clasped between his knees. "I hope you'll give us your blessing, Mr. and Mrs. Sampson. I'll do my best to take good care of Lilly and I won't… I won't allow anyone to disgrace her."

"You already have."

Lilly tried to form words to defend Tommy, but Uncle Henry jumped in.

"Well then, I guess we're having a wedding. You have our blessing."

Lilly finally raised her head. Uncle Henry sent her a sad smile.

Mrs. DeWitt reached across and placed one hand on Tommy's knee. "This isn't what we wanted for you, not yet." She took a deep breath. "But—" She nodded slowly.

Tommy wrapped a protective arm around Lilly and rested his hand on her shoulder. "It'll be okay, Lilly."

His mother inhaled deeply and let it out slowly. "A baby is always a precious gift." She looked at Aunty Margaret. "We're going to be grandparents together!"

Aunty Margaret let out a long, slow breath and nodded. "Can't say I didn't see this coming. We'll make the best of it."

• • •

The six of them talked and planned until midnight. By the end of the evening, a wedding date had been set for three weeks away—Saturday, December 3. The ceremony would be small, the reception in the church basement. Uncle Henry agreed to arrange it with the pastor. Mrs. DeWitt would bake the wedding cake. Aunty Margaret wanted to sew Lilly's wedding dress—but not white, of course.

"We'll shop for fabric tomorrow, Lilly." She began gathering cups. "Think about what color you'd like to wear. Blue suits you."

Mr. DeWitt knew of an apartment one of his co-workers had available for rent above his garage. "I'll check into that first thing tomorrow morning. Might be perfect for a young couple just starting out. And close to Danny's Hardware. You could walk to work in ten minutes, Thomas."

"I'd appreciate that, Dad. And I'm sure I can get work on a farm, too. Mr. Arnold has been asking if I had any time to spare. That'll bring in some extra money." Tommy turned toward Uncle Henry, who nodded his approval.

Lilly placed a hand on her abdomen as she regarded each of the others in the room. Somehow it all seemed a little too easy.

Chapter Twelve
Diana

Well, well. My father was "conceived out of wedlock," as they used to say. Funny what a scandal those situations created back then. It still doesn't explain the mystery in my DNA test, though.

Dad is completely exhausted when we reach home, and to be honest so am I. I give Mouse some much-needed attention and she settles at my feet. Still, I lie awake thinking about my grandmother and how different things were in her day. I think about Lilly giving up her dream, her education. I sure hope she considered it worth it.

When I finally fall asleep, I have the wedding dream again. As usual, it ends with Ryan taking the pen to sign the register and I wake up, my head pounding.

• • •

In the morning, I suggest to Dad that he'd be a lot more comfortable if we attend the early church service, the one where they stick to the hymnbooks and pass silver offering plates down the rows.

He raises an eyebrow. "I want to go to whichever one you normally attend."

"You do?" I set a plate of toast and a cup of coffee in front of him.

"I'm here to see your life, Princess. Your world. I'm not here to be comfortable."

Oh, how I love that man. "All right then. But you might want to turn your hearing aids off until the sermon time."

• • •

The music from the worship band is already thumping in the church lobby as we enter. I introduce Dad to a few friends and we make our way to the auditorium to find seats near the middle of the room.

"Will Shane be joining us?" Dad shouts over the music, cupping a hand over his ear as he awaits my answer.

I lean in. "It's Canada Day. The fire department has to supervise the fireworks setup and all that. He'll be tied up all day and most of the night."

Dad nods. "Bummer."

"Don't feel sorry for him. Shane loves that stuff."

The worship leader invites us to stand and join in the singing. I've come to rely on this Sunday morning worship time to help wash away the cares of my week and prepare my heart for what God might want to say to me.

As wonderful as it is to have my father next to me, I'm soon focusing on my heavenly Father. He has been truly good to me. I raise my hands in gratitude for all his blessings and let the music wash over my heart and soul.

The last song repeats its tagline for what probably feels like the fortieth time to Dad, and I once again become aware of him, thinking he might be annoyed. However, when I turn toward him my father is singing along wholeheartedly. Eyes closed and tears escaping down his cheeks, he raises his face in humble and honest worship.

The speaker is one of the female members of our pastoral team, and again I wonder if Dad will find this hard to get used to. He certainly didn't grow up with women in the pulpit. Nor did I. But when I glance over at him a few minutes into her sermon, Dad has pulled out a pen and is taking notes on his program.

The scripture displayed on the projection screens is 2 Chronicles 7:14 and the pastor has us read it aloud together: *"…if my people, who are called by my name, will humble themselves and pray and seek my face and turn from their wicked ways, then I will hear from heaven, and I will forgive their sin and will heal their land."*[2]

She pauses a moment to let it sink in. "If ever our land needed healing, it's now."

She lists sobering statistics from across the country for crime, suicide, drug addiction, poverty, teen pregnancies, abortions, divorce, mental illness, and other diseases on the rise.

"Jesus called us, his church, to be his answer to our world." She speaks with passion, rising from the stool on which she's been perched, Bible in hand. "And the four-step recipe is given right here in this verse."

She outlines what it might mean for us to follow the four steps. To truly humble ourselves. To pray. To seek God's face. To turn from our wicked ways, and she isn't talking about a long list of external don'ts we've been taught to avoid. She challenges us to look inward, at the judgment, anger, pride, and envy we carry around. The prejudices we ignore in our own hearts.

"Jesus hasn't called us to sit in our comfy pews and sing pretty songs while the world suffers and destroys itself," she says. "He tells us, 'Even as the Father has sent me, I'm sending *you*.'

"We're going to close today by singing our national anthem. Did you know that *O Canada* is one of the few national anthems in the world written as a prayer? The first verse, the one we all know by heart, is not obviously a prayer until you reach the chorus: 'God, keep our land glorious and free.' But are you familiar with verse four?"

The words come up on the screen:

> Ruler Supreme, who hearest humble prayer,
> Hold our dominion in thy loving care.
> Help us to find, O God, in Thee
> A lasting, rich reward;
> As waiting for the better day
> We ever stand on guard...

"In a moment, we're going to sing this verse together, along with the one we all know. The words will be on the screen, and please agree in prayer as you sing. If ever there were a prayer for our country, this would be it. *O Canada* in both official languages gives testimony to our rich spiritual heritage. I am saddened that too often we forget our roots. We have been given so much, the best of natural resources and freedoms others can only dream of. We remember the valor that bought us this freedom, but we ignore the 'steeped in faith' part. Yet etched into the Peace Tower on Parliament Hill in Ottawa are three verses from the Bible."

A photo comes up on the screen, and she reads aloud the inscription.

"'He shall have dominion from sea to sea.' I can think of no more appropriate prayer this Canada Day than that. God, have dominion from sea to sea."

We sing through both verses while beautiful videos from across our country roll behind the words. When the final "We stand on guard for thee" fades, Dad and I are not the only ones wiping away tears.

• • •

After church, we take part in various activities and celebrations around city parks. We buy burgers from a food truck, listen to bands, watch a magician and at least three different ethnic dance troupes. Everything culminates in fireworks at the legislature grounds at sundown. By the time we head home, the clock is inching toward midnight.

Dad buckles his seatbelt and relaxes against the headrest. "Too bad Shane couldn't join us today."

"Dad." Seriously, between him, Becky, our co-workers... when will they let up? "You and Shane are obsessed with each other. He asked if he could come along when I take you to the airport tomorrow."

"He did?" Dad is all smiles.

"He did. I said no. I want you all to myself."

Dad feigns complete outrage. "You had me to yourself all day today!"

I start laughing so hard that I almost miss my turn-off. "I'm just kidding, Dad. He's meeting us at my place at eleven."

"Oh, good. I like that young man."

"Well, the feeling is mutual. Not sure how you managed it, but—"

"Oh, it's just my natural charm. You've got it, too, ya know."

I snort. "Right."

"Now tell me the truth. Why are the two of you so bent on staying just friends? What are you afraid of?"

I don't know what Shane is afraid of. If anything, he's one of the most courageous men I know. But as for me, well... I pause until Dad begins staring at me over the top of his glasses.

"I can't speak for Shane," I say.

"Fair enough."

"Although... his parents' marriage failed. Maybe he knows we've got a good thing going as friends and he's afraid to mess it up."

"But doesn't he realize the best marriages are when the couple start out as friends?"

I shrug.

He pushes some more. "So what's *your* excuse? Your parents had a great marriage, if I do say so."

I pull into my driveway and stop the car. "I think you know what I'm afraid of."

Dad pauses, staring out the windshield. "It was a long time ago, Princess."

"Does that change anything?"

"Seems to me you've made an agreement with the devil."

"An agreement with the devil? Don't you think that's just a tad dramatic?" I shut off the engine and unbuckle.

Dad seems in no hurry to unbuckle or get out. "No. I don't. I think you agreed with him when he whispered that you could never trust another man, never give your heart away again. And you've been keeping that agreement, collecting evidence as you go along."

"Evidence?"

"Evidence that the agreement is worth keeping. Once we make up our minds about something, it's not that difficult for us to turn every little thing into evidence to support our position. But sometimes agreements need to be broken."

I sigh as I gather my purse and phone. "Dad. You're meddling."

• • •

Dad and I take turns in the bathroom, showering away the heat of the day, mosquito repellent, and sunscreen. When I come out in my bathrobe and slippers, I expect Dad to be sound asleep. Instead he's made a pot of herbal tea and even arranged a few cookies on a plate.

"Thought you might be ready for some more of Mother's story." He sets the cookie plate on the coffee table and settles himself in the armchair. Mouse quickly hops up to join him.

"You sure? I thought you'd be pooped." I notice his yellow pad and a pen on the coffee table.

"I'm fine if you're willing to do the writing." He strokes the cat, who immediately purrs like a little motorboat. "Besides, I'm heading home tomorrow. Whatever we can't get through tonight will need to be sent in more emails."

"I'm all ears." I stick a cookie in my mouth and grab my laptop. "But I'm using this. It's faster."

Dad talks for another hour or more, which I'd have never predicted. But then, I would never have guessed the next chapter of Lilly's journey.

CHAPTER THIRTEEN

Lilly

WINTER 1938–1939

"They say rain on your wedding day is good luck, so maybe snow is too." Aunty Margaret gazed out the kitchen window in her pink chenille bathrobe, curlers in her hair, hands clutched around a coffee cup.

Lilly leaned against the bathroom door in case she needed to return for one more bout of morning sickness, grateful her uncle had installed the indoor plumbing last year. The blustery day did not bolster her confidence.

Aunty Margaret turned toward her. "Want any breakfast?"

At the mere word, Lilly felt a new wave of nausea. She gripped the doorframe and held on, shaking her head.

"Maybe you should go lie down for a bit. There's plenty of time to get ready."

Lilly only nodded and returned to her room where the pretty royal blue dress hung on the window curtain rod, waiting. The wedding had been set for eleven o'clock, to be followed by a light lunch for around twenty guests. From there, she and Tommy would go to their new apartment, already outfitted with a hodgepodge of hand-me-down furnishings. A bridal shower had been hastily thrown together by the church ladies. After the last gift was opened, Lilly had stood to thank everyone. Though she felt genuinely grateful for the dishes, towels, and other household goods, the questions remained. What would they think if they knew? How many would be counting the months from her wedding date until her baby's birth?

Aunty Margaret and Mrs. DeWitt had helped her clean the apartment. Yesterday she'd made up the bed with new sheets and hand-embroidered pillowcases. The quilt under which she and Tommy were to sleep had apparently belonged to Lilly's mother. Aunty Margaret had tucked it away and saved it for her all these years.

By nine-thirty, Lilly felt fine. While she'd have preferred a sunny day, the dismal weather was probably all she deserved. Or maybe it truly was good luck.

When she went downstairs for her bath, she ate the toast and tea Aunty Margaret gave her. Then she scrubbed herself from top to bottom in the claw-footed tub. She'd gone to see her local physician, Dr. Ramsey, who confirmed the pregnancy and noted her weight gain despite morning sickness. Once that passed, he'd said, she would start to see a bump in her belly, and not long after that feel movements of the baby.

Perhaps it would start to seem real when she felt the baby move.

Thirty minutes later, Lilly stood in front of Aunty Margaret's big dresser-top mirror.

"Beautiful," Uncle Henry announced from the doorway. "Absolutely beautiful."

Lilly smiled at the image before her. Her blond tresses were swept up and pinned to the top of her head in a mass of tight curls. Her face glowed with the help of a little face powder and a light touch of rouge and lipstick. The dress pattern she and Aunty Margaret had chosen wasn't the most stylish, but its clever design would allow room for expansion and the shiny blue fabric accentuated Lilly's eyes. The hem hung just below her knee, and on her feet she wore the black Mary Jane shoes she'd bought new for graduation.

"Now then, seams are straight." Aunty Margaret almost seemed to be enjoying this as she double-checked the back of Lilly's stockings. "The dress is your something new *and* your something blue. We need something old... and something borrowed." She opened the jewelry box on top of her dresser. Then she pulled out a delicate chain from which hung a single blue gemstone in the shape of a teardrop. She smiled as she held it up for Lilly to see. "This is old. My mother received it from my father long before I was born. I'm glad you agreed to a blue dress, because I think this would go perfectly. What do you say?"

A tear escaped and slid unchecked down Lilly's cheek. "Oh, Aunty Margaret. It's beautiful. I don't deserve it."

"Well, I'm not giving it to you to keep, silly girl." Her aunt cleared her throat. "I want it back after the wedding. It can be your 'something borrowed,' too."

Lilly laughed and allowed Aunty Margaret to fasten the clasp at the back of her neck. They stood side by side, gazing into the mirror. The necklace really did complement the dress and complete the outfit.

"Perfect." Aunty Margaret gave one firm nod and turned to tidy the room.

Uncle Henry wiped away a tear. "And I don't want to hear any more talk about deserving or not deserving. You're our girl and we want the best for you."

"Thank you." Lilly's voice cracked.

"Now come on, ladies. Thomas will think Lilly chickened out if we don't get on our way."

• • •

Twenty minutes later, Lilly walked down the short aisle of Summervale Community Church clutching an enormous bouquet of Aunty Margaret's dried hydrangea blossoms in her left hand, her right looped through Uncle Henry's arm. The front two benches on each side were filled with immediate family of the bride and groom. The remaining pews sat empty.

Front and center stood the pastor, Bible in hand. Beside him waited Tommy in his graduation suit, tall and handsome and shaking. When their eyes met, Lilly gave him the biggest smile she could, and he appeared to relax.

The pastor's wife sat at the pump organ, pounding out "Here Comes the Bride." When they reached the front, the song finished abruptly and long before its ending.

"Dearly beloved," the pastor began. "We are gathered here today to unite this man and this woman in holy matrimony."

Lilly tried to stay focused, though her mind drifted in a thousand directions. How was Tommy holding up? Was he glad this day had come? Were they going to be all right?

"Who gives this woman to be married to this man?"

"Her aunt and I." Uncle Henry carefully withdrew his arm from Lilly's grip and placed her hand in Tommy's.

Tommy stepped forward and looped her hand into his arm. Together, they took another step closer to the minister.

The shuffling of Uncle Henry taking his seat behind her, followed by sniffling sounds from both sets of parents, flooded Lilly's heart with guilt. This was not what any of them wanted for her and Tommy. Eventually, yes. But not now. Not in this order. Her aunt and uncle had taken her faithfully to church, read the Bible at home. Their sons had all married virtuous women, as far as

Lilly could tell. At least none of them had given birth in the first nine months of marriage.

Now she, the adopted one—the one they'd chosen—had let them down.

The pastor was reading scriptures about marriage, but Lilly couldn't stay focused. She clutched Tommy's hand. What was going on in his mind? Was he glad it was she standing here beside him? Was he wishing he'd done things differently?

For a fleeting moment, the image of William Tidsbury crossed her mind. Thank God for the small gathering. William's presence would only have accentuated the wrong deeds Lilly was trying so desperately to forget and make right.

When the pastor asked them to turn toward each other for their vows, Tommy's parents were visible in the front row. Mrs. DeWitt sniffled and dabbed her eyes with a dainty handkerchief. Her husband stared, sober-faced, at his son. They'd always treated Lilly like family. They represented one more piece of the pie she did not deserve.

"Repeat after me."

Lilly did, her own thoughts filling in the blank spaces between phrases.

"I, Lillian Grace Sampson, take thee, Thomas James DeWitt, to be my wedded husband. To have and to hold from this day forward. For better, for worse." *It'll never get worse than the night of the fire.* "For richer, for poorer." *We are poor now. Things can only improve.* "In sickness and in health, as long as we both shall live." *One of us will be the first to die. God, let that be a long way off.*

Tommy repeated the vow and they signed their names to the register, with the pastor's wife signing as a witness. The minister gave Tommy permission to kiss the bride, which he did ever so gently.

"I now pronounce you man and wife. Ladies and gentlemen, I present to you Mr. and Mrs. Thomas DeWitt!"

The pump organ started up again and Lilly and Tommy led the little group back down the aisle and to the church basement. Lovely food, warm wishes, and more gift-opening filled the next two hours.

• • •

After spending three weeks in rapid wedding preparation, Lilly now found herself with time to fill. Over the years, Aunty Margaret had done her utmost to teach her housekeeping, cooking, and sewing skills. The little apartment wasn't hard to keep clean, and she dutifully swept and dusted daily. She washed clothes every Monday and baked bread on Tuesdays and Fridays. Her least favorite task was the weekly washing and waxing of the floors, down on her knees. Was it really necessary? One week she decided to skip it. When nothing happened, she ignored the ritual for another week.

Tommy certainly didn't notice. He was home only to sleep anyway. He worked long hours at the hardware store, then evenings and Saturdays for a local farmer. Lilly fought back tears when the loneliness weighed heavy, then chided herself for not feeling grateful. At least Tommy was a hard worker and good provider.

On Sunday mornings, they attended church together. Sunday afternoon, Tommy usually slept, exhausted from his work hours. Lilly's energy had returned, and she used the time to work on a maternity dress she was sewing for herself to go along with the two Aunty Margaret had made.

Hours were spent in Aunty Margaret's living room preparing tiny baby garments—Lilly with knitting needles, Aunty Margaret at her sewing machine, and Mrs. DeWitt with a crochet hook. The stack of diapers, nightgowns, sweaters, booties, and caps grew by the day.

"It's hard to keep the secret," Mrs. DeWitt admitted one evening as the three of them sat together. "But it won't be long now, and you can start telling folks."

"I pray every day for a tiny baby," Aunty Margaret added. "That way, folks will assume it's premature."

Lilly kept quiet. If her baby arrived on schedule, he or she would have to be at least ten weeks premature to have been conceived after their wedding. No baby that young could survive.

"I'm just praying for a healthy child." Tommy's mother glanced at Lilly over the top of her eyeglasses before returning her gaze to her needlework.

"Well, yes, of course," Aunty Margaret agreed. "It's just that people do the arithmetic. And they can be cruel."

"Remember when Belinda Hawkins's first baby arrived in July, after a January wedding, and weighing nearly ten pounds?" Mrs. DeWitt shuddered. "Mothers would steer their little girls away from her, lest her immorality rub off."

Lilly remembered another girl named Helen, who'd been even less fortunate. She'd never married, and the identity of her baby's father was never revealed. When Helen had been expected to stand up in front of the congregation to confess her sin and ask forgiveness in order to be welcomed back into the fold, she'd chosen instead to leave the church. The practice was supposed to serve as a caution to other girls.

Lilly kept focused on her knitting. *The warning clearly didn't work on me.* As far as Lilly knew, Helen had never stepped foot in that or any other church since.

• • •

One Monday morning in mid-January, Tommy left for work after downing the hearty breakfast of oatmeal, scrambled eggs, and toast Lilly had made him. She kissed him at the door and watched him walk down the street toward the hardware store. When she turned back to her kitchen, a sharp pain in her lower abdomen made her double over. A gasp escaped as the sudden cramp gripped her. She leaned with both hands on the table until the pain subsided, but just as quickly as it had come, another followed. When that one lifted, she made her way to the living area and lowered herself to the couch. She'd no sooner maneuvered into a prone position than a third pain hit her.

What was going on? Should she try to get to the doctor? She and Tommy had agreed not to install a telephone yet, to save money. Their nearest neighbor had one—could she make it down the stairs?

Each time Lilly tried to sit up, she was overcome with pain. Finally, she curled onto her side, shivering and soaked in sweat. What had she eaten the day before? Suddenly the blanket beneath her felt soaked. Had she wet herself? How embarrassing.

She reached down to feel the wetness. When she drew her hand away, it was red with blood.

• • •

Tommy was calling her name. "Wake up, Lilly. Dr. Ramsey's here."

The doctor's voice came to her as though through a long tunnel. "What time did you find her?"

"About five minutes after twelve. I came home for lunch. I don't always come home for lunch, but—"

"Well, it's a good thing you did today, son. You may have saved your wife's life."

• • •

The next time Lilly was aware of anything, she found herself tucked into her own bed, wearing a clean nightgown. Aunty Margaret was there, holding a cool washcloth to her forehead. Tommy sat in the corner, a worried expression on his face.

"Hey, Lil." He stood and approached the bed. "Gave us quite a scare, but doc says you'll be all right."

"Of course she will." Aunty Margaret still leaned over her. "I went through this myself once. It'll take a little while for her to get her strength back, but she'll be right as rain soon."

Lilly swallowed. "We lost the baby, didn't we?" Her voice was barely above a whisper though she tried to speak at a normal volume.

Aunty Margaret looked at Tommy, and he nodded just once. No one said anything more for a long time.

Aunty Margaret finally rose and turned to Tommy. "Would you like me to stay the night, just in case you need anything?"

"We'll be fine. Won't we, Lil?"

Lilly nodded. "Go get a good sleep in your own bed, Aunty Margaret. Thanks for coming." But just before Aunty Margaret crossed through the doorway, Lilly called her back. "Can you please take the maternity clothes from my closet? Oh, and the baby clothes, too? Take them home with you. They're all piled on the little table in the corner of the living room."

"Oh, but Lilly, there'll be other—"

"Please. I don't want to see them."

Aunty Margaret's eyes locked with Lilly's for a moment. Her lips parted as if to speak, but she said nothing. She found the dresses in the closet and left the room without another word. A few minutes later, Lilly heard the door to their apartment open and close. Aunty Margaret's footsteps gradually faded as she made her way down the staircase on the outside of the garage.

"Mum brought over some soup earlier. Want some? I can bring it to you." Tommy's eyes were rimmed with red.

Lilly just shook her head.

"You should try to get some rest. I can sleep on the sofa."

Lilly wondered whether the sofa was soaked in blood but said nothing. Only when Tommy turned off the lamp did she discover it was nearly dark already. He left the door open. The clatter of dishes being washed stifled her sobs.

The next time she awoke, soft voices drifted in from the kitchen. She recognized her father-in-law's voice.

"Well, I'll be heading back home. Your mother just wanted me to check on you and bring these cookies over."

"Thanks, Dad."

"I'm real sorry, son."

"I know."

"Sometimes these things happen for the best."

Next came the scraping of chairs and footsteps. Then Tommy spoke with a crack in his voice. "Nobody would have known, Dad. I know I shouldn't think like that, but… I can't get it out of my mind. We didn't have to get married. I could still be living with you and Mom, saving up for my own place. Lilly could be in school now just like she planned, if we'd known this was going to happen. Nobody would have known there was ever a baby."

CHAPTER FOURTEEN

FEBRUARY 1939

A red foil heart decorated the front door of Gordon's Grocery when Lilly pushed it open and stepped inside, but the Valentine's Day spirit had passed her by. The changes she'd expected to see with the end of harvest had not played out. She still rarely saw her husband. Tommy had convinced his boss at the hardware store that he needed to work Saturdays.

"We don't seem like newlyweds," she'd complained once when Tommy came home to a cold supper at nine in the evening. "We're never together."

He'd only shrugged, but it was enough for her to reach a decision. She would get a job of her own. If there wasn't going to be a baby to look after, she could easily hold down a job and take care of their little apartment. She'd start at the grocery store where she'd worked part-time during her last year of high school.

"Lilly!" Mrs. Gordon greeted her from behind the counter. "Nice to see you. Congratulations on your marriage!"

"Thank you."

The woman wiped her hands on a towel. "I guess I'm usually out when you do your shopping."

"Actually, I'm not shopping at the moment." Lilly smoothed her hair. She'd pulled it back into a French roll, hoping to look more professional.

"No? What can I do for you?"

"Well, I was hoping for my old job back."

Mrs. Gordon's eyebrows came together. "Your old job? Why, I'm surprised. That strapping husband of yours not bringing home the bacon?" She grinned as if to say she was only teasing.

Lilly didn't laugh. "Oh! Yes, of course he is. He's working very hard. I just… I miss being out and… I thought you might be looking for help. Part-time, perhaps?"

Mrs. Gordon smiled but shook her head. "Oh, Lilly. We like hiring young single gals, but I'm a firm believer that a married woman's place is at home. In my case, of course, this *is* my home." She pointed upward with one finger, indicating the living quarters over the store she shared with Mr. Gordon. "And our children are all grown and gone, of course. Don't need me anymore." She pulled an apron down from a hook, tugged it over her head, and tied the waist strings in front of her midsection. "Besides, if I hire a young newlywed like yourself, we'd just nicely get you back on track when you'd be telling us you're in the family way. It's happened more times than I can count. Not to *us*, thankfully, because I don't hire married gals." She chuckled as she turned and began rearranging shelved goods behind her.

Lilly took a step back from the counter. The woman's opinion seemed ridiculous, and she had no idea how to respond. Tommy's words to his father rang in her head for the hundredth time: *Nobody would have known there was ever a baby.*

"You just stay home and keep that young man happy, Lilly girl. In no time at all, you'll be busier than a one-armed paper hanger." Mrs. Gordon stayed focused on her shelves and products, her back facing Lilly. "And you could always do some volunteer work in the meantime. The church is gathering clothing for the little African children. Oh, and have you heard? It's terrible what's happening with the Nazis over there."

"In Africa?"

"No, no. Germany. Their president or prophet or whatever he is, Mr. Hitler, wants to send the Jews to Africa. You could help sort clothes and get them ready to ship over. Maybe keep a little dress or two for your own little ones when they come."

Lilly mumbled a weak thank you and left the store. She would find a job somewhere else, but for now she made her way to the cemetery and found the grave shared by two. She brushed snow away from the dead grass and sat down, pulling her legs up under her coat.

"Hi, Mama. Sorry I haven't come for so long. I just wanted you to know there's not going to be a baby after all. Maybe you already know that. Do little ones who die before they're born go straight to heaven or what happens to them? I wanted to ask Uncle Henry, but to be honest, I'm not sure he knows either. I like to think it's true. I can't ask the pastor. He doesn't know I was pregnant. Nobody knows I was pregnant except for Doc Ramsey, Aunty Margaret, and Uncle Henry… and Tommy's parents." She picked up a twig and twirled it between her fingers. "And Tommy of course. I think he's relieved. Well, maybe not so much relieved as… feeling like he was duped or something. He's sorry we ever got married, I'm sure of it.

"And if I'm totally honest, I suppose I am too. I could be in school now like I planned. On my way to becoming a nurse. Are we being punished, Mama? I guess it's no less than we deserve. Our dreams dashed. And now, no baby either. Aunty Margaret says I'll have another. Maybe lots of babies. I haven't told her—or Tommy—what Dr. Ramsey said when I went back for a checkup. He really doesn't think I'm capable of having another child. Something got wrecked inside me. I can't bring myself to tell Tommy. I will. I know I should. I just can't do it yet. Everything still hurts too much to talk about, so we just don't talk at all.

"Anyway. If my little baby is there with you and my baby brother, I hope you give her a name. I feel like it was a girl. I had sort of picked out Victoria for a girl. I know it's a big name. You could call her Vicky if you want. Tommy and I didn't discuss names either, but I don't suppose he'd care. He'd probably say it's silly to name the baby now. A waste of a name. But I want her to have a name. And if I'm wrong and it was a boy—then Victor, I suppose."

A chill wind swept through the cemetery, causing Lilly to shiver. She rose to her feet and pulled her coat tight around herself.

"I guess I'll be on my way. I just wanted you to know, so that you can be looking out for my baby there and maybe… maybe I'll get to meet you both one day. I'm not a very good Christian, though. As you know. Uncle Henry says it doesn't matter. That God forgives. But he doesn't know all the things I need to be forgiven for."

• • •

The next stop was the library to ask if they were hiring. Lilly was surprised when the first person she saw was William Tidsbury. She waited while he stamped three books for a little girl and slid them across the counter toward her. "There you go. Due in two weeks. Enjoy!"

The girl clutched the books to her chest and left. William lifted his eyes toward Lilly.

"Lilly!"

"Hi, William. What are you doing here? I thought you were in university."

"Mid-term break. Between my time here last summer and now over the break, I can earn credit toward my librarian's certificate. Maybe eventually a bachelor's degree in Library Science." William picked up a stack of books from the counter and limped over to a cart behind him where he began sorting them. "How are you? How's married life?"

"Fine." Lilly forced a smile. "Actually, I find I have a lot of time on my hands and stopped in to see if the library might be hiring."

"Hm. Well... not that I know of, but you could talk to Miss Wallis."

"That's what I was afraid you'd say," Lilly whispered with a grin. Miss Wallis was notorious for being cranky. She'd been in charge of the library for as long as Lilly could remember, and the kids were all afraid of her. William seemed to get along fine with her, though. "Maybe you could put in a good word for me?"

"That I can do, for what it's worth. Hey, Lilly, follow me. I want to show you something." William pushed the cart out from behind the counter and over to the nonfiction section of the library. He paused before the shelves labeled *Science*, pulled down a thick book, and then added one more before handing both to Lilly. "These are used, but not out of date by any stretch."

Lilly accepted the two books and looked down to read the covers: *Introduction to Nursing* and *Anatomy 101*. "Textbooks?"

"Sure. I know you're out of school, but you like to study, don't you? Or does marriage change all that?"

Lilly smiled. "No. I'll take them. Thanks."

William began reshelving books from his cart but pointed his chin toward the counter. "There's Miss Wallis now. She'll check those out for you."

Lilly laid the books on the counter and placed her library card on top.

"These are due back at the end of the month." Miss Wallis stamped both books with the due date. "But you can renew them if no one else is waiting for them." Before sliding the books back toward Lilly, the librarian perused the covers.

Lilly cleared her throat.

"Is there something else I can do for you?" Miss Wallis raised an eyebrow.

"I was just wondering... do you have any openings? Maybe part-time?"

Miss Wallis looked Lilly up and down. "Not at the moment, no. Not that we couldn't use more help. We could always use more help. We just don't have the budget. Now if you're interested in volunteering, I'm sure I could put you to work."

Lilly nodded. "I'll… give that some thought. Thanks."

• • •

"Guess who I saw at the library today?"

Tommy forked up mashed potatoes. "Miss Wallis?"

"Well, yes, her too. But I meant William. He's home for mid-term break."

"Already?"

Lilly nodded. "That's what he said."

"So… he's doing well? Liking it?"

Lilly shrugged. "I guess so. We didn't really talk about it. I went in there looking for work and came out with two nursing textbooks."

"What?"

"I said I went in there looking for—"

"I heard what you said. I just can't believe it."

"Which part? Looking for a job or bringing home textbooks?"

"Either one. You don't need textbooks anymore—that ship has sailed. And what do you need a job for?"

Lilly shrugged. "I guess I don't, really."

"Darn right. I don't want people thinking I'm not providing." Tommy cut a bit of meatloaf with the side of his fork and put it in his mouth.

"No, that's not it at all, Tommy. I just… could use more to do. I asked at Gordon's first, but they don't hire married girls. Mrs. Gordon and Miss Wallis both suggested I could do some volunteer work, so… maybe I'll look into that."

"Sure. Why not?"

"Although if I'm going to volunteer, I'd just as soon it was something I care about, you know?"

"You gonna read those textbooks?"

"Already started." Lilly had opened the *Introduction to Nursing* book and left it face up on the kitchen counter while she'd prepared supper.

"Maybe you could volunteer at the hospital."

Lilly looked up. Why hadn't she thought of that? "Maybe I could."

"I still find it hard to believe you went looking for a job without even discussing it with me first. And now the Gordons know."

"I'm sorry, Tommy."

They finished their meal in silence, but it was the longest conversation they'd shared since the night of the miscarriage.

CHAPTER FIFTEEN

"Wait." I'm getting sleepy and nearly miss it. "So Lilly wasn't pregnant with *you.*"

Dad shakes his head. "I'm old, but not quite that old."

"And she was told she couldn't have more children? Wait. Dad—were you *adopted?* Is that why—?"

"I wish I could keep going, but it's been a long day." He yawns and stretches.

"Dad!"

"I can assure you, Princess, Lilly DeWitt gave birth to me. And it was a miracle in more ways than one."

Something Dad wrote in his first letter, way back when I started asking him about all this, jumps to mind. *"For you see, Diana, neither you nor I would be here at all if my mother had succeeded with her plan back in 1941."* What plan? Had she been planning to leave Tommy?

I really want to know, and I'd drag it out of him if he didn't look so weary.

"I'm turning in. I got a plane to catch tomorrow. Can you do that thing where you check me in from your computer?" Dad rises from the chair with a grunt, dumping Mouse unceremoniously onto the floor. He makes his way to my room.

"Sleep in a bit, Dad. We don't have to leave until eleven."

I go online to check him in, print the boarding pass, and make sure he's got it before he turns out the light. Then I spend another hour typing up his newest chapters.

• • •

When Dad still hasn't emerged from the bedroom by ten the next morning, I decide he's taken me too literally. I rap on the door. "Dad?" I knock again. "You up?"

I hear a soft moan.

"Dad?" I open the door and peer around it. "Dad!"

His face is as pale as the pillowcase and he looks at me with a glazed stare.

"Dad, what's wrong?" I rush over, my heart racing. He seems to be having trouble breathing. "Can you sit up?"

"Too weak," he whispers.

Lord, how long has he been trying to get up? Has he been trying to call out?

"Dad, stay right there. Try to relax. Do you need a sip of water?" I'm already on my way back to the kitchen where I grab my phone and press 9-1-1.

A business-like female voice comes on the line. "What's your emergency?"

I rush back to the bedroom, phone in hand. "It's my father. I think he might be having a heart attack or stroke or something." I give my address and answer questions as best I can. "Are you dizzy, Dad?"

Dad nods. He's sweating through his pajamas.

"He says yes… she's asking if you have any chest pain."

"Yes."

Oh no. Lord, please. I can't lose Dad yet.

"Leg pain?"

Dad nods again. Does he even know what I'm asking? He begins to cough and I lay my phone on the nightstand so I can help him roll onto his side. When he does, he coughs up a streak of bright red blood.

"He's coughing blood!" I shout into the phone.

"The ambulance should be there in two minutes. I want you to stay on the line until they arrive, okay?"

Someone knocks on the door and I run to open it. "They're here!" I holler into the phone, swinging the door open.

It's Shane.

"Oh my gosh, Shane." I'm hollering at the person on the other end of my phone and at Shane simultaneously. "They're *not* here. It's Dad… his heart or something… ambulance is on its way—"

"Give me your phone." Shane takes the cell and speaks with the operator in a far calmer fashion than I did.

We leave the front door hanging open and move to the bedroom, where Shane describes what he sees in paramedical terms. I have never been so glad to have him around. I take a long, slow breath while I run water over a washcloth to wipe Dad's face.

Before I finish the task, the ambulance arrives. The paramedics get his blood pressure, pulse, and temperature. They listen to his chest, asking questions the entire time. Past medical history? Any cardiac or lung issues? Does he have a history of heart failure? What meds is he on? Allergies? How long has this been going on? Last oral intake? Events leading up to this?

My head is swimming as I try my best to answer. I'm not sure how many times I repeat "He's a doctor," as though that somehow makes him immune. It seems to be taking forever, and my eyes plead with Shane to make them hurry.

He gives me a comforting nod. "They're doing their job, Di."

They hook Dad up to oxygen and start an IV before finally loading him into the ambulance in a half-sitting position. They take off, sirens blaring.

"C'mon, I'll drive." Shane hands me my phone. "Got your wallet?"

I grab my purse and lock the door on my way out. Trying to blink back tears, I climb into Shane's car and he drives off in the same direction as the ambulance.

"Deep breaths, Di."

I close my eyes and focus on breathing slowly until my heartrate feels normal again. "Thanks for being here."

"Should we be calling the airline?"

Shoot! "I don't know. I can't think about that now. If I know Dad, he bought insurance."

At the hospital, we rush inside. The nurse at the desk assures me that Dad is in good hands, but as an out-of-province visitor there will be time-consuming paperwork to fill out.

"Need this?" Shane holds out Dad's wallet. "Grabbed it off the dresser."

"I can't believe you had the presence of mind—thank you, Shane."

Inside the wallet, we find Dad's Manitoba medical card and I fill out the forms. I know of no pre-existing conditions. Dad has been healthy all his life. Mom often teased that he really needed to get sick once in a while so he'd have more empathy for his patients.

With the forms turned in, the woman at the desk tells us someone will come to get us as soon as we can see Dad. Shane finds Dad's boarding pass in his wallet and calls the airline.

There's nothing left to do but wait.

"You hungry?" Shane raises his eyebrows. "Thirsty?"

"I couldn't eat." I shake my head. "But you go ahead and get something if you want. I guess I could use something to drink."

Shane walks away and I pull out my phone. How can it be only eleven o'clock? Haven't hours passed since I first knocked on Dad's door?

I call Becky.

"Hey!" She never answers with hello. "You at the airport?"

"No, Beck. There's a problem. We're at the hospital."

"What?"

"Something's wrong with Dad. I'm not sure what it is yet."

I spend the next five minutes describing the last hour to Becky and promise to call her as soon as I know more.

Shane returns with two cans of ginger ale. Setting his own on a low table, he pops the tab on the other and hands it to me.

"Thanks. I don't know what I'd do without you, Shane. Thanks for being here."

"Hey. Quit it. This is kind of what I do. Besides, I had this timeslot booked for you and your dad already. I'm just sorry he's in there and I'm stuck with you."

I swat his arm. "Dad's got a man crush on you, you know."

Shane chuckles. "He's got good taste. Maybe that's why I'm fond of him, too." His smile fades. "I'm sure he's going to make it through this just fine, Di."

I take a big breath and blow it out as slowly as I can. "I'm glad he approves of you. He got too nosy last night, though. Wants to know what you're afraid of."

"Really? Me?" Shane takes a swig of his drink. "Lots of things. Snakes creep me out. Not a fan of any reptile, really."

"Funny."

He gazes out the window, saying nothing at first. Then he turns back to me. "So did you give him an answer?"

Tempted to tease him back, something about the look in his eyes stops me. "I… basically said he'd have to ask you, but… I thought it might have something to do with your parents' divorce and not wanting to ruin a good friendship." I pause for a swallow of the ginger ale. "Was I close?"

"Something like that, yeah."

We sit quietly until panic wells inside me again. "Shane, what if this is really serious? What if he doesn't make it?"

He takes my left hand in his right and squeezes. "Shh. If that were the case, they'd be calling you in to say goodbye. Hey, did he give you more of the story yesterday?"

I know what Shane is doing, but the distraction works. I fill him in on what Dad told me last night.

"I begged for more, but he was too tired and—oh my gosh! Do you suppose that's what caused this? I've been keeping him going and staying up late ever since he got here. We shouldn't have taken that trip to Jasper on Saturday. What if it's too much? Shane, I'll never be able to live with myself if Dad—"

"Stop, Diana. Just stop. Your dad is nearing eighty. He's bound to start having some health issues."

"Yeah, but—" My phone pings, and I swipe it. "Oh, shoot."

"What?"

"I'm supposed to be hanging out with Carly tonight. I'm going to have to reschedule."

When I explain to Carly, she expresses genuine concern for Dad, which touches me.

I'm still on that call when a nurse approaches.

"You can see your father now, if you'd like to follow me." She doesn't ask whether or not Shane is family, and I don't volunteer. He follows as the nurse leads us down a hallway. "Your father has suffered a pulmonary embolism," she explains as she walks. "He's stable now. His doctor will be in shortly to answer your questions."

She pushes open the door.

My poor father lies hooked up to an IV on one side, a blood pressure monitor on the other. He appears to be asleep.

I go over to him and touch his hand gently. "Dad?"

His eyes flutter, then close again.

"He'll be pretty drowsy for a while, but he can hear you. Dr. Lee will be with you in a minute." The nurse leaves quietly.

"Dad, it's me, Diana. Shane's here, too. Don't try to talk or open your eyes. We're at the hospital, and they're taking good care of you. You're going to be fine." I stroke the back of his hand. "I'm so sorry this happened to you, Dad."

Dr. Lee is a tiny woman with a commanding presence. She sweeps into the room and introduces herself without shaking our hands.

"Your father's blood test results reveal lower than normal oxygen and higher than normal D dimer, both of which could indicate an increased likelihood of blood clots. The CTPA confirmed it—"

"Wait." I give my head a little shake. "The what?"

"CT pulmonary angiography," Shane murmurs.

"—and I've ordered a compression ultrasonography on his thigh."

"My father's a doctor," I explain. "He'll want to know all this, but for now can you please just dumb it down for me?"

"He has a pulmonary embolism, which means a blood clot has reached his lung, likely coming from his leg. He has no previous heart or lung issues, is that correct?"

"Right. As far as we know."

"Has he flown lately?"

There it is.

I nod slowly. "Yes. He flew here from Winnipeg three days ago."

"It's possible that—"

A sound out of Dad stops her mid-sentence. He clears his throat and speaks a little above a whisper. "Hey there, Princess. Is there still time to make that flight?"

"Dad!" I reach down and put my face next to his in an awkward attempt at a hug. "You gave me a scare."

"Did not mean to do that." He looks at Shane. "Sorry you had to see all this, young man. Thanks for being here."

"No problem." The look of relief on Shane's face makes me realize he's been more worried than he let on. "I'm just glad you're still with us."

Next, Dad looks at Dr. Lee. He's still whispering. "You the one I have to thank?"

"Hello, Dr. DeWitt. I'm Dr. Lee. You have a—"

"Yeah, I heard. Cut to the chase. What's in the bag? Heparin?"

"Yes." She shines a flashlight into his eyes, feels his throat, and listens to his chest with her stethoscope. "We're going to keep you for a couple of days, maybe more, so we can keep an eye on things. You'll need to be on medication for at least three to six months."

"Warfarin?" Dad asks, and all I can think about is rat poison.

Dr. Lee nods. "Or possibly one of the newer oral anticoagulants. Let's take this one step at a time. And I don't want to hear any more about catching any flights. You won't be doing that anytime soon."

My mind begins to whirl. I've been so concerned about whether Dad will live that I haven't thought ahead. I'm due back at work tomorrow. I'll need to figure a few things out.

After the doctor leaves, I call Becky and listen to her cry with relief.

Shane and I stay until Dad falls asleep, then we cross the street to a coffee shop. When I push open the door, the aroma of freshly baked bread makes me suddenly ravenous. I order a Reuben sandwich with fries.

"I know I should be eating something healthier, especially in light of what's just happened," I admit.

"Actually, that sounds good." Shane folds his menu and hands it to the waitress. "Make it two."

When the food comes, Shane offers to say grace.

"Lord, thank you that Dale is going to be okay. Thank you for good and swift medical care. Please bring healing to his body and peace to his heart. Amen."

"And thanks for the food," I add. "Amen. Oh, *shoot*."

"What now?"

"Mouse. I saw her dash under the couch when the ambulance arrived at the house. I hope she's okay."

Shane speaks around a mouthful. "Her food and water bowls were full. She'll be fine."

I stare. Who is this man who takes time to notice such a thing?

I don't know when I've enjoyed a meal more. Does relief make everything twice as tasty? Shane and I talk and laugh. I call my boss and arrange to take the rest of the week off.

"Using your 'sickness in the family' leave?" Shane asks when I finish the call.

"You bet." After eight years at this job, I've long since reached my maximum accumulated sick days. They can, alternatively, be used for when an employee has a sick family member who needs their care. "I never dreamed I'd need to."

"It's a blessing."

• • •

Dad's color is returning when we get back to his room. I take his hand again.

"Wish I could come home with you." His voice is stronger, but he's still having a hard time catching his breath.

"You of all people should know better, Dad."

"Yeah, yeah."

A volunteer in a pink vest comes in carrying a bouquet of flowers. "Dr. Dale DeWitt?"

"Yes."

"These are for you." She places the arrangement of lilies, roses, daisies, and carnations on Dad's cart and rolls it closer so he can see the card.

Dad pulls the card away. "You read that, Princess. I don't have my glasses."

I look at the little card. "It's from Becky and family. 'Get well soon. We love you and miss you.'"

Dad closes his eyes and breathes in the fragrance of the flowers. "Well, what do you know about that? Beautiful, aren't they? That's real thoughtful."

Dad watches the young volunteer walk away, then turns to me.

"Say, did I ever tell you my mother volunteered at the Summervale Hospital?"

CHAPTER SIXTEEN

Lilly

SPRING/SUMMER 1939

Nineteen thirty-nine marched on. Newspapers and radio announcers warned of pending war in Europe, but it all seemed so far away. Lilly paid little attention.

At Tommy's encouragement, she began to volunteer at Summerville's small hospital. Since it served a wide area, the facility offered a surprising range of services and had a larger number of staff than Lilly expected. Within a month, her duties came to include delivering meals and books to patients, feeding and reading to patients, changing linens, cleaning rooms, and restocking supplies.

One afternoon, her supervisor called her away from the supply room. "Lilly, we're short-staffed in the nursery. Could you please report there today and see how you can help? Maybe just rock some babies?"

Lilly swallowed. Was she ready to hold a baby? She thought hard, frantically trying to come up with an excuse. But her supervisor was already gone.

She made her way to the nursery. Within minutes, she was wrapped in a hospital gown, seated in a rocker, and holding a tiny, crying newborn. Lilly's chest felt weighted with grief as she stared down into the little one's face. Her own baby would have been this exact age right now.

She closed her eyes and sighed. "Don't cry, don't cry," she murmured, talking to herself as much as to the child. Gradually, the baby settled down and went to sleep.

Lilly reached a conclusion. *If I can learn to give comfort to other people's babies without the pain of my own loss searing my heart, I'll know I've paid for my sin.*

How long would it take?

• • •

Several days later, she passed through the staff room to get her coat and purse at the end of her shift. Co-workers flocked around Irene, the admissions clerk, congratulating her and showering her with gifts. Lilly stopped to watch, and a nurse handed her a slice of cake.

"What's the occasion?" Lilly asked.

"Didn't you hear? Irene's getting married! She'll be leaving us in a couple of weeks."

Lilly ate the cake and went over to congratulate Irene, who had been two or three years ahead of Lilly in high school.

"Thanks, Lilly." Irene leaned in. "Say, you should think about applying for my job. They haven't filled it yet."

Lilly raised her eyebrows. "Me?"

"Sure! The nurses have nothing but good things to say about how helpful you've been around here and your great attitude. Can you type?"

"Yes." Lilly had taken both typing and shorthand in high school, after Aunty Margaret had insisted they would provide her with skills to fall back on. "But I'm married."

"So?"

"I doubt they'd hire me. Aren't you leaving because you're getting married?"

"No. I'm getting married, but that's not why I'm leaving. I'm leaving because I'll be moving to Winnipeg where my husband's job is. Shucks, I might even find work at another hospital there."

Lilly smiled. "How progressive."

"You should apply."

• • •

By the following week, Lilly sat in an interview for the position of admissions clerk. This time, she'd discussed it with Tommy first, appealing to his yearning for a car before he could suggest that her returning to work would be an insult to his manhood. She knew her tactic was a success when she watched his eyes light up at the possibility of owning an automobile.

"You're at the hospital most of the time anyway," he said. "Might as well get paid for it."

Five minutes later, he was perusing the auto section of the newspaper and adding up numbers.

Lilly gladly accepted the offer when it came and began training. As Irene had predicted, she caught on quickly and enjoyed the work. Tommy wasn't complaining, and Lilly worked harder than ever to make sure nothing at home suffered.

But as summer evolved into harvest season, not everyone shared her enthusiasm for her new career. She stopped in unannounced at Uncle Henry and Aunty Margaret's one evening but didn't get further than the doorstep.

"Can't visit with you tonight." Aunty Margaret stepped out, pulling on her gloves. "The Ladies Aid Society needs me. We're meeting to roll bandages or whatever's on the agenda." She pulled the door closed behind her, leaving Lilly no choice but to back down the steps. "You should spend your evenings with your husband. You two don't see nearly enough of each other." Aunty Margaret headed down the sidewalk, all but dismissing Lilly. "I'll walk you home since it's on my way."

Lilly blinked several times. True enough, she and Tommy hardly saw each other. The farmer he usually helped during harvest, Mr. Arnold, had fallen from a hay wagon and broken his arm. He was paying Tommy to complete his early morning and evening chores. In between the two, Tommy worked his usual hours at the store. Plus, he still volunteered at the fire hall and responded to calls whenever there was a fire. Recently, there had been three—all of them grass fires.

She scrambled to catch up to Aunty Margaret. "Tommy isn't home. He doesn't usually get home from the Arnolds' until nine or so."

"He's working too hard. Doesn't even get to church anymore."

Lilly couldn't disagree, but it seemed Tommy didn't want to be around her any more than necessary. After a fire had called him out of church one Sunday morning, he'd suddenly realized he could survive without church too. Now he came with her only occasionally. Would she be better off staying home as well?

She returned to her own apartment as Aunty Margaret continued on to the church.

• • •

The following Sunday, Lilly walked the three blocks to church alone again. *If I stayed home, he'd likely attend without me just for spite.*

Aunty Margaret stood with two friends on the front steps. One of them, Mrs. Hardy, greeted Lilly at the door.

"I hear you're working at the hospital, Lilly." Mrs. Hardy peered over the top of her eyeglasses. "That must leave quite a load for poor Tommy to carry."

The other woman chimed in, giving Aunty Margaret an accusing look. "Really? How come you never said anything, Margaret?"

"Oh, it's only short-term." Aunty Margaret gave a weak flutter with her hand.

"Actually," Lilly said, tightening her grip on her purse, "I just finished my probationary period and am looking forward to some additional training. They're sending me to Winnipeg for a day."

Lilly lifted her chin to appear confident in the face of the thinly disguised criticism.

Aunty Margaret's face turned an interesting shade of red. She grabbed Lilly by the elbow. "Let's find our seats before the service begins."

Lilly followed her to their pew and sat down obediently, but then she turned to her aunt. "Do you agree with your friends? I should be staying home and not working?"

Aunty Margaret pursed her lips together and shook her head. "It's not my decision."

"I know. I'm asking your opinion. I value your point of view."

Her aunt smoothed her skirt and picked a piece of lint from her lap. "Oh, I don't know, Lilly. It's just... it doesn't look good. That's all."

"Since when do you care about how things look?"

A heavy sigh escaped Aunty Margaret's lungs. "Maybe I should have cared a little *more* before—well, before... you know. Now shh. The service is starting."

Lilly heard little of the sermon. Instead she stewed about the gossips and their old-fashioned opinions.

When church ended, she marched directly home, stomped up the stairs, and flung open the door to their apartment.

"Tommy, what on earth are you telling people?" She tossed her hat and handbag aside. "The way they talk, you'd think I've left you with six starving children while I'm off on a holiday or something."

Tommy looked up from the firefighters manual he was studying. "Don't listen to 'em, Lil. You know better than to let it bother you."

"Well, maybe I *should* know better, but it still bothers me. Do you agree with them? Do you feel abandoned?"

Tommy shrugged. "Maybe sometimes, but hey, we agreed to this."

"Maybe sometimes? Like when?"

"Forget it, Lil." He raked a finger through his hair. "Let's have lunch."

With a huff, Lilly pulled eggs from the icebox and set a frying pan on the stove. "I can cook and talk at the same time. Tell me when you feel that way."

Tommy found a cutting board and began slicing bread. "Mother came over last week when you were working the evening shift. I'd been home just long enough to finish my supper—the stew you made—and I was washing up my dishes when she walked in."

"And…?"

"Well, she started in about how I shouldn't have to do that. Then she came and took the dishrag out of my hand and said she'd finish up."

Lilly glared at her husband. "Which you were glad to let her do."

"Well, sure. Shucks, Lil, who wouldn't? It was no big deal."

Lilly slapped some butter onto the pan, but she missed. A lump of butter hit the floor. A nasty word escaped her lips as she reached for a rag to clean it up.

"I'll get it." Tommy took the rag and bent to wipe the floor.

"Because you're the perfect gentleman." Why was she picking a fight? Something egged her on from deep inside and she didn't know how to apply the brakes.

Tommy threw the rag into the basin and crossed his arms over his chest. "What's that supposed to mean?"

"Everybody thinks you're so perfect, Thomas DeWitt." Her pitch rose as she mimicked the gossiping women. "'Look at Tommy, he's so wonderful. Such a hard worker. Tommy the fireman. Poor Tommy, stuck with that woman. What did he ever see in her, anyway?'"

"Lilly! Stop it. Nobody's saying that."

"Aren't they? 'Poor Tommy, marries Lilly and now he's stuck supporting her while she traipses off to do whatever she wants as if she were free as a bird.'"

Tommy crossed the room. "I said stop it, Lil. I mean it. What's gotten into you?"

"If they only knew the truth, Tommy. They'd change their minds pretty quick if they knew your deep dark secrets, wouldn't they?"

Tommy gaped at her. "Is this about the baby?"

"The baby, the fire—take your pick! Maybe there's more. How do I know there's not more?"

Tommy's brown eyes turned cold and fierce. "How do I know there's not more about *you*?"

Lilly glared back. "I guess you don't. How could you when we never talk? Don't you think maybe it's time we did? Time we told?"

"Told? Told who?" Tommy glared at her, his jaw set. When she didn't have an answer, he abruptly grabbed his coat, opened the apartment door, and slammed it behind him.

CHAPTER SEVENTEEN

FALL 1939

On September 10, Prime Minister Mackenzie King declared that Canada was at war with Germany. The announcement seemed fitting, given the war going on in Lilly's home and heart. While she continued to find her job a wonderful distraction from her troubled marriage, home was usually a place of cold silence with rumblings of explosions under the surface.

Within weeks, newly enlisted soldiers were in basic training. The government was encouraging citizens to save their resources, conserve fuel, and invest in war bonds. Trains increased their runs to discourage private transportation.

On October 6, the Friday before Thanksgiving, Lilly boarded the early morning train to Winnipeg for her day of training. The timing couldn't have been more perfect. She needed to get away from the hospital for a little while. She rested her head against the back of her seat and began to drift, reliving the disturbing incident of the previous day when an ambulance pulled up to the front doors with two burn victims from a barn fire twelve miles from town.

She'd walked around her desk to hold the front door open for the stretchers. A young mother and her ten-year-old son, their burns too severe for the Summervale hospital to handle, were almost immediately rerouted to a bigger hospital in Winnipeg. Lilly's heart sank as the two patients were loaded into separate ambulances. The stench of burnt flesh and hair assaulted her senses. Her legs grew weak. One of the nurses had noticed her pale face and helped her back to her chair.

Lilly shook off the memory and stared out the train's window. She'd have to toughen up if she was going to keep this job. She spent her training time soaking in everything, scoring a hundred percent on the quiz at the end of the day.

When she boarded the train to return home, the first passenger she saw was William Tidsbury.

"Hello, William. Going home for the long weekend?"

William nodded and removed his coat from the seat next to him. "You bet. Sit here if you like."

"Thanks." Lilly took the seat and tucked her bag under the seat in front of her. "Haven't seen you in weeks. Don't you normally stay in the city on weekends?"

"Yes. I got a job in the university library."

"Good for you. Been quite the start to a school year, eh?"

"I'll say. So far, classes are status quo. I'm grateful for that."

"I bet."

After explaining her day in the city and sharing news of who among their classmates had joined the military, they rode along in silence. The gentle rocking of the train and steady rhythm of the tracks lulled Lilly into a sleepiness she hadn't felt all week. She rubbed her eyes and blinked several times.

"Sleepy?" William closed his book.

"Can hardly keep my eyes open."

"Must be challenging. Being a married woman and holding down a job, too."

"Not really."

"Well… I'm sorry about the rumors. And proud of you for ignoring them. Both you and Tommy."

"Rumors?" Lilly's throat tightened. She and Tommy had been married over a year now. The miscarriage had been nearly a year ago, too. Had someone found out about her pregnancy? Were people talking about it behind her back? Why now? "What rumors?"

William hesitated. "I'm sorry. I shouldn't have said that." He shook his head. "Not thinking."

"No, I want to know. What rumors?"

William let out a long sigh. "Oh, it's silly. My mother's probably the worst culprit. She should know better."

"Go on."

"Last time I was home, Mum said you and Tommy were—how did she put it? 'Headed for destruction'? Apparently, the gossip mill is feeling sorry for Tommy, having to fend for himself while you work."

Lilly snorted. "You're right, that is silly. Tommy encouraged this. He's set his sights on buying a car."

William nodded. "I knew you wouldn't do this without his support. Just a bunch of jealous, old-fashioned biddies." He raised the pitch of his voice several notes to imitate said biddies. "'What is she thinking? Lilly should be at home where she belongs, scrubbing floors and growing vegetables!'"

"Is that what they say?" Lilly giggled harder when William shook a finger in the air for emphasis.

"'Putting up tomatoes and changing diapers.'"

Lilly chuckled, but at the word "diapers," her laugh quieted. "Well, I can assure you, if it's jealousy, there's not much to be jealous of."

"Not yet. Wait 'til you buy your husband that shiny new car."

"Well... we'll wait and see, I guess. Who knows what's going to happen with this war and everything?"

William nodded. He looked out his window for a bit, then turned back to Lilly. "Have you and Tommy discussed the possibility of his being drafted?"

Lilly nearly spluttered. She and Tommy had discussed nothing about anything. "The prime minister says there won't be a draft."

"I think they may have promised that last time, too. I hope it doesn't come to that. And even if it does, I think they wouldn't draft married men unless they get desperate."

"What about you?"

"Me?" William sniffed. "They'd have to be awfully desperate to want the likes of me."

Lilly could feel the heat rising in her face. How could she have forgotten, even temporarily, William's bad legs? She, of all people? "Sorry."

"Don't be sorry. If they do end up drafting fellas, they'll be marching off to their deaths and I'll be back here holed up with more books than I can read in a lifetime. Pretty lucky if you ask me." William spoke with bravado, but the sadness in his eyes betrayed him.

"Do you... still have pain sometimes?"

"Nah. Nothing worth complaining about."

"It must have been awful." Why was she torturing herself?

"At first, yes. There were days I didn't want to survive. But... I'm glad I did."

Lilly nodded. "I'm glad you did, too." *More than you know.*

She rested her head against the back of the seat, her jacket tucked in for a pillow, her thoughts on her husband. Though they hadn't talked about anything significant, Tommy had simmered down from the anger that had prompted him to stomp off the previous Sunday.

Now she was struck by the irony of sitting here next to William even as she mulled over the note she had left Tommy early that morning.

Dear Tommy,

I'm not sure whether to be sorry for my harsh words or glad that we've finally had a fight, because at least it means we were talking. Seriously, I am sorry for speaking to you that way. Can you forgive me? I'm under a lot of stress and I was taking it out on you. Even your mother seems to have turned against me. I know this hasn't been easy for you and I do appreciate your support. Here's the thing, Tommy. We need to talk about things. Yes, even the "big thing." Sometimes I wonder if it's time we told someone, before it eats us both alive. Would you consider it? Can we talk about it? Please think about it. Telling someone might do us both a world of good.

She'd paused over how to close the note. Somehow, adding "Love, Lilly" felt wrong. Especially if she wasn't sure it was even true. But with or without love, she and Tommy were bound to each other in ways she couldn't begin to describe.

Finally, without losing any more time, she'd completed the note.

See you tonight,
Lilly

Her heart lifted when she found Tommy waiting on the platform at the Summervale station. A light dusting of snow covered the whole town, but Tommy wore a warm smile as they made eye contact through the window.

She said goodbye to William before stepping down from the train.

When she reached Tommy, she wrapped her arms around him, kissing his neck. He took her satchel and kept one arm wrapped around her shoulders.

Lilly was vaguely aware of William stepping down somewhere behind her. Tommy nodded to him and turned his attention back to Lilly.

"Welcome home."

"Thank you. I'm so glad you're here. I thought you'd still be working."

"I've been off since four. Got a surprise waiting at home." Tommy waggled his eyebrows and smiled.

Lilly hustled to keep pace with Tommy's brisk step. "You got my note?"

"I did. Thank you."

"So... you've forgiven me?"

"I have."

No more was said. Lilly was content to tuck her arm through his as they hurried home to their little apartment. Tommy had swept the stairs free of snow, probably just before he headed to the station.

The closer she got to the top, the more delicious something smelled.

"Did you cook?"

Tommy only grinned, reaching around to open the door for her. She stepped into the most delightful atmosphere she'd seen in ages. The oven had warmed the apartment to a cozy temperature, and something smelled wonderful. Their best dishes graced the little table, along with the tablecloth and napkins embroidered by Tommy's mother. Two tall, tapered candles stood waiting to be lit.

"Tommy!" Lilly squealed. "This is amazing! What a wonderful surprise."

Maybe this meant Tommy agreed that it was time for them to really start talking and share their deep secret with someone.

Like the ultimate gentleman, Tommy seated Lilly at the table and lit the candles. A shiver went down her spine like it always did at the sound of a match striking and a flame bursting to life. Tommy then pulled a beautiful roasting chicken from the oven, surrounded by onions, potatoes, and carrots.

"Wow! You did this all by yourself?" Lilly couldn't stop grinning.

"Don't be so shocked." Tommy cut some meat and dished it onto her plate, along with some of the steaming vegetables. After filling his own plate, he recited a hasty grace and dug in.

"Delicious! I didn't even realize how hungry I was."

"I wasn't sure I should cook the chicken, given that we'll be having Thanksgiving turkey at my parents' on Monday. But then I thought, why not? We're both making money, we can afford it. And... I have some news."

"You do?"

Tommy nodded, his face glowing. Was he finally ready to talk?

"So... when you said you had a surprise waiting for me... it wasn't just this fabulous meal with the pretty candles and everything?" Lilly waved a hand around the room. "Because I'm already a little overwhelmed here."

"In a good way, I hope."

"Yes, of course."

"Good." He dished chicken onto Lilly's plate. "But I'm saving my news for dessert."

"There's dessert, too?" Lilly looked around.

"Yes, but I can't take full credit. Save room for a slice of my mother's apple pie. I stopped in there today to ask for her advice on the chicken and she sent two pieces of pie home with me. I think she'd have given me the whole pie, but Dad wouldn't hear of it."

Lilly laughed. "Sounds great. I don't know if I can stand the suspense, though."

"Tell me what you learned today."

"Well... today was good. I learned a lot about record-keeping and filing, mostly. I'll find it useful. Had a little visit with William on the ride home."

"I thought as much. He doing okay at school?"

"Yes." Lilly hesitated. "He loves what he's learning."

Tommy cut into his chicken. "Guess you heard about the barn fire yesterday."

"You helped with that?"

"I did. We saved the house." Tommy's voice held a note of pride. "Bob Kolinski and Matt Tucker went into the barn and got the mom and the kid out." He hesitated.

"You could have done it, though. Right?" Lilly watched his face.

Tommy took his time with a forkful of potatoes, chewing it thoughtfully. He swallowed and shrugged one shoulder. "Sure. I could have. I can't very well stay on as a firefighter if I couldn't have done it. Could I?"

Lilly sighed. "I wish *I* could get past it."

"What do you mean?"

Lilly shared her reaction to the injured patients. "I just sort of froze. I don't know how else to describe it." She left out the part where she'd eventually thrown up in the ladies' room. "Tommy, do you think it's time we told somebody what we did? For our own sakes, if nothing else?"

Tommy stared back at her. "You really think telling someone would make it go away?"

"Well... no. Not go away. I mean... I don't know. I'm just wondering."

"Telling would make matters worse, Lil. Trust me on this. We'd only be inviting someone else to share a burden they don't need. It would be unkind. Cruel, even."

Lilly studied her husband's serious face. He was probably right. If they told someone, that someone would then need to struggle with whether *they* needed to tell someone. Whether justice needed to be exacted somehow.

"Yeah. I guess so. I never really thought of it that way."

"Besides, what makes you think we deserve to have our burden lifted? Maybe carrying it is our penance. For everything."

Was he including their premarital sex and the loss of the baby in his assessment? She chewed her bottom lip. "Is that really how it works?"

"Think about it. If we got away scot-free, it wouldn't be right. So we live with our guilty consciences and all the crazy quirks that go with it—until we've suffered enough or done enough good to outweigh it."

Lilly was too tired to argue, even though nothing Tommy said brought her any peace. They finished their main course in silence.

Tommy made a show of clearing their plates and then ushering her into an armchair in the living room area. He brought her a cup of coffee and a serving of pie.

"Ready for my news?" He stood straight and tall.

A little good news would certainly redeem the conversation. Lilly nodded. "Finally. What is it?"

Surely, he was about to reveal that he'd found a car for them, or possibly even brought one home already. Maybe it was parked in the garage below them this very minute. She smiled back at him expectantly.

"Okay. Don't be shocked. I know we didn't exactly discuss this, but…" His smile broadened. "I've enlisted."

Lilly nearly dropped her cup. "Enlisted?"

"This will be good for us, Lil." Tommy sounded completely convinced. "'Absence makes the heart grow fonder,' and all that. When I come back, we can make a fresh start on a clean slate."

Maybe he was right. "But what if you don't make it back?"

"Then you can make a fresh start with some other fella."

He ducked when Lilly picked up the nearest thing, an embroidered pillow, and hurled it at him.

"What a horrible thing to say!"

But as the news sank in, it brought relief. Perhaps time apart would do them good. Surely the war would be over in a year at most. Tommy could return home having had his adventure and probably feeling like he'd completed his penance.

Now if Lilly could only find a way to serve hers.

CHAPTER EIGHTEEN

Diana

I'm so lucky. Dad exchanges medical lingo with Dr. Lee. She treats him as a respected colleague while I sit back, not having to figure out her explanations and then interpret them for an aging parent.

By the end of his third day, Dad is impatient to leave. Becky books him a flight home for the following week, and I buy him two pairs of compression socks.

Shane helps Dad pack while I sign forms and get his prescriptions filled.

Back at my house, Dad heads straight to the recliner to rest. I put Mouse in her pet carrier so she leaves Dad alone. She meows her complaints for a minute, then settles down to sleep. Suppertime is approaching, and I'm glad I threw a stew in my slow cooker before leaving the house this morning.

Shane isn't impressed. "You shouldn't leave those things unsupervised."

"Then what's the point of having one?" I can imagine what he'd say if he knew I frequently leave the clothes dryer running when I leave for work in the mornings.

His superior grasp of fire safety doesn't stop him from enjoying my stew.

Shane agrees to stay with Dad while I meet with Carly. Dad argues that he doesn't need babysitting, but I can tell he's pleased to have Shane here. The two of them are into a cribbage game at the kitchen table when I leave.

I take Carly to the theater and tell her she can pick any movie she wants as long as it isn't R-rated. I try to disguise my pleasure when she chooses a recently released Christian film.

"I've heard about this one." She peruses the poster in the theater lobby. "Sounds good."

I buy our tickets while she stands in line for popcorn and drinks.

Oh Lord, please don't let this one be preachy or cheesy, I pray as we walk through the theater doors and find seats.

I needn't have worried. The story captivates us and is well done. So well that I feel guilty about my arrogant prayer. We both shed tears when the main character is reunited with her sister after being separated in different foster homes. God draws them to himself in unique ways, and they become sisters in Christ as well as through blood.

On the way home, we discuss the movie, which is inspired by a true story.

We talk for a bit longer after I pull up in front of Carly's building. I turn the radio down to a barely perceptible volume. "How's it going with Josh?"

She slurps the last of her drink through her straw. "Okay."

"Am I going to get to meet him sometime?"

Carly giggles. "That depends. You won't embarrass me, will you?"

I feign complete mortification. "*Moi*? When have I ever embarrassed you? I am so offended right now."

"Okay, okay. Maybe next week."

"Your mom's met him, right?"

"Yeah. Hey, can I ask you something? You talk about your church sometimes, but you've never invited me to go with you. Why not?"

"Oh. Uh… I guess I never really thought about it. Never thought you'd be interested."

"Are you embarrassed to take me?" She looks me in the eye when she asks, a huge step for her. Best not to mention that, though.

"Are you kidding me? Just the opposite! Do you have any idea how cool you are? How gorgeous? Who wouldn't want to be seen anywhere with you?"

She blushes and looks down.

"Would you like to come?" I ask. "Just say the word. As long it's okay with your mom."

"Yeah, I think she'd be cool with it. I'd like to learn more about God and stuff. We've never gone to church."

My heart is suddenly convicted. "Oh, Carly, I would love to take you. This Sunday?"

"Sure."

"My church has a youth group, too. I'm sure they do cool stuff."

"Whoa. Church first."

"Okay. I'll call your mom to make sure, and then pick you up around ten-thirty Sunday morning."

I watch until she is safely inside, then pull into traffic.

Oh Lord, forgive me. I could be doing so much more for Carly.

I make up my mind to buy her a Bible in a modern translation and give it to her at the next opportunity.

• • •

When I get home, Dad and Shane have put away the cribbage board and are watching a hockey game. Dad is once again petting my cat. He turns off the TV.

"Don't do that on my account, Dad. Watch the rest of the game." I kick my shoes into a corner and put the kettle on for tea.

"Nah. It's nearly over. My team's losing and Shane's team isn't even playing."

I've never known Dad to have time for sports. "I didn't know you had a team, Dad." I put air quotes around the word *team*.

"Well, the Jets of course. Like any good Manitoba boy. Shane here likes the Oilers. That's only right." Dad's breathing still isn't back to normal, but I'm impressed with the improvement.

Shane nods. "How was your evening?"

I tell them the whole story. "I can't believe I was so oblivious to Carly's interest in spiritual things. In fact, I think I was being overly careful to avoid talking about my faith lest she write me off as a religious fanatic or something. I feel horrible."

"Don't feel bad, Princess. You've done something right, or she wouldn't be asking."

Shane removes his feet from the coffee table and sits forward. "Your dad's right. Carly sees something in you that she figures is worth investigating. You've shown her Jesus with your life instead of your words."

"Mm." I throw a teabag into my teapot. I'm not convinced, but it's nice of them to say so.

Once we all have a mug of tea in our hands, I settle into my favorite chair.

Dad looks at us both expectantly. "Well? You two ready for more of Lilly's story? Where did we leave off?"

I look at Shane, unsure.

Shane settles back against the sofa again. "Tommy told Lilly he'd enlisted."

"Ah, yes. So he did."

I'm not sure I like this grandfather I never met. "Did he really not discuss it with her first?"

"It was a different time." Dad pushes the recliner into a more comfortable position, prompting Mouse to hop down.

"I'll say. Poor Lilly."

"You might change your mind when you hear the next bit."

Intrigued, I grab my laptop and open a fresh page to start typing while Dad talks.

CHAPTER NINETEEN

Lilly

1940–1941

Tommy had been gone for nearly two months when Lilly received his first letter. When she hurried over to Tommy's parents to share it, she was taken aback to learn they had already received two.

"How are you holding up, dear?" Mrs. DeWitt pulled out a kitchen chair for Lilly.

She sat down with a sigh. "I'm all right. Worried for Tommy, of course."

Lilly couldn't very well admit the whole truth. While it was true she held concern for Tommy's safety, she enjoyed having their little apartment to herself. She slept better at night and had more energy for her job. In fact, she was looking for new ways to fill the long evenings.

They read each other's letters. Tommy couldn't reveal his location, only that he was safe, meeting interesting people, and seeing remarkable places. If not for his complaints about the bad food, it would seem as though he had gone on a pleasure trip.

• • •

One Saturday afternoon, Lilly walked to the library to stock up on books. She was perusing the fiction shelves when a familiar, imperfect gait at the end of the row grabbed her attention. William Tidsbury was instructing a volunteer on the proper way to shelve books.

Curious, she selected her books and waited for him at the checkout counter. "Hello, William."

"Hi, Lilly."

Lilly laid her books on the counter. "I didn't know you were back in town. Did you finish your course already?"

"No, I still have a semester to go, but it's on hold for now."

"Oh?"

"Both my brothers enlisted and... well, Mother's been having a tough time with it. When this job came up for a full-time librarian, I decided to apply. Just started last week."

"And is your mum doing better?"

"She always does better if she has at least one of us under her roof."

Another patron approached the counter. "Excuse me?" He held up two books. "These books weren't where they were supposed to be. It took me thirty minutes to find them."

"I'm sorry, sir." William reached for the man's books. "Are you ready to check out? I can do that now if you like."

William shot an apologetic glance in Lilly's direction and she slid her stack of books over a few feet to make room for the other patron. William stamped the due date in the man's books and apologized again.

The man left, and William turned his attention to Lilly's books. "Sorry about that, Lilly."

"Not a problem, I'm in no hurry. In fact, I was thinking of staying here awhile to read."

"Were *your* books shelved properly?" William took her card and stamped her books.

"I think so."

"We've been having so much trouble with that. People take them down, peruse them, then stick them back any old place. We sure could use another volunteer or two. You're not looking for more to do by any chance, are you?"

"Really?" Lilly didn't have to think about it long. "I need to fill my evenings and Saturdays. Sign me up."

• • •

By February, Lilly was helping at the library Tuesday and Thursday evenings and every other Saturday morning. She loved the work and the opportunity to acquaint herself with more books and periodicals. She kept abreast of the headlines, most of which had to do with how the war progressed—which was rarely good. Her friendship with William grew as they discovered they enjoyed the same books and music. Lilly began to realize she was looking forward to her time with William more than anything else.

In May, when William invited her to see *The Philadelphia Story* starring Cary Grant, Katharine Hepburn, and James Stewart, Lilly didn't hesitate.

"We're just friends" she explained to her reflection in the bathroom mirror as she applied her lipstick.

So why did you fib to Aunty Margaret when she asked if you had plans for tonight? She pushed her conscience down. *Aunty Margaret wouldn't understand. A girl needs some fun.*

By July, William and Lilly had become Saturday night regulars at the movie theater in a neighboring town. The newsreels before each feature film reminded Lilly that her husband was in danger, fighting valiantly along with so many other young men she knew and many she did not. But it all seemed so far away. Other than the rationing of certain foods and supplies, the war had little effect on her daily life. Besides, the news was always depressing. She could do her bit by bringing a little joy into William's lonely life.

One warm September night, William shared a secret.

"You probably know I always had a crush on you." The slight blush made his face even more handsome. "As far back as I can remember."

Lilly smiled. "How would I know that? You were always so quiet and absorbed in your books."

"You were always with Tommy, so I never acted on my feelings. But I figured you could tell anyway." He stopped and turned toward her. When he took both of Lilly's hands in his, she could feel her heart pounding. "Here's the thing, Lilly. This past year, as I've gotten to know you better… well, my feelings have only grown stronger. You're a wonderful woman. Beautiful and smart. Fun to be with. I feel like you understand me."

This is wrong.

Lilly tamped down her guilt like she was putting out an ember under her shoe. Being admired and hearing William's words filled a massive hole deep inside.

"I know you belong to someone else." William turned and continued leading her down the sidewalk but still held tightly to one hand. "Yet I don't think I could forgive myself if I never told you. So… I'm risking it. If you decide we can't be more than friends, I still want you to know how I feel. No matter how much I wish things were different. I love you, Lilly."

Lilly could hardly breathe, let alone speak. They reached the bottom of the staircase leading to her apartment.

"Good night." Without another word, William turned and limped away.

"Wait!"

William stopped but didn't turn. "Don't make me turn around right now. Just think about what I said. What I can't believe I just said."

He kept going, leaving Lilly more confused than ever.

She couldn't sleep that night. What was William saying? Was he ending things or was he inviting her into something illicit? Should she stop volunteering at the library so she wouldn't see so much of him? Her heart ached at the thought of not seeing him. And soared at the knowledge that she was loved.

She returned for her regular library shift right on schedule.

• • •

By October, friendship and flirtation had spiraled into a full-fledged affair. Lilly stopped attending church altogether and avoided her family as much as possible, especially Tommy's parents. For the first time in her life, she felt complete and loved. William's attentions were romantic, his passion for her undivided. She refused to let God or anyone else take that away.

Twice, Lilly came near to telling William about setting the fire. Unbearable turmoil pulled her back and forth. One side argued that he would leave her, hate her, if he knew the truth. The other side argued that she could never know true intimacy with him until he knew everything.

In the end, fear won. She couldn't bear to lose him, not now. If Tommy didn't make it home, William would marry her in a heartbeat. She could cross that bridge then.

If Tommy did make it home, the affair would end, and it wouldn't really matter anymore. William would be better off not knowing. For now, she would enjoy his attentions and live one day at a time. What else could anyone do during a war anyway? By tomorrow, they might all get blown to bits.

• • •

But in January, everything changed when a familiar dread plagued Lilly. This time, she knew enough not to ignore the clues. Rather than seeing Dr. Ramsey, her local doctor, she bought a train ticket and sought out a doctor in the city who didn't know her.

"Congratulations, you're expecting." The doctor's wide smile confirmed Lilly's fear. "Is this your first pregnancy?"

Lilly hesitated. "No… my first was… I had a miscarriage. My regular doctor said I wouldn't be able to conceive again."

"Well then, I'm happy to be the one to tell you that you've proven him wrong. I recommend you see him as soon as possible and set up a schedule for prenatal appointments. But so far, everything seems fine. Baby should be coming in September. Any questions?"

Lilly was too stunned to speak. She had prayed all the way to Winnipeg that her hunch was wrong. But why should it be? She'd made another really stupid choice and now she would pay the consequences.

"If not, I'll leave you with Nurse Rogers. She can fix you up with some vitamins." The doctor handed his clipboard to a nurse standing off to the side and left the room.

Lilly clutched her stomach. What was she going to do? If she had a baby, everyone would know it wasn't Tommy's. How could she do that to him? To his family? To Aunty Margaret and Uncle Henry?

The nurse handed Lilly her clothes. "Am I right in guessing this isn't the happy news you were hoping for?"

Compassion radiated from the dark-haired woman's eyes. Lilly squeezed her own shut to pinch off the tears. She needed to talk to someone, someone who didn't know her. "My… husband… has been overseas for over a year." Lilly stared at the floor, shame flooding her body and soul until she thought she'd choke.

"I see." The woman's voice held no condemnation.

Lilly took a deep breath and let it out with a shudder.

"I might be able to help you. Go ahead and get dressed." The nurse left the room.

Lilly pulled her clothes on. She buttoned her coat as she walked slowly down the hallway toward the reception area.

The same nurse waited at the front counter. As Lilly approached, the nurse caught her eye. Without a word, she slid a slip of paper across the counter toward Lilly. As soon as Lilly took it, the nurse called her next patient, turned, and disappeared around the corner. Lilly glanced down at the paper to see the name of a doctor and a phone number. She plunged it deep into her pocket and nearly ran out of the clinic.

That night, Lilly sat at her little kitchen table with the slip of paper in front of her. Who was Dr. K. Wall? Discussions had come up at work about doctors who terminated pregnancies even though the procedure was illegal. Any doctor caught doing such a thing would immediately lose his license and probably face prison time.

Maybe I'll lose this baby like I did the last. That horrible day returned in a flash. Someone would still find out. Or she could bleed to death, alone in her apartment.

And if she waited too long and didn't miscarry, it would be too late to call this Dr. Wall.

Oh God, what do I do?

Just as quickly as the question came, so did an answer. *How dare you even ask for God's help? You got yourself into this, and you deserve whatever comes.* The voice sounded a lot like Aunty Margaret's.

Lilly tried to play out both scenarios. If she had the child, everyone—including Tommy—would know she'd been unfaithful. He would probably divorce her, but what if he refused out of spite? Where did that leave William?

Aunty Margaret and Uncle Henry would be devastated regardless. How could she do this to them?

If she went ahead with the procedure, no one would ever have to know. Not even William. What he didn't know couldn't hurt him, just like he didn't know about the source of the house fire. She'd break things off with him to ensure she never revealed either secret.

Then another thought plagued her. Dr. Ramsey would probably say it was a miracle she was pregnant at all. What if this were her last chance to have a child?

Some miracle. What she needed right now was the kind of miracle that would take her back in time and erase her stupid actions. But that wasn't going to happen. Better to end this now and live with whatever pain she deserved.

By the end of the week, Lilly had ended things with William, quit her volunteer position at the library, and booked an appointment at a Winnipeg residence.

CHAPTER TWENTY

1941

March blurred into April. Lilly put in extra hours at the hospital without pay, calling it her contribution to the war effort. In truth, she knew it was a somewhat successful attempt to forget about William and the termination of her pregnancy.

When the April 14 issue of *Life* magazine arrived for the waiting room, she flipped through it to see photo after photo of soldiers, sailors, and airmen. She stared hard at a picture of German sailors whose cargo ship, the *Arauca*, had been captured and repurposed into the *USS Saturn*. Its original crew would probably spend the remainder of the war imprisoned in Florida.

Lilly quickly flipped the page, not wanting to think about young men being held prisoner anywhere. Her last letter from Tommy had indicated he was hoping to be deployed for an active mission soon but couldn't say where. Lilly wasn't sure if that was because he didn't know or simply wasn't supposed to reveal the information. Her letters to him were short, describing the weather and latest developments at the hospital. Though she did not wish any ill on him, to say she missed him would have been one more lie to add to her growing pile.

She turned another page. In the top corner, a photo of an attractive young woman caught her eye. The caption said:

> Marjorie Myers, Oberlin College co-ed, wrote last fortnight in
> the Oberlin Review: "Marriage should not necessarily demand

sexual fidelity." Last week Marjorie was 1) investigated by postal authorities, 2) accused by a priest of writing "unadulterated filth," and 3) confined to her room after 7:15 p.m. for the rest of the year for necking.[3]

Lilly stared at the student's pretty face, her lips and eyes projecting a sassy attitude. Marjorie was probably close to the same age as Lilly.

I guess she'd like me really well. Apparently, I don't see marriage as demanding sexual fidelity either.

During the day, it wasn't difficult to stay busy and focus on work. In the evenings, she took care of her apartment and read novels, making sure to visit the library only on William's day off. But after she went to bed, the turmoil assaulted her. She kept reliving the procedure she'd undergone in the city, yearning to tell someone about it. When Saturday dawned warm and sunny, she walked to the cemetery she hadn't visited since the previous summer and found the familiar grave.

"Well, Mama. Here I am again. Your disgraceful daughter. I know I should have stayed away from William, but I really care about him. It hurts to not be able to talk to him, laugh with him. To tell him this big, awful secret. Tommy never made me feel like William does. *Did.*

"It's over now, and the poor man is probably confused. I told him I just couldn't deal with the duplicity anymore, the guilt. He bought it. He has honored my request and hasn't tried to contact me, even though part of me wishes he would. I know it was the right and best thing to do, but it feels horrible.

"Turns out the doctor I went to see is a woman, and she told me Wall isn't even her real name. I don't know what her real name is, but she assured me she'd performed the procedure many times. She gave me a sedative, so I don't remember much. She took care of it. I bled some, but it wasn't really that bad. I walked out of there so relieved, like a truckload of worry had been lifted off my back and I could breathe again. They charged me a whole paycheck, but I learned from it, Mama. I won't let it happen again. If I never get to be a mother, well… so be it. I wouldn't be very good at it anyway.

"I just needed to tell somebody. And since I know you can keep a secret, you get to be the somebody. You must be so disappointed in your daughter. I know Uncle Henry would be if he knew.

"I'm sorry. I'll try to do better, I promise. I'll go back to church, too."

• • •

As the days passed, Lilly wished she had thought to ask Dr. Wall when she could expect to feel normal again. She continued to feel nauseated much of the time. Fatigue plagued her, though she chalked that up to not sleeping well. Could she have contracted an infection?

One day at work, Dr. Ramsey paused as he was walking past her desk. "Are you feeling all right, Mrs. DeWitt? You look a little pale."

Lilly dabbed at her forehead with her handkerchief. "Could be a touch of the flu. I hear it's going around."

"If it is, you should stay home. Stop by my examining room when you finish your shift and we'll take a quick look at you."

Lilly did. Blood and urine samples were taken along with blood pressure and temperature. Dr. Ramsey used his stethoscope and felt her abdomen, then dismissed his nurse and told Lilly to get dressed.

When she came out from behind the curtain, he was scribbling notes at a small desk.

"Have a seat, Mrs. DeWitt."

Lilly sat, wondering if Dr. Ramsey could tell she'd undergone the termination procedure.

"Your husband is overseas, is that correct?"

Lilly nodded.

"When's the last time you saw him?"

"November of '39, so…" She did a quick addition with the aid of her fingers. "Seventeen months, I guess. Eighteen?"

Dr. Ramsey stared at her. Lilly broke into a sweat. *He must know. Will he report me? Try to find out who did this? What's going to happen?*

"Well, the good news is you don't have the flu. But… I'm not sure you want to hear that you're pregnant."

Lilly stared. "What?"

"Almost four months along, I'd say. I'm not sure whether to congratulate you or—"

"But that's not possible!" Lilly shook her head.

Dr. Ramsey waited, closing his eyes a moment as if trying to determine how best to continue. "I've been caring for expectant mothers for twenty-five years. I haven't been wrong about a pregnancy yet."

"But you are this time! You *must* be wrong."

"I heard the baby's heartbeat, Mrs. DeWitt."

Lilly swallowed hard and sank back into her chair. *Heartbeat.* The procedure had failed.

"Look, you don't have to tell me anything, unless you want to." Dr. Ramsey made a note on the form in Lilly's file. "Anything you wish to say will be kept in strictest confidence—unless of course, there's been a crime committed. This isn't the result of a rape, is it, Mrs. DeWitt?"

Slowly, without raising her head, she shook her head. What would he do if he knew what she'd done?

"I'll take care of you and be happy to deliver your baby without judgment in any case. Delivery should happen in…" he twirled a pinwheel chart on his desk. "…middle of September or so. Meanwhile, let's get you on some vitamins, shall we? Those dark circles under your eyes concern me."

• • •

The next morning, Lilly called Dr. Wall's number. The long-distance operator told her the number was not in service. On Saturday, she caught the early train to Winnipeg and made her way to the same house where she'd gone for the procedure. She went around to the back door like she'd been instructed the first time and knocked. A man came to the door and looked at her without saying anything.

Lilly cleared her throat. "I'm here to see Dr. Wall."

"Ma'am, this is my home. There are no doctors here." The man started to close the door.

"No, wait!" Lilly lowered her voice to a whisper. "I know that's not her real name. She treated me a few weeks ago. I really need to see her."

"Look, lady, I don't know what you're talking about. There is no doctor here. Are you sure you have the right address?"

Lilly knew it was the same place. She recognized the door, the rug the man stood on, the color of the kitchen walls behind him. "Yes. I was here."

"Well, I'm sorry, but I've never heard of a Doctor Wall. I can't help you." He closed the door. Lilly heard the deadbolt click into place.

Lilly had read *Alice's Adventures in Wonderland* when she was twelve years old. Now it seemed she herself had fallen down some strange rabbit hole and would never surface. She walked around to the front and checked the house number again. She stared at the house, then studied the houses on either side and the one across the street. She walked to the corner and double-checked the street name. Nothing had changed except the occupant of the house.

Clearly, she'd been duped.

Lilly took her time on the long hike back to the train station, each step feeling as though she was pushing through a thick fog, despite the sunshine. Should she return to the original clinic and look for the nurse who had given her Dr. Wall's number? But it was pointless. She was too far along now anyway.

Maybe this was meant to be.

Up ahead and to her right, a church with a tall steeple pointed toward heaven, one of its front doors hanging open as though beckoning Lilly inside. Feeling shaky, she made her way up the steps and through the foyer. Rows of wooden pews filled the sanctuary, and Lilly slipped into the back row. Waiting for her eyes to adjust from the bright daylight to the darker room, she rested her forehead on the back of the pew in front of her and let out a shuddering sigh.

Oh God. Do you see me here? Do you care? Her silent prayer turned audible. "I don't know what to do. Please tell me what to do."

When no answer was forthcoming, the sobbing began. Alone and lost, she crossed her arms under her face to absorb the sound and the tears. She simply could not imagine a future for herself. She'd have to quit work. Tommy's paycheck arrived every month and she could live on it, but how dare she when she was carrying another man's child? And how could she turn to Uncle Henry and Aunty Margaret now? Two of their own boys were off fighting in the war, too. Lilly couldn't add more to their burden, not when it was a result of her own recklessness.

"Foolish, foolish, foolish!"

The words escaped her lips just before a sound in the room made her raise her head. A woman stood near the front with a scrub bucket and mop, staring at Lilly.

Oh no. Lilly quickly wiped her eyes and stood to leave.

"Wait!" The woman set her mop and pail aside and started toward Lilly. "Please don't leave."

The closer she came, the more obvious it was that the right side of the woman's neck and face were badly scarred.

Burn scars. Lilly wanted to run, but the woman's warm smile compelled her to stay where she was.

"I'm s–sorry," Lilly stammered. "I'm probably not supposed to be here."

"No, it's fine. I left the door open for fresh air, but anyone is welcome to come in and pray. Or just sit and rest."

Lilly tried not to stare at the woman's scars. "Well... I can see you have work to do, so I'll get out of your way."

"Nonsense. I'm a volunteer, so I can take all day if I want to." The woman chuckled. "I couldn't help noticing your... distress. Would you like someone to talk to?"

The last thing Lilly wanted right then was a pastor or priest. "No. I'll be fine."

"Are you sure? I'm a good listener... on this side." She chuckled again, pointing to her left ear, opposite the scarred side.

The warmth in the woman's eyes and voice touched a tender spot inside Lilly. Fresh tears sprang up.

"Here, honey. Sit by me." The woman slid into the row and sat, patting the spot from which Lilly had just risen. "We don't even have to talk if you don't want to."

Lilly took a deep breath, let it out, and eased herself onto the edge of the pew. Maybe she should dump her whole story on this stranger. She'd surely be glad to see Lilly leave the premises once she heard it.

The woman touched Lilly's arm ever so gently. "I'm Lilly."

What? She must have heard wrong. "Lilly?"

The woman nodded. "Lillian, really. Never been called that, though. Just Lilly. What's *your* name, honey?"

Should she say? This Lilly woman probably wouldn't believe her, and Lilly wasn't sure she wanted her knowing her name anyway.

She gazed at a stained-glass window that featured a red rose with a thorny stem, then blurted out the first name that came to mind. "Rose."

"Oh, that's beautiful! We're both flowers." The woman took Lilly's hand and held it between her own two. "Precious flowers made by God's own hand. Did you know that, honey? You were made by God and he loves you more than you will ever know. You are a treasure to him."

Lilly stared back at her. Tears dripped off her chin and she swiped at them with her free hand. "I... doubt that's true."

"Oh, but it is, Rose. Doesn't matter what you've done. Doesn't matter how you feel about him. Doesn't matter if you're scared or confused... if you feel like you did something stupid."

"You heard me, didn't you?"

The woman tipped her head to one side. "Kinda couldn't help hearing you, honey. Even with only one good ear."

Lilly smiled, looking down at her feet.

"Did you do something stupid?" asked the woman.

"I've done nothing but stupid things. One bad choice after another. All my life."

"Oh, now, I doubt that. I bet you've done lots of things right, too. Why, you walked into this church, didn't you? You know what that tells me?"

Lilly shook her head.

The woman pushed some graying hair up under the kerchief tied around her head. "It tells me you're seeking God in some way or another. And honey, there's no better place to start looking for help, any kinda help. Take it from me. I'm fifty-five years old and seen far more in this nasty ol' world than most. Done my share of stupid, you better believe it. But I can tell you right now, Rose… beyond any doubt." She thumped her fist against her chest once for each of the next three words. "God. Loves. Lilly. God's got Lilly in his hands, and he's never gonna let her go. No matter what."

CHAPTER TWENTY-ONE

Diana

"Oh Dad." I kneel beside his chair and take one of his hands in both of mine. "That was *you*, wasn't it? You were almost aborted?"

Dad nods slowly, his eyes glistening with tears. I look over at Shane, who is wiping his eyes with his sleeve. In that moment, I am such a jumble of compassion for Lilly and gratitude for my father's life, I can't process it all. I reach my arms up and Dad wraps his around me.

"This is what you meant when you said neither of us would be here."

"Yep. And I'm glad my mother told me. It's given me a deeper appreciation for my life every day. I'm here. I've got two wonderful daughters and three beautiful grandkids. And I like to think I've made a bit of a difference in this world."

"Of course you have, Dr. DeWitt." Shane moves to the edge of the couch and leans in. "You've made a difference in *my* life and I've only known you a week."

Dad takes in Shane's tender words with a nod. "Every time I hear of one of my young interns taking a clinic job at a remote posting or the mission field, I stop and thank God for leaving me here, so I could teach them. Did I ever tell you about Sarah? She worked with me for five years. Now she's doing breakthrough research, writing papers. Giving the medical community hope for ending pandemic-level viruses." Mouse hops up onto Dad's lap and Dad cuddles her close, clearing his throat. "I just feel so proud and so humbled at the same time. I wonder what might have happened if I hadn't been born?"

We hear no more about Lilly's story tonight. Shane has to work in the morning, so he says his goodbye to Dad and leaves. While I help Dad pack up, he pesters me more about Shane.

"You need to snag that man before it's too late, Princess."

I shove his freshly laundered socks into his suitcase. "Meddling, Dad."

"Only because I love you." He arranges the clothes he plans to wear in the morning on the chair. "I know you're scared. But don't you think it's time to leave that old hurt in the past where it belongs?"

"It's not that simple. It was the ultimate rejection, Dad."

"Was it, sweetheart?"

I just shrug. "I guess… I suppose the ultimate rejection would be from God himself. My creator."

Dad nods slowly. "I think you're right. And that's never going to happen. Not ever."

• • •

In the morning, I drive Dad to the airport and hug him tightly.

"Dad, thanks so much for coming. I wish your visit had turned out differently for you."

"I don't. I got a wakeup call, a new appreciation for my life, and lots of time with you, Princess. What more could a guy ask?"

I hug him again and watch him go through security. On the other side, he turns and waves to me one last time. He heads off to his gate and I drive to my office, using the thirty-minute commute to mentally transition to work mode.

Four hours later, Becky texts to say Dad is with her and all is well.

As nice as it is to sleep in my own bed again, the house feels empty.

• • •

Sunday morning, I knock on Carly's door. She answers it, ready to go. Her mother and brothers are watching TV.

"Bye, everybody!" She heads out the door, but I hold it open and step inside.

"Hi, Tonya. You're okay with Carly coming to church with me, right?"

"Oh sure. It'll do her good." She laughs. "Maybe some of it will rub off on me."

"You're welcome to join us."

She waves us away. "No, thanks. You two go ahead. I'll stay here with these hooligans."

"Okay. Another time, maybe."

Look at me, turning into quite the evangelist.

• • •

I observe everything at church as though experiencing it through Carly's eyes and ears. What does she think? Does she like the music? Are the greeters trying too hard? Does she understand the scriptures? Is anything offensive? Is the sermon boring? Does anybody act stuffy or condescending?

On the way to the car afterward, I realize I've been so busy worrying about everything that I can't even say what the message was about.

We climb into my car and do up our seatbelts.

"So? What did you think?" I immediately second-guess myself. Maybe I should wait for her to volunteer something.

Her answer stumps me. "I like those announcements on the screen."

The announcements on the screen? That's what impressed her? "What do you mean?"

She shrugs as if she's already forgotten.

I drive out of the parking lot and onto the street. "Where would you like to go for lunch on this gorgeous day?"

"Can we get subs and go to the park?"

"You know my picnic blanket is always in my trunk."

Thirty minutes later, we're sitting cross-legged on it, munching sandwiches and chips in the shade of some linden trees. Squirrels and chipmunks scamper around, scolding and chasing each other as though they've been specifically assigned to entertain us.

"I'm really glad you came with me to church." I hope Carly will share some insight she picked up, or maybe ask a question about Jesus.

I pray silently. *Lord, help me communicate your love and truth to her.*

But she is still on about the announcements on the screen. "So one of those slide-thingies said there was a pregnancy support place. What's that about?"

I need to think a bit. "Oh. Yeah. Um... well, our church helped start a pregnancy support center, along with several other churches. That way we can combine our resources to help young women in a tough spot. I don't know that much about it, but... I've seen their brochures."

I stopped at their info booth at church one Sunday to drop off a couple of baby afghans I'd crocheted last winter and grabbed some of their printed materials. Now I wrack my brain to remember all the services they provide.

"I know there's counseling available, as well as support for young parents," I say. "Baby clothes and supplies. Classes on health and parenting. Sexual health and integrity. Grief counseling for infant loss. That sort of thing."

"Is it free?"

"Yes. Do you know someone who could use their help?"

Carly focuses on the fountain in a nearby pond. "Maybe. Do they do terminations?"

I need to pause a second to grasp her meaning. "No. It's not a medical clinic, so they don't refer or prescribe or anything. Although they *are* raising funds to buy an ultrasound machine. They educate women about their options. I know they do a lot of post-abortion care and counseling for those who need it."

Carly stares off into space for so long that I begin to worry. Is God nudging me?

"Carly?" I venture. "Have you... have you had an abortion?"

She shakes her head, but tears well up. "No. I think I'm pregnant."

I swallow, even though my sandwich is long gone. I've never felt so keenly out of my league. What do I have to offer Carly? I am an "old maid," older than her mother, never been pregnant, never dealt with anyone in her situation. The only things I know for certain are that Carly needs to take a pregnancy test and she has to tell her mother. She doesn't need me berating her or her boyfriend, no matter how much I might want to wring the boy's neck.

"You won't tell anyone, will you?" she says without looking at me.

I take a deep breath and let it out slowly. "On one condition."

She looks at me, waiting.

"You agree to meet me at the pregnancy support center tomorrow."

She nods.

I spend the night praying for wisdom.

• • •

I leave a little early for my lunch break and hurry to the pregnancy center. Carly sits on a bench outside and we walk in together. At the counter, she makes me proud by speaking for herself, explaining that she thinks she is pregnant and that I'm her big sister, along for support. I'm impressed with the level of respect and compassion extended to her by everyone we see.

When we walk out an hour later, Carly has completed two separate tests, both of which show positive for pregnancy. Our purses are loaded down with every educational pamphlet the center has to offer.

Speaking of offers, I know before we reach my car which one I need to make next.

"Want me to go with you to tell your mom?" I secretly hope Carly says *no*.

"Yes, please. The sooner the better."

My heart sinks. Will Tonya find a way to blame me? I was supposed to be a role model, a mentor. Instead I've turned out to be a miserable failure.

I am also grown up enough to know this isn't about me. "Now?"

"Mom's at work now. But she'll be home by five-thirty. Can we do it then?"

I nod. I'll be off work by then, too, but I'll have to give up my house church meeting which Shane agreed to join me at for the first time.

"All right." I sigh. "You're smart to not put it off."

I drop her off and return to work. My feeling of dread grows heavier as the afternoon ticks by, making it hard to concentrate. If I feel this way, I can only imagine what Carly is going through.

God, help me. Help Carly. Help Tonya. Help us.

My pleas grow into a repeating mantra in the back of my brain.

• • •

When I arrive, Carly opens the door. "C'mon in."

Tonya enters the room, turns off the TV, and shoos her two boys into their bedroom before turning to me. "So, what's this about? Carly said you were coming over and she has something important to tell me. Have a seat."

At least Carly has made an effort to prepare her mom. Has Tonya already guessed? We all sit in separate chairs.

Carly's hands shake, but she doesn't beat around the bush. "I'm pregnant, Mom."

Tonya stares at Carly while the words sink in. She glances at me, then back at her daughter. "You sure?"

Carly nods.

"How far along?"

"Six and a half weeks." Carly is staring at a spot on the floor.

Tonya turns to me. "How long have you known about this?"

Oh dear. Tonya is hurt, and who can blame her? "She... we... just confirmed it this afternoon. We went to the—"

"Get rid of it."

What? My eyes dart back and forth between the two of them.

Carly looks up at her mother. "Mom, it's… it's a big decision. I need some time to—"

"You heard me. The sooner you do it, the easier it'll be. I'll call right now and set it up." She reaches toward the coffee table and picks up her phone.

"Tonya, wait." I fumble for words. "Shouldn't this be Carly's choice?"

"Well, it sure isn't yours." She stands and points at the door with one hand while her thumb scrolls her phone with the other.

"Mom, I invited Diana here."

"And I'm inviting her out." With a huff, she walks over to the door and holds it open. "Look, I appreciate all you've done for Carly these last few years, I really do. I guess it was too much to expect you could keep her from making the same mistakes I made. But now it's my turn to keep her from making another mistake I made."

Immediately, Tonya realizes what she said and turns to Carly. "I'm sorry, I didn't mean it like that. It came out wrong."

The pain on Carly's face tells me it's too late.

I have to say something. "Tonya, I can only imagine how hard being a single mom is… I… can't pretend to know. But Carly is a wonderful, beautiful, smart girl. She's made a mistake, but she has the legal right to choose for herself—"

"Do you think I'm an idiot? I can't force her to do anything, I know that. But I'm her mother, and unlike you, I have been in her shoes, okay? You have no idea how hard it is. I love my daughter. I want her to go to university, not be caring for a child while she's still a child herself."

"Mom, I'm not—"

"—I'll guide my daughter through this decision. Now you need to leave. Don't make me call the Big Sisters people on you."

I give Carly a long, solid look through my tear-filled eyes, unsure she can even see me through her own. I leave, quite certain she will no longer be pregnant the next time I hear from her.

• • •

The meeting with Tonya ended so quickly that I could easily make it to house church. But I arrive home exhausted. I kick off my shoes, relieved to be staying in. I put the kettle on, muttering to God the whole time. "What do I do next, Lord? I feel so helpless and inadequate."

I grab the mail out my mailbox and sift through it. One bill, three pieces of junk, and a thank-you letter from Big Brothers/Big Sisters for my five years of service. Great.

I warm up some leftovers in the microwave and plop down in front of my laptop to check email. My father's name pops up and I click on it.

Hey Princess. I'm writing up a storm. Have fun typing up this next installment and tell me what you think of it.

Please, God, let this next chapter of Lilly's story be a happy one.

CHAPTER TWENTY-TWO

Lilly

1941

Lilly managed to keep her secret for another month. She went to work, did her job, and walked home. On Saturdays, she purchased what she needed from Gordon's Grocery, avoiding Mrs. Gordon's scrutiny. Once a month, she paid her rent, deposited her paycheck, and collected Tommy's pay of $37.50. This she placed in a separate account, determined that it be waiting for him upon his return. Last, she'd stop at the library for as many books as she was allowed to borrow.

As May turned to June, it was becoming impossible to squeeze into her clothes. Standing in front of the mirror one Saturday morning, she tried on every skirt and dress she owned, desperate for something that would conceal her growing body.

When she took her eyes off her reflected shape long enough to notice her face, a sad and much older-looking woman gazed back.

"What are you going to do now, Lilly? Go out and spend money on larger clothes? Let the seams out of these?"

Neither solution would hide her shape for long. Somewhere in Uncle Henry and Aunty Margaret's house was a box of maternity and baby clothes.

"It's time to face them. Just do it and get it over with."

She raised her chin for confidence and pulled her hair back into a ponytail for youthfulness. Even her face was growing rounder.

With her roomiest skirt safety-pinned, she grabbed a pale blue shirt from Tommy's side of the closet and pulled it on. She was able to button it up. By letting it hang outside the skirt, it covered her half-closed zipper. To make the ensemble more feminine, she rolled the sleeves to her elbows and added a silk scarf around her neck. She grabbed her purse and headed over to see her aunt and uncle.

"Lilly!" Aunty Margaret scanned Lilly's outfit in the second it took to open the screen door. "Come on in." She scurried around while she talked. "I'll put on a fresh pot of coffee—or would you like something cold? It's going to be a hot one out there, I think."

She stepped from window to window, pulling blinds closed against the morning sun.

"Oh, don't waste your rationed coffee on me. A glass of water will be fine." Lilly entered the familiar kitchen and took a seat at the table where it was easier to hide her midsection. "Is Uncle Henry around?"

"He's mowing grass at the cemetery."

"Oh." Lilly's heart sank. Should she try again later?

Aunty Margaret filled two glasses with water and sat down opposite Lilly. "I bet your little apartment gets hot on days like this."

"It's not bad. I have a fan." Lilly took a sip.

"So what brings you by? Did you get a letter this week? Tommy's parents didn't."

"No. I didn't either."

"Work going all right?"

Lilly nodded. "Yes." She looked around the room nervously, her eyes drawn to her aunt's clothing. She was clearly dressed for gardening. "I'm sorry, Aunty Margaret. I'm keeping you from your garden, aren't I? You probably want to be out there before it gets hot. I should help you."

"Nonsense. I mean, you're welcome to stay and help if you want. In fact, there's spinach and lettuce ready for you to take home if you like. We'll never eat it all. Maybe radishes, too."

Lilly's heart was pounding. She really couldn't put this off any longer. "Aunty Margaret, do you still have the baby clothes and maternity clothes we made?"

"Of course! I saved them together in a box upstairs. Why?" She picked a crumb off the table.

"Well… I… need them."

Aunty Margaret looked up. "For who? Anyone I know?"

Lilly took a deep breath and let it out, then looked her aunt in the eye. "For me."

"Well, of course, you can have them back whenever you want, they are yours after all—" Suddenly, her expression changed. She focused on the manly shirt Lilly was wearing for a moment, then tipped her head to one side. "What are you saying?"

Lilly swallowed. Too late to turn back now. "I'm going to have a baby. In September."

"September." The color drained from Aunty Margaret's face. "That's not—" She stared at her until Lilly had to look away. "Oh, Lilly. What have you done?"

Lilly studied the surface of the table. "I think it's obvious what I've done."

"With whom?"

Lilly knew this would be the first question and had already decided she would not tell. "Does it matter?"

"Well, of course it does. Especially if he forced himself on you. He did, didn't he?"

Lilly rested her elbows on the table and hid her face behind her hands. "No, Aunty Margaret. I'm… I'm sorry. You must be so disappointed in me and I'm sorry for my behavior. It's over, if that helps."

"How can it be over if you're having his baby? It will never be over. Oh, Lilly."

"I know. I just… I need those clothes. Nothing fits anymore."

"And here I thought it was sweet that you were wearing Tommy's shirt. That you were missing him. Clearly, you're not missing him at all."

Lilly let out a big sigh and rose to her feet. "Can I just go upstairs and find the box myself? I won't trouble you with it." She was beginning to wish she'd gone shopping for fabric instead, but she didn't want to spend any more money than necessary. Besides, it would have meant borrowing Aunty Margaret's sewing machine.

She wouldn't be able to keep this secret forever. Or even for another week.

"Wait a minute." Aunty Margaret wasn't done. "What about work? They're not going to let you keep working."

"No. Likely not."

"When are you planning to tell Thomas? What about his parents?"

Lilly had been trying hard not to think about Tommy's mom and dad. Tears welled up at the mention of them. "I don't know. I… I haven't figured any of that out yet. Right now, I just need something to wear."

With a long slow huff, Aunty Margaret pulled herself to her feet and turned toward the stairs. "Follow me."

From a closet at the end of the upstairs hallway, Aunty Margaret pulled out a box labeled "Maternity and Baby Clothes—Lilly." A lump formed in Lilly's throat at the sight. She accepted the box with a murmured "Thank you" and turned toward the stairs.

At the top of the stairs, Aunty Margaret gripped Lilly's arm. "Here. Let me." She took the box and carried it down, then laid it on the table. "How am I going to tell your Uncle Henry? He practically worships the ground you walk on."

"Do you want me to tell him?" Lilly's voice was barely above a whisper.

Aunty Margaret's eyes smoldered. "No. I'll tell him. This is going to break his heart all over again, but far worse this time." She picked up their water glasses and carried them to the sink. "You know, my mother tried to warn me it was hereditary, but I didn't want to believe her."

Lilly stared at her aunt's back. What was hereditary?

"Henry convinced me that just because his sister was a... an *immoral* woman... it didn't mean anything about you. But he was wrong. I should have listened to my mother."

Lilly picked up the box and stepped toward the door. What else could she expect? Better get out before Aunty Margaret changed her mind about the clothes.

"I'm really sorry. You and Uncle Henry deserve better." She doubted the words meant much, but Lilly truly was sorry to be bringing pain to others.

As she opened the door, Aunty Margaret had one last word. "I'll tell Henry. But you need to tell the DeWitts yourself, and the sooner the better. I won't bail you out of that one."

Lilly returned home without any garden produce, feeling more alone than ever.

• • •

After changing into one of the maternity skirts and blouses, Lilly faced her next challenge. May as well get it all over with in one day.

From her mother-in-law's back door, she could see Aunty Margaret kneeling in her garden, yanking weeds with a vengeance, her back to the DeWitts' home. She knocked on the door lightly and Tommy's father opened it.

"Lilly! Great to see you. Come on in." He opened the door wide, clearly not noticing anything different about her. "Doris, come down! Lilly's here."

As before, Lilly made her way quickly to the kitchen table to sit just as Tommy's mother reached the bottom of the stairs. "Hello, dear. I hope this means you got a letter this week?"

"I'm afraid not. I was hoping maybe you did." Lilly already knew the answer.

"Nothing here either. It's so hard, isn't it?" Mrs. DeWitt placed a few cookies on a plate and brought them to the table before sitting across from Lilly. "Hungry? I used up my sugar rations this week, but it was worth it." She slid the plate toward Lilly.

Mr. DeWitt moved toward the back door, grabbing his hat off a hook. "I'll leave you two ladies to visit."

"Wait." Lilly tried to choke back the desperation she felt. "Can you stay? I really need to tell you something. Both of you."

Her father-in-law slowly returned his hat to the hook. "All right." He joined them at the table and sat next to his wife.

Mrs. DeWitt's face registered nothing but concern. "What is it, Lilly? Do you need something? Money?" Suddenly she gasped. "You haven't received a telegram, have you?"

"No!" Lilly needed to reassure them as quickly as possible. "Nothing like that. It's about me. I… I've done something horrible. I don't expect you to forgive me, but you need to know. The news will be all over town soon."

"Lilly, whatever are you talking about?" Mrs. DeWitt reached across the table and placed her hand over Lilly's wrist.

Lilly fought to hold back the tears. "I'm so sorry. I'm pregnant."

Several seconds ticked by while the information sank in. Once it did, Mrs. DeWitt retracted her hand. She glanced at her husband. Stared at Lilly some more. Then the inevitable two questions. The first came from Tommy's dad.

"Who? Who did this to you?"

Lilly shook her head. "He's not to blame. I am."

The second from Mrs. DeWitt. "Are you sure?"

"Completely sure. The baby is due in September."

Tommy's parents sat speechless for so long, Lilly wondered whether she should just leave. She didn't know what more to say.

When she finally raised her eyes to her mother-in-law's, she saw tears. The woman was trembling.

"How could you do this to our son?" Mr. DeWitt's clenched fists rested on the table. "Thomas does not deserve this. He's off fighting for our country, for cryin' out loud. For our safety. For you! How could you… how could you disgrace us all like this?"

"I'm sorry." Lilly stood to leave. "I'm so sorry. You're right, Tommy does not deserve it. Neither do you."

Mrs. DeWitt took in Lilly's clothes and stared at her midsection. "Oh, Lilly." She wiped at the tears on her cheeks. "Have you written to Thomas yet?"

"No, ma'am. I… don't want to make things harder for him than they already are."

Mr. DeWitt rose to his feet so abruptly that his chair fell over backward. "And you think it will be easier for him to come home from the war and discover you have a child that isn't his?"

"No. I… I haven't thought it through."

"I'll say you haven't. All you've thought about is your own lust!"

"Fred." Mrs. DeWitt grabbed her husband's sleeve. "Settle down."

While Tommy's father stormed into the living room, Mrs. DeWitt stood. "Lilly. I want you to go home right now and write to Thomas. Tell him everything, including who the father is. He deserves to have all the information so he can decide what he wants to do before he comes home. You owe him that much."

Lilly nodded, though the idea of confessing to Tommy made her weak in the knees. It couldn't be harder than what she'd already been through today, though. "I will."

"I need you to promise. Because if you don't, he's going to hear about it some other way. You don't want that. Promise me you'll do it."

"I promise."

• • •

That afternoon, Lilly sat at her kitchen table and made good on her word. She revealed everything, ending her letter with a cry for mercy.

> Please don't blame William. I take full responsibility and
> I have not seen him since I ended it with him in March.
> I don't blame you if you want nothing to do with me ever
> again. I hope for your own sake you can find it in your
> heart to forgive me, Tommy. You don't deserve this, and I

am so, so sorry. I would say it a thousand times if I thought it could change the situation or how much this will hurt you. I beg you to take some time before you respond. If you wish to divorce me, I won't fight it. But I will not make any moves in that direction on my own.

Lilly sealed and stamped the letter and walked to the post office to throw it in the mail slot before she could change her mind. The baby could arrive before Tommy ever saw the letter. As she stepped back out into the bright sunshine, a familiar figure greeted her on the front step. The irony of seeing William now, after all these weeks, was not lost on her.

"Lilly!" He sounded as surprised as she.

"Hello, William." She brushed past him as quickly as possible. Had he noticed her changed figure? She could feel his eyes boring into her as she kept walking without turning back.

She didn't leave her apartment for the rest of the weekend.

• • •

At work the following week, Lilly stayed behind her desk as much as possible and tried every trick she could to keep hiding her pregnancy. When no one had said a word by Friday, she returned home and collapsed onto her bed in relief. She'd bought herself a short reprieve and another week's pay.

A knock at the door pulled her back to her feet. When she opened it, there stood William.

She stared at him, waiting for her tongue to release. "You can't come in here."

"I know. I don't need to. I just—needed to see for myself." His eyes quickly scanned her body. "I see it's true."

Had the gossip started or was this a result of their encounter at the post office? What could be going through William's mind?

He glanced around. "Is this why you called things off with us?"

"Only partly. What we were doing was wrong, William, whether I got pregnant or not."

"When were you planning to tell me?"

"I'm sorry. I should have told you." She started to close the door. "But it wouldn't have mattered. Telling you wouldn't have changed things."

William pressed his foot against the door, preventing her from shutting it. "I've been sleepless ever since I saw you at the post office last week, Lilly. Does Tommy know?"

"He will as soon as he gets my letter. Probably take several weeks."

"What do you think he'll do?"

Lilly shrugged. How could she admit she didn't know her own husband well enough to predict how he might respond?

"I'm sorry, too, Lil. I didn't… you told me you could never conceive again."

Lilly had shared with William about the rushed wedding and miscarried baby. "That's what I was told. Guess Dr. Ramsey was wrong."

Lilly's next-door neighbor opened her back door and started shaking dirt out of a rug, watching Lilly and William the whole time. William grimaced at the flying dust and turned back to Lilly, lowering his voice. "Fine. I'll go. But listen to me. If you and Tommy decide to divorce, I will marry you, Lilly. You hear me?"

Lilly's eyes welled up. She nodded, not trusting herself to speak.

"I will, Lilly. Just say the word." William turned to limp his way down the steps, but before he was halfway down, a bicycle bell jingled repeatedly from the sidewalk.

Lilly looked up to see Clarence Cambridge in his Canadian National Telegram uniform pedal to the bottom of the staircase.

"Mrs. Thomas DeWitt?" His eyes darted to William, then back to Lilly. "Sorry, Lilly, but I'm supposed to ask."

"Yes." Lilly's heart began to pound.

Clarence got off his bike and leaned it against the garage. "Telegram for you, ma'am." He climbed the stairs, passing William who had stopped halfway down.

"Should I stay?" William asked.

"Please do." Lilly placed one hand on the railing and let the door close behind her. "Read it to me, Clarence." Her hand was shaking.

Clarence pulled the telegram from his pocket and cleared his throat.

FROM: CANADIAN ARMY OTTAWA ONTARIO

TO: MRS. THOMAS DEWITT SUMMERVALE MANITO-BA

REGRET TO INFORM YOU YOUR HUSBAND PRI-VATE THOMAS JAMES DEWITT ON EIGHTEEN MAY

WOUNDED IN LONDON AIR RAID STOP YOU WILL BE ADVISED AS REPORTS OF CONDITION ARE RE-CEIVED. PRIVATE DEWITT TO RECEIVE HONOR-ABLE DISCHARGE.

Lilly sank to the top step. Tommy was coming home.

Chapter Twenty-Three

1941

By July, Lilly's pregnancy was obvious to everyone she encountered, and word had spread about Tommy being wounded. The day of the telegram had become a blur. Lilly could vaguely remember Clarence reading it aloud, then handing it to her and leaving. William helping her into her apartment and leaving. Walking to Tommy's parents' house and showing them the telegram... and leaving. Sending notice to the hospital that her husband had been wounded and that she would not be returning to work.

At least she was spared the humiliation of being fired.

She kept to herself as much as possible. William hadn't come around again. She fell asleep most nights with his words replaying in her heart: *"I will marry you, Lilly. You hear me?"*

No further telegrams or letters about Tommy's condition arrived, nor did she hear from him herself. Divorce, unless Tommy insisted on it, was now out of the question. Whatever his wounds, decency obligated Lilly to care for and stick by him. Would he want her by his side once he knew the truth?

Dr. Ramsey assured her the baby was healthy but said she should be drinking milk each day and eating meat two or three times a week. As her bank account dwindled, she began to draw from Tommy's to make ends meet. Though Uncle Henry and Aunty Margaret didn't invite Lilly to visit, Uncle Henry delivered baskets of fresh garden produce every week. The last one had included a loaf of freshly baked bread.

Expecting another such delivery, she wasn't surprised to hear someone climbing the stairs to her apartment and knocking on the door. But when she opened it, Tommy's parents stood there instead.

A soft "Oh" escaped her lips. "Come in."

"Oh my Lord, you're as big as a house." Mrs. DeWitt stepped into the apartment, followed by her husband. "Sorry. That just slipped out. Haven't seen you since... that day."

"It's okay." Lilly tried to smile. "You're right. I'm very heavy."

She didn't have to wait long to find out why they'd come.

"Thomas called." Mr. DeWitt removed his hat. "He's in Winnipeg."

"Winnipeg?" Lilly's hand went to her heart. "He's home?"

"He'd have called you if you had a phone," his mother explained. "He's catching the evening train home. He wants you to meet him at the station. Just you."

Lilly swallowed. "Did he say how he was wounded? Or... where?" She had tried to imagine every possibility. Would he be without an arm? A leg? In a wheelchair, perhaps? Blind? Clearly he could still hear, or he wouldn't have been able to telephone his parents.

Mr. DeWitt answered. "I asked, but he refused to say. I offered to come pick him up in the car, but he said that wouldn't be necessary. So he must be able to walk."

"Did you tell him?" Lilly laid one hand across her burgeoning belly. "Did you tell him about me?"

His father shook his head. "That was *your* job."

"I know." Lilly pushed down the panic rising inside. "I wrote to him, but... I don't see how he could have received my letter yet. He should be warned before he sees me. Don't you think?"

Her in-laws stared back, Mrs. DeWitt once again releasing tears of her own. Tommy not wanting them to meet him at the station must have stung deeply. And they were still angry with Lilly, no doubt.

"You made your bed." Mr. DeWitt replaced his hat and left the apartment without turning back.

Mrs. DeWitt handed Lilly a slip of paper and leaned toward her with a whisper. "I didn't speak with Tommy, only his father did. I would have tried to find out whether he got your letter. I would have given him some warning. I would have tried to find out how bad his wounds are and tell him how glad we are that's he alive and coming home—"

A sudden sob escaped her.

"It's okay." Lilly took the paper and looked at it. The time of the train's arrival was scrawled across it in large penciled numbers: 10:35 p.m. She placed a hand on her mother-in-law's arm. "Tommy knows you're on his side, no matter what."

"Thank you for saying that." She turned to leave.

"Mrs. DeWitt?"

Her mother-in-law looked back.

"Can you get Tommy's old bedroom ready for him? Just in case?"

Mrs. DeWitt nodded. "I already did."

• • •

Lilly had little confidence that her husband would be coming home to their apartment with her that night. There could be only one reason he was eager to have his wife meet him at the station. Like any man, he would want his sweetheart to throw her arms around his neck and shower him with welcoming kisses. Whatever his injuries, he would want to know she'd stuck by him and would continue to do so.

But he would change his mind the moment he saw her.

She took time to bathe and wash her hair. While it dried, she put on her best maternity outfit—a navy dress with white collar and buttons. With shaking hands, she applied her makeup as best she could, then fussed with her hair as long as she dared.

The evening grew dark. At ten-fifteen, she picked up her purse and began the ten-minute walk to the train station.

A handful of others waited on the platform. Lilly found a bench away from the moths and bugs that fluttered around the light. As she sat at the dark end, she imagined how this scene would play out if she'd remained faithful to Tommy. As though she'd been in love with him all along.

The train pulled in at exactly ten-thirty-five. Two young women climbed down and were greeted by parents who hugged them and carried their bags as they walked away together. An older gentleman came next, then a middle-aged couple. Finally, a soldier in uniform.

Tommy.

He stepped onto the platform and stood there on both legs. No crutches, no cane. From one arm hung a duffel bag which he deftly hoisted to his opposite shoulder with both hands. He could clearly see. Why on earth had they sent him home?

He looked off to his right, then left toward where Lilly sat in the relative darkness. She couldn't move. No matter how much she wanted to rise to her feet, to call out his name, she felt paralyzed and mute.

Tommy took two steps toward the door of the station.

Finally, she cried out. "Tommy!"

He turned in her direction and at that moment, Lilly saw it. The light from the station house landed squarely on Tommy's face. His right side no longer looked like Tommy at all. The lid of his right eye drooped and seemed to melt into a scarred cheek, jawbone, ear, and neck. The scars were shiny and red.

She'd seen this before. Tommy had been burned.

"Lilly." He let his duffel bag drop to the platform and took a few steps toward her.

Whether it was compassion for her husband or something else, Lilly didn't know. But she felt herself being pulled to a standing position at last. If Tommy thought she'd be shocked to see his face, it was he who was in for the bigger shock.

She made no attempt to conceal her condition. Might as well get it over with.

"Lilly," he repeated, picking up his pace. Then, just as quickly, he froze.

They stared at each other. Lilly wanted to weep at the carnage she saw on her handsome husband's face and the pain he had no doubt endured. She couldn't get any words out. Apparently, neither could he. She raised her hands, clutching them together at her chin and biting down on the side of her forefinger.

When tears dripped onto her hands, something finally shook loose.

"Hi, Tommy." It came out like a weak croak.

Tommy's eyes scanned her figure, registering utter bewilderment. "Lil, what on earth—?" He shook his head as if to clear the vision before him. "Oh, Lilly. Why?"

Lilly pressed her lips together tightly. "I'm so sorry, Tommy. I am so, so sorry. I'll understand if you want nothing to do with me."

Tommy's confusion turned to smoldering anger. "This is what you were doing while I was fighting Nazis?"

"I wrote to you, Tommy—"

"—Running from bombs, getting my face half burned off? Trying to rescue innocent women and children from a similar fate?"

"Tom, please—"

"*This* is what you were doing?" He waved his hand in the general direction of her abdomen. "With *who*, Lilly? Who did this to you? When were you going to tell me?"

"I wrote you, Tommy."

"Well, I didn't get it."

Clearly.

"Tommy, I am so sorry. I ended it. I explained in the letter. If… if you want a divorce, I won't fight it. I'm so sorry for all you've been through. You must have suffered so much. Is it still painful?"

Tommy glared. "Worst pain I've ever had in my life. And yes, it still hurts. But it's nothing compared to coming home and seeing this."

Lilly focused on taking one breath in, one out. She could have spared Tommy. She could have spared herself, William, their families… so much pain.

Tommy still hadn't so much as blinked. "They tell me it will hurt more if I have other surgeries, which I am advised to do if I don't want to look like a monster the rest of my life."

"Oh, Tommy, you don't look like a monster."

"We're in the dark, Lil. We're standing here in the dark and you can tell I'm disfigured. And I can tell you're pregnant. What are we going to look like when we step into the light, huh? How far along are you, anyway?"

Lilly swallowed hard. "Seven. Seven months."

"Seven months. Who did this, Lilly?"

Now or never. Lilly took a deep breath and looked straight into Tommy's eyes. "William Tidsbury."

Tommy's lips formed the word William, but no sound came out. He swore softly. "Does he know about this?"

"Yes. But… I ended things with him."

Tommy swore again as he turned and picked up his duffel bag. "Does *every*one know? My parents?" He walked to the end of the platform and Lilly followed.

"They know I'm pregnant—"

"Obviously."

"—but no one knows who the father is. You're the only one I've told. And I'm certain William hasn't told anyone."

"Of course not. William Tidsbury." Tommy stepped down off the platform. "Why didn't Dad say anything on the phone? Warn me?"

"He didn't want to be the one. Said it was my job."

Tommy kept walking. "You coming?"

Lilly hustled to keep up, not even certain where they were going.

• • •

Ten minutes later, with no further conversation, they reached their little garage apartment. At the bottom of the stairs, Tommy stood aside. "After you."

Lilly climbed the stairs. Did Tommy have any intention of following her or would he carry on to his parents' house?

He followed.

Lilly had opened the windows and left a fan running to cool their space, but it was still warm compared to the night air. She poured two glasses of water and set them on the table.

"Are you hungry?" she asked.

"No." Tommy took a seat. "Not tonight. Maybe not ever."

In the light of the overhead bulb, Lilly got a clearer image of the extent of Tommy's injuries. "The telegram didn't say what happened, only that you were wounded. We... didn't know what to expect. Your parents are pretty worried."

"I wanted to warn them when I called. I just... I couldn't find the words. I thought it would be better if they were at home when they first see me than at the station with other people around, gawking. I'll head over there in a minute."

"I'm not sure I understand why you asked me to come. You could have just shown up here."

Tommy studied her face for a moment. "I wanted to give you the chance to return home without me, once you saw me. I thought it might be too much for you." He let out a snort. "Then I saw you, and... I guess I forgot all about my face."

Lilly kept standing, staring at Tommy's scars while he stared at her belly. Slowly, she moved toward him and raised a hand to touch his burned cheek. Gently, she felt the ragged ridges and ran her finger softly over the area where his ear should be. She tried to remember all she'd read and studied about burn wounds, but all she could see was an eight-year-old Tommy lighting William Tidsbury's shed on fire.

Tommy lifted his hand to her abdomen. He held it there firmly, his fingers spread. At that moment, the baby moved—one of those huge barrel-rolls that had been keeping Lilly awake most nights. Tommy jumped, removing his hand.

"What was *that*?"

Lilly couldn't help smiling. "That was the baby. He gets restless this time of night. Or she."

Tommy put both hands on her stomach to feel the motion again.

Lilly stroked the short hair that remained on one side of Tommy's head. "Tommy, I'm so sorry this happened to you. I'm so sorry you had to come home to this. You deserve better."

"I doubt that." His hands slipped around to her back and he leaned his head against her. "I'm one of the lucky ones, Lil. At the hospital, I saw fellas who'd lost their hands, their vision, their noses and lips. Some of them had these bizarre tubes made from their own thigh skin attached to their noses and connected to their shoulders until enough skin could be grown to rebuild a nose. They called themselves the Guinea Pig Club because it was experimental. They nicknamed me Handsome, if you can believe it."

"I do. And I think you're still handsome."

"Well, I think we both know that's not true, but thanks for saying it." Tommy sighed. "Look at the pair of us. What are we going to do, Lil?"

"I don't know. But I wouldn't blame you if you want a divorce. Nobody would."

He looked up at her. "Is that what you want?"

Did she even know what she wanted? Slowly, she shook her head and stepped away. "No. I think you're going to need me, Tommy."

He stood and moved toward the door. "I think you're going to need me, too. Maybe what we deserve is each other, Lilly DeWitt." He opened the door and put his hat on. "I'm going to see Mom and Dad. Don't worry about waiting up."

• • •

By the end of the week, Tommy had secured his old job at Danny's Hardware. By the end of July, he'd been so rude to customers who stared at his face that his boss moved him to the back warehouse where he wouldn't have to deal with people.

And by mid-August, Tommy's frustration had escalated. He came home from work one morning at ten o'clock.

"What are you doing home so early?" Lilly looked up from the laundry she was rolling through the wringer before carrying it out to the clothesline.

"I'm done."

"What do you mean?"

"Danny doesn't have enough work to keep me busy in the back. Said he really needed me in the front, doing my old job. He asked if I could return to the front and try being nice to people. 'Don't worry about them staring at you,' he says. 'They're the one with the problem, not you. It's only your problem if you get rude.'

"So I tell him, 'Okay, I can do it. I'll be nice.' But I can't, Lil. Every stinkin' person who comes through that door, even the ones who have already seen me before. They should be used to it, but they come in and they stare like I'm some kind of freak show at the circus. So I try to ignore it. Keep my cool. But I can't do it. Somethin' just comes up from inside my gut and I say something insulting.

"'Apologize,' Danny says. Sometimes I do and sometimes I don't, but I never mean it. Customer complains again. Danny says, 'Look, kid, I don't want to have to fire a veteran. You've always been a good worker, but maybe this isn't the job for you no more.'"

Lilly's hopes sank. The baby was due in a month. Tommy needed steady work. "He fired you?"

"I quit before he could."

CHAPTER TWENTY-FOUR
Diana

I now understand why the only photograph of Tommy DeWitt I've ever seen is his army picture, one of those old black-and-whites where the uniformed men all looked so handsome. The photo would have been taken shortly after he enlisted, before the explosion. I piece together that Lilly and Tommy, if not happily ever after, at least managed to stick together.

Though the coincidence of Tommy and William both experiencing burn wounds is uncanny, I feel satisfied that I've now heard the whole story and know why the Tidsbury surname shows up in my DNA test results.

On our next Friday movie night, I ask Shane if we can skip the movie and just talk.

"Sure."

We meet at a park near his place where we can stroll. I bring him up to speed on Dad's latest chapter.

"Wow." Shane leads me to a bench where the breeze off the lake can cool us off. "That's a lot of drama for one family."

"At least now my little ancestry mystery is solved." Which is good because I have Carly's crisis to think about. I desperately want to fill Shane in on that too, but I don't have Carly's permission to tell him. I texted her earlier, asking if she reached a decision. No reply. I called her mother, leaving a message asking if I could come see Carly. No answer. I even called the pregnancy support center to ask if she'd returned, only to be told they couldn't divulge client information.

I need to tell Shane *something*, though.

"Carly needs our prayers, Shane. I'm afraid maybe I've been shut out of her life."

The tears start flowing then. When I reach into my purse for tissues, the bag flips over, landing on the ground in front of the bench and spilling its contents. The wind begins picking up random tissues and papers and suddenly Shane is running around, laughing and chasing down paper while I stuff my wallet, pens, and makeup back into the purse.

When he returns to the bench, Shane hands me a fistful of brochures from the pregnancy center. I take them from him and awkwardly stuff them into my bag.

"Is there… something you need to tell me?" he asks.

"What? No!" I chuckle at the idea.

Shane is no dummy. "Do those brochures have anything to do with why Carly needs our prayers?"

I nod, tears starting again. "I can't really talk about it. I've already said too much, but I feel so… helpless. I love that girl, Shane."

"I know." He puts an arm around me. With our heads together, he begins to pray. "Lord, you know what's going on. Whatever's happening, it sounds like Diana needs a lot of wisdom. And Carly's going to need a lot of support." He pauses, as though listening for something. "Father, I pray that your Spirit would prompt Carly to go to the pregnancy center. And to contact Diana soon. Please give them both peace. Amen."

"Thanks," I mumble, pulling away from Shane.

We don't speak any more about it, but I feel like the weight has lifted a bit. God is perfectly capable of guiding and protecting Carly and her baby whether I'm allowed back into the picture or not.

• • •

At work on Monday, my boss walks into my office with a surprise. She's sending me to a ten-day conference in Winnipeg. Months ago, she registered herself for the event. I booked her hotel and flight. Now a family crisis is keeping her home and she asks me to attend in her place.

With only two days to get ready, I call my neighbor about taking care of Mouse while I'm away. Then I text both Shane and Carly to let them know I'll be out of town for nearly two weeks.

Only Shane replies. *Say hi to your dad for me.*

I'll miss you, too, turkey, I text back.

As I pack, I decide the time away from Shane will be good for me. For both of us. As much as it bugs me to admit, Dad and Becky are probably right. My relationship with Shane is nice, but what is the ultimate outcome? The image of us in thirty more years, a little old man and a little old lady, still going to the movies on Friday nights—worse yet, pushing our walkers down the hall to the TV room at the nursing home—does not fill my heart with joy. Since neither of us wants romance and marriage, spending time with other people, maybe meeting some new friends, seems like a good and logical plan.

But landing in Winnipeg, my first impulse is to text Shane and let him know I arrived.

• • •

The next five days keep me crazy busy in sessions at the conference hotel, so I often don't make it back to my room until nine in the evening. The first night, I resist the urge to call Shane. The second night, he calls me, and we talk for an hour.

On Friday, I catch myself scrolling through pictures on my phone, looking for his face. Every time I find one, his eyes look more attractive. Each time we talk, his voice sounds warmer. Every time he texts, my heart does a little flip.

Good grief. This is not how this was supposed to go.

I rent a car for the weekend and make the one-hour drive to Becky's as arranged. Her noisy household helps me focus on other things. My niece and nephews have grown to an impossible height, giving me the definite sense that life is passing me by.

Face it, Di. You're old.

On Saturday, Dad comes over and I don't feel quite so ancient. I love seeing him interact with his grandkids as everybody pitches in to help with the ridiculous abundance of garden produce. We sit around shelling peas and snapping beans, filling bags for the freezer, talking and laughing the whole afternoon. At supper time, my brother-in-law grills steak which we eat with fresh corn on the cob, tomatoes, and cucumbers.

"I think I'm too stuffed to move," I groan.

"Not me." Dad licks his fingers. "I was hoping you girls might go with me to the cemetery this evening."

His request isn't the kind you turn down. Besides, it gets us out of dishes. Leaving the kids and their dad to clean up, Becky and I take time to cut some white daisies and red roses from her garden. We pile three abreast into Becky's truck and drive the two miles to the Summervale cemetery.

"I'm ashamed to say I haven't been back to Mom's grave since her funeral," I confess.

"That's okay." Dad pats my knee. "She's not really there."

"And she knows you love her," Becky adds.

Their grace warms my heart. As does the sight of Mom's lovingly maintained grave. The simple headstone is flanked by tiny, artfully trimmed shrubs. The grass is well-watered and weedless. I stand by in respectful silence as my sister places the vase of flowers in front of the stone.

After we stand quietly a few moments, Dad moves. He indicates the space next to Mom's.

"Here's where my remains will go when the time comes. And over here…" He walks a few graves over. "Here's where my parents are buried."

I've seen these graves before, of course. But now the names Lilly DeWitt and Thomas DeWitt mean much more to me. I feel as though I know them, at least a little. I see them as deeply troubled people, making unfortunate choices and getting stuck in the consequences of life's harsh realities.

Dad pulls some weeds out from around the headstones, then keeps leading us around. He shows us the graves of Henry and Margaret Sampson and Fred and Doris DeWitt, all of whom Dad remembers as his grandparents. Oddly, none of them actually are.

"Would William Tidsbury be here somewhere?" I look around.

"No. I'm sure he's buried in Winnipeg."

Curious as to why Dad isn't more interested in his biological father, I let it drop. We find the headstone of Lilly's biological mother, its etchings barely discernible:

Nora Sampson
December 16, 1902–August 5, 1923
Baby Boy Sampson
August 5, 1923

Suddenly, all I can think about is Carly. This great-grandmother of mine died in childbirth at only twenty years of age, buried with her dead newborn and leaving tiny Lilly behind.

On the ride back to Becky's, I text Carly again. This time, a reply comes almost immediately: *When are u coming home? Need to talk.*

I text her back: *Talk now? Call me.*

By the time we reach Becky's place, my phone is ringing. I stay in the truck while Dad and Becky climb out.

"Hey, Carly, I'm so glad you called. I've been trying and trying—"

"I know, I'm so sorry. Mom said I shouldn't try to contact you and I remembered how you're always careful to follow Mom's rules, so… I didn't want to get you in trouble."

I feel touched that she's been thinking of my good. "Aw. How are you?"

"Well… I'm still pregnant, if that's what you mean."

"Okay…" I feel myself relax a bit.

"I'm just… struggling. A lot. I wish you were here, Di."

"I wish that, too. But you can talk to me now. Tell me what's going on." I open one door to let in some air.

"I read all those pamphlets. Mom still wants me to terminate, but I don't know if I can go through with it. Did you know my baby's heart is already beating?"

"Was that in one of the brochures?"

"Mm-hmm. It also says they—the pregnancy center staff and volunteers—are… 'committed to providing you with caring emotional support, no matter what you decide.' Do you think that's true? They'll still be there for me if I terminate?"

"Of course they will. I will, too."

"I just don't know if I could live with that. I keep thinking about how Mom chose life for me. Right now, this little one inside me has no choice. No voice. But if they did, I'm sure they would choose to live." Carly lets out a long sigh. "I wish I lived in the olden days, like your grandparents who got married right away."

I realize then that Carly has only heard a small part of Lilly's story, the day of our road trip. "No, I don't think that's what you want. That solution didn't work out so well for my grandparents."

"Well, Josh is out of my life now anyway." Another sigh. "I just keep staring at this picture of an eight-week-old embryo. It's only the size of a bean, but already has little arms and legs. Fingers. How will I ever get that image out of my head if I end this now?"

I doubt she ever will but say nothing.

"But if I have it... I want more for my baby than I can give right now. I would want him to have a good life, but I have things to accomplish before I'm ready to parent."

I send up another quick prayer for wisdom. "Well... there are lots of families wanting to adopt."

"I'm thinking about that, too. But what if that family doesn't take good care of my baby? Or what if I live the rest of my life wondering what happened to my child?"

I take a deep breath before answering. "Those are really great questions, Carly. They show that you already have maternal feelings for the baby inside of you. That you are already becoming a loving mother, whether you decide to raise your child or entrust him to another family."

Carly sniffles. "I just don't know if I could give a baby away."

"I'm sure it would be the most difficult thing you'd ever do." I can hardly imagine giving away my cat, let alone a child. "But adoption has changed. Your baby isn't just taken away and you have no say in where he goes or... or never have contact again. You have choices." I climb out of the truck and walk around the yard, phone to my ear.

"Would you help me, Di?"

"Of course I will, you know that. I'll do whatever—"

"No, I mean... would you consider..."

Where is she going with this?

"I want you to adopt my baby."

My knees suddenly feel weak and I lean against a fence rail. *Oh God. What do I say? What are you asking of me?* If I say no, even if I tell Carly I need time to pray and consider it, she might go ahead with the termination.

But there is no way I am ready to say yes.

"Oh honey." I swallow. "Carly, I feel so honored that you would ask. But... wouldn't you want your child to have two parents?" I'm treading on rocky ground. Carly has never known anything but a one-parent home. "Two parents who are committed to each other and can work together as a team. You've seen how challenging it's been for your mom, right?"

"Are you saying no?"

"No! I'm not. I just... you caught me completely by surprise. This would be the biggest commitment of my life. You wouldn't want me to make that decision lightly, would you?"

"I guess not."

Whew.

"So does that mean you'll think about it?"

I pause too long.

"Di? You still there?"

"Yes. I'm here. Listen... I promise to think about it... if you promise you won't do anything until I get back."

"Okay. I promise."

"I promise, too. And Carly—however this goes, whatever happens, I'll support you, okay? If something comes up I can't handle, I'll help you find someone who can."

Am I making an impossible promise? I'm already in over my head.

We say goodbye. I lean against the fence, watching a horse grazing in the distance until my heartrate settles down and I can breathe normally again.

Oh God, what have I done?

• • •

In the house, Becky's family sits around the kitchen table eating rhubarb crisp topped with ice cream. Becky hands me a bowlful and a cup of coffee. "Here. Your ice cream is melting."

I look around the room. "Where's Dad?"

"He's out on the back deck where it's cooler and quieter. Join him if you want."

I find Dad, his dessert finished, writing on the yellow pad that has become his ever-present companion. A tabby cat swirls herself back and forth around his feet. He looks up and smiles. "Was that Shane on the phone?"

"No, it was my—it was Carly." I take a seat and dig into my dessert. "She needs our prayers."

He nods but doesn't ask for details. "She's already on my list. How *is* Shane doing?"

I'm not about to tell him Shane and I have been talking nightly or that I miss him like crazy. "He's fine, I guess. He wanted me to tell you hi. He still has questions about the rest of your mother's story."

"Well, there's a whole lot more to tell."

"Really? I figured the mystery was solved. Lilly had her baby. Which was *you*. And she and Tommy raised you together as if you were his. Right?" I take a big mouthful of tart sweetness.

Dad shakes his head. "Not nearly that simple. You forget there were still some pretty heavy untold secrets." He slides his writing pad across the glass-topped table toward me.

As the day gradually closes with a gorgeous Manitoba sunset, I read still more of Lilly's story.

CHAPTER TWENTY-FIVE

Lilly

SEPTEMBER 1941–JANUARY 1942

Mr. Arnold offered Tommy work on his farm, but his doctor advised against it, reminding him that he was still subject to infection and the dust and dirt of harvest time could lead to disaster.

When Lilly encouraged him to visit the fire hall, he found an excuse not to. He began sleeping until noon. Afternoons, he'd poke around the yard or go visit his parents. He'd come home for supper but often leave again only to return home smelling of liquor.

One night he drove up in a battered, gray 1932 Ford. "Took it off George Randall's hands for a hundred bucks."

Lilly stared at the car. "How on earth did you pay for that?"

"Don't worry about it. We'll need it to get you to the hospital when it's time to have the baby, right?"

Lilly couldn't very well argue with that.

On Sunday, September 20, her labor began. As promised, Tommy drove her to the hospital like any good father would. Whether he stayed in the waiting room or went home, she had no idea.

Her labor dragged on through the night, the pain growing increasingly worse until finally, at six o'clock on the morning of September 21, 1941, her baby boy was born.

When they brought him to her, clean and wrapped in a blue blanket, her tears began to flow. The little boy was the most beautiful she'd ever laid eyes on. For the first time in her life, her heart swelled with more love for another person than she could contain. She stroked his downy soft hair, weeping with the knowledge that she had nearly ended his life.

Frantic that her actions might have damaged him in some way, she examined his entire little body, counting fingers and toes.

"He's perfect," Dr. Ramsey declared.

Lilly wept some more. The reality of what she had tried to do fell on her like a heavy black cloak. A fresh wave of grief for the loss of her first baby swept in along with it, and she held her little son close. Overwhelmed with both grief and gratitude, she couldn't sort it out.

Oh God, thank you for sparing this boy's life. I don't deserve him.

As he nursed with gusto, she studied his tiny face, searching for any resemblance to William but seeing only her own coloring and features. Perhaps Tommy would be spared the pain of seeing William in the boy and be able to love him as his own. God had indeed been merciful to her.

Tommy came in that afternoon. "You okay? Was it hard?"

"Yes to both." Lilly partially unwrapped the baby so Tommy could get a good look.

He peered at the little face. "Well done, Lil."

"Do you want to hold him?"

"Not yet." Tommy walked over to the window and looked out.

A nurse came in carrying a clipboard. "How's everyone? Do we have a name yet?"

Lilly hesitated. She and Tommy had not discussed any names. "We're... not sure yet. Can you give us some time?"

"I'll leave the paperwork here with you to fill out. If you can name him today, it would be great." She placed the clipboard on a rolling metal stand and left the room.

Lilly stared at her husband's back. "I was thinking about calling him... Dale Thomas."

At this, Tommy turned around.

She tried to interpret his expression. "That okay with you, Tommy?"

Tommy focused on the baby a moment, then looked away again. "I guess he's your kid. You can name him what you want."

I deserve that.

Though the barb stung, Lilly refused to argue. Tommy would come around once she'd given him time to process. How could she expect him to love this child right off the bat?

She put a smile on her face. "Dale Thomas DeWitt has a nice ring to it, don't you think?" Maybe if he was reminded that the boy would carry his name, his heart would soften.

· · ·

Tommy tried. As those initial weeks went by and she learned to care for Dale, Lilly could tell Tommy was making an effort. At least most of the time.

One exhausting night when little Dale refused to settle, Tommy carried him back and forth across their living room and kitchen, bouncing him and humming. Lilly fell asleep despite the baby's howling. When she awoke, Dale was asleep beside her and Tommy was gone.

Late the next morning, Lilly opened the door to see her father-in-law and Tommy standing there, one of Tommy's arms draped across his father's shoulder. She opened the door wide and, without a word, Mr. DeWitt helped his son into the room. Tommy bumped into a kitchen chair, causing it to fall over with a crash.

The baby started screaming. Odors of whiskey and vomit filled the room. Tommy's dad steered him over to the sofa and let him drop into a heap. He pulled off Tommy's shoes and lifted his feet to the couch. With a sigh, he gave Lilly a look of resignation and left.

Lilly tended to Dale first. Once the baby was asleep, she faced Tommy. Helping him out of the soiled shirt, she listened to him mutter.

"Sorry, Lil. Now you've got two babies to look after. Shouldn't be too much for a gal who can handle two men at once."

She said nothing, cleaning him up as best she could. She washed out his shirt and hung it outside to dry. When she returned to his side with a cup of black coffee, Tommy had fallen asleep. He slept through the afternoon. That evening, he was back to the kind of person who washed the supper dishes and rocked the baby.

And so it went. Day in and day out, Lilly had no idea what to expect from her husband. Abusive words would occasionally escape his lips. The next thing she knew, he'd be repentant. Sometimes he cried, apologizing to her. Other times he'd call her cheap names and tell her to take her son and leave.

"Go back to William Tidsbury. Let him raise his own kid." Then he'd suggest it would be better for her if he'd died in that blast back in London. Never did he give more details about his war experience than that. "That blasted blast in blasted London," he'd say with a chuckle after a few beers.

When Tommy was scheduled for more facial surgery in early December, Lilly looked forward to it. The skin-grafting process would get him out of the house for a few weeks, improve his appearance, and with any luck help heal his heart and soul, too.

She waited a week to go see him. A neighbor agreed to babysit while Lilly took the train to Winnipeg with Tommy's parents. Walking through the hospital corridors brought back memories of her brief stint in nursing school. If she'd stuck with it, she could be so much more useful to Tommy now. Then again, it was as much Tommy's fault as her own that she had not completed the training.

A lifetime ago.

They entered Tommy's room to find him sitting up in bed, his face bandaged but his spirits light. He showed Lilly where skin had been taken from his thigh to use on his face.

"I won't be winning any beauty pageants. But maybe little kids will stop running away when they see me."

• • •

Nineteen forty-two arrived with record cold. The news headlines gave little hope of an end to the war anytime soon.

Tommy returned home from the hospital optimistic, but within days depression settled in again. His scars had diminished somewhat. While his looks had improved, his disposition had not. Lilly thought he must be disappointed even though the doctor had warned him they still had a long way to go and more surgeries to endure.

Too tired to go out, he begged Lilly to bring him a bottle of whiskey.

"I need it for the pain." He hung on to her wrist.

"I can't, Tommy. We need the money for food."

He squeezed tighter. "Just do it."

Trembling, Lilly glared back at the cold glint in his eye. When he let her go, she bundled up Dale and let him cry while she put on her own winter coat, boots, mittens, and scarf. Then she picked the baby up and stepped out onto the landing. Snow had fallen overnight and the stairs were covered with it. Step by step, she worked her way down, brushing snow aside with her foot while clutching the wailing baby and gripping the railing with one hand. By the time she reached the bottom, she was exhausted and near tears.

She soldiered on. Thankfully, the movement of her body lulled Dale to sleep. When she reached the grocery store, she pushed the door open and closed it behind her as quickly as she could. The overhead bell jangled, announcing her arrival. The warmth of the room cradled her in relief, only to be followed by the entrance of Mrs. Gordon. The woman's presence turned Lilly cold in an old but familiar way.

"Lilly!" The woman singsonged as though she couldn't be more delighted at Lilly's arrival. "It's about time you brought that little one around."

Lilly had come for groceries numerous times with Dale since his birth, but until today she'd managed to pick days and times the woman would not be minding the store.

"I only need a few things," Lilly murmured. "Can't carry a whole lot and hold onto the baby, too."

"You need a little sled is what you need," the woman said in a baby voice. She hustled over and wagged her face so close to Dale that Lilly could smell her breath. "You need a sled, yes-you-do, yes-you-do! Oooh, let me hold you while Mama shops. Come on over here, big fella."

Lilly surrendered the baby to Mrs. Gordon. Maybe the woman didn't mean any ill will toward them. She had to know the baby was not Tommy's, but she still acted friendly.

"Oh, look at this precious little tyke. He favors you, Lilly. How lucky is that?"

There it was. The old gossipmonger had probably been hoping to see a resemblance to one of the men on her list of possible candidates so she could spread around her newly formed suspicions.

Lilly chose to ignore the dig. She lifted a container of oatmeal down from a shelf and placed it on the counter, then began perusing the limited supply of fresh produce. Mrs. Gordon followed, talking baby-talk to Dale as she went along, clutching him to her amble bosom.

"What did you name him?"

"Dale. Dale Thomas."

"Oh isn't that nice. Is Dale a family name?"

"No. I—we just like it." Lilly selected four apples and placed them in her shopping bag.

"I don't think I know anyone named Dale, at least not around here. Do you?"

"Just this one." Lilly reached for the baby. She'd forfeit the other items on her list in the interest of getting away from this busybody.

Mrs. Gordon gave Dale back and moved around the counter to ring up Lilly's order, but she wasn't through. "And I don't think I've had the chance to tell you how sorry we were to hear of Thomas's injuries." She lowered her voice to a whisper even though no one else was in the room. "I haven't seen him, but I've heard it's awful. Awful, awful. Must be so hard, looking at that every day. Pretty young woman like you."

Lilly slid some money across the counter without comment.

Mrs. Gordon returned to her normal volume, but this time she added a sickeningly sweet tone of caring. "How is he doing?" Her eyes turned compassionate, imploring Lilly for just a hint at how horrible it all must be.

Lilly would not grant her the satisfaction. "He's doing really well. Thanks for asking."

"Glad to hear it." The woman handed her a receipt.

Lilly forced out her biggest smile. "Good day, Mrs. Gordon. Please give my regards to Mr. Gordon."

As she picked up her shopping bag, the bell over the door rang again and Lilly felt the cold blast of air before she turned around. When she did, she immediately recognized the new customer.

William.

She'd not seen him in months. Painfully aware of the surprise on William's face, the baby in her arm, and the gossipy woman behind her, Lilly froze for a moment. Her brain scrambled. How did one normally greet an old classmate in a casual setting?

"Hello, William."

William looked past her at the store's proprietor, then back at Lilly. "Hi there, Lilly. Happy new year."

"Same to you."

"I see you've got your little one with you. A son, right?"

Lilly nodded. "Yes."

"I heard. May I have a peek?" He limped forward and waited while Lilly peeled the blanket away from Dale's face. Father and son gazed into each other's eyes for the first time.

William swallowed. "Congratulations." He gave Lilly a quick nod and carried on past her. "Good morning, Mrs. Gordon."

"Morning, William. Sweet baby, isn't he?"

"Yes."

"I told his mama she needs a little sled so he can ride in style."

Lilly left the store without turning back, her heart pounding.

Having bought so few groceries, she had enough cash left for a bottle for Tommy. She paused briefly in front of the door to the pub. Yes, she could go in and bring him some relief for a little while. Buy herself a bit of peace while he slept it off.

But she kept walking.

I can't do that. I would only be contributing to his problems. Besides, I will not take my son into that place.

A fight ensued when she got home.

"Who needs you? I can go get my own drink." Tommy pulled on his coat.

"Fine. Do it then. And on your way, you can grab that snow shovel and clear the stairs."

Lilly went into the bedroom to change Dale's diaper. She waited to hear the door open and close, but it didn't. With one hand on the baby, she peered around the corner.

Tommy stood at the mirror she'd hung beside the door, staring. The glass reflected a grim and hollow expression.

When Lilly finished the diaper change and returned to the living room, Tommy had hung up his coat and hat without leaving and was seated at the table reading a magazine his father had brought him the previous week.

• • •

By that evening, Tommy had still not stepped outside. After Dale was settled, Lilly bundled herself up again and went out to shovel snow in the dark, puffing with frustration and resentment with every scoop she pushed off the stairway. At this rate, they'd never be able to afford a house. How could they raise a child in this tiny place? How could they keep living on Tommy's meager veteran's pay? The car had been parked for weeks, its engine needing repair and its tank needing fuel.

Thoughts of leaving Tommy disappeared as quickly as they arose whenever Lilly tried to envision supporting herself and Dale all alone. And if she'd already disgraced herself in the community, she could only imagine how they would shun her when they learned she'd abandoned a poor, wounded war vet.

Her father-in-law's words were never far from her mind: *"You made your bed."* The rest of the old saying automatically followed, and Lilly was now lying in the bed she had made. Mr. DeWitt was right. She would simply have to make the best of it. She and Tommy had tied themselves to one another long before. Theirs was a tie with many tangles, and those tangles made it impossible to undo.

As she neared the bottom step, something bright red caught her eye. She stopped the shovel in mid-swing and stared.

Leaning against the base of the stairs stood a brand-new child's sled.

CHAPTER TWENTY-SIX

1942

Although certain it was William who'd left the sled, Lilly offered a different suggestion when Tommy asked about it the next day. "It was probably left by someone whose children have outgrown it."

"Looks new, though." Tommy sized it up from the window.

"I'll ask Uncle Henry. Seems like something he might do." While Uncle Henry had continued to stop by with gifts of food and had taken a polite interest in the baby, Lilly loved him all the more knowing he did so without Aunty Margaret's knowledge or approval.

She could imagine the conversations around the table if and when the four parents ever got together. Tommy would come off looking like a hero for staying with Lilly and being a father to Dale. Lilly would come off as a spoiled brat who never appreciated the good opportunities she'd been granted. They would question whether she could be trusted to stick it out with Tommy and his disfigured face or if she'd run off with the first handsome man who showed interest.

In any case, it would be best to let Tommy believe one of them had brought the lovely gift.

Tommy turned from the window and sat at the table with the newspaper. "I'll ask Mom and Dad."

"Don't grill them about it," Lilly advised. "If they wanted us to know, they wouldn't have just left it."

• • •

January's cold tempered as the calendar turned to February. Tommy seemed more settled about his appearance and began going out again, though he never said where and Lilly didn't ask. Sometimes he came home smelling of liquor, other times not. With gasoline rationed, he made no effort to repair his car.

The sled made an enormous difference. Lilly bundled Dale into it daily, sometimes going for groceries or to the post office, other days just out for some exercise and fresh air. The baby loved it, and Lilly's heart swelled with gratitude. Convincing herself she owed William a thank-you, she deliberately ventured to the library one afternoon. She looped the sled's rope over the end of a bicycle stand in front of the building and carried Dale inside. She'd stay only as long as necessary.

William stood behind the counter, helping a patron. Lilly waited until she caught his eye, then walked past and made her way to the farthest corner of the room, hoping Dale would stay quiet for as long as it took. At five months, he slept less and babbled more each day. She sat him on the floor at her feet with a stuffed monkey she'd made from a pair of Tommy's socks. Then she began to peruse the bookshelves, feigning interest in political history and the biographies of long-dead inventors.

Sure enough, within five minutes she could hear the uneven sound of William's limp growing closer. He came around the corner of the tall shelving.

"Are you finding what you're looking for?" His voice sounded strained and a little too loud.

Lilly closed the book in her hands. "I just wanted to say thank you. For the sled."

William neither acknowledged nor denied it. He squatted down to take a closer look at Dale. "Hey there, little fella. My goodness, you've grown!"

Dale's face immediately scrunched up and he began to cry, reaching for Lilly's leg and clutching at her stockings with his chubby fists. She handed William the book and picked up the baby.

"Shh. It's okay." She stroked Dale's back gently.

The baby turned to look at William even as he leaned into his mother. His cries turned to soft sobs and then quieted completely.

William stood. "I'm sorry. Sure didn't mean to make him cry."

"Oh, don't worry about it. He's like this with everyone these days."

William looked at the book in his hand and wiggled it. "Did you want this?"

"No."

He replaced the book and leaned down to pick up Dale's toy. Then, using the monkey, he tried again to befriend Dale.

"Hi there." He bounced the monkey up and down. When Dale rewarded him with the hint of a grin, he gently moved the toy toward Dale's tummy and pulled it away again, making the monkey chatter while still trying to maintain a soft library volume. He repeated the action until a genuine giggle escaped the baby. "Well, I do believe I've made a friend."

When the baby wrapped his arms around the toy, William let him keep it. He reached out and stroked Dale's soft hair and ran a finger gently down one cheek.

"Like velvet." He looked at Lilly. "He's wonderful, Lilly."

Lilly smiled. "He really is. I had no idea…" A lump formed in her throat. "No idea how mothers really feel about their children. Until now."

William watched as Dale squirmed and Lilly placed him on the floor again. "Can he crawl?"

"Not yet. He's only been sitting up like this for a few days. Being able to set him down and know he'll just sit there comes in pretty handy. I'm going to be a lot busier when he figures out how to get around."

A soft chuckle escaped William's lips. Then a whisper. "I want him in my life, Lilly."

Lilly didn't know what to say. "I know it's unfair, but… as long as Tommy is willing to stick with us, to be a family—"

"But you're not a family. Not really."

"—it's the right thing to do. It would be wrong to abandon Tommy."

"Because he's got burn scars?"

Lilly understood William's point immediately, and it felt like a knife between her ribs. She winced. Few people ever saw William's scars, but his limp would always mark him as disfigured.

"Because he's my husband."

"Dale is *my* son, Lilly." William's whisper grew even softer as he inched his face closer to hers. "He may be the only child I ever have."

"I'm sorry, William."

He drew away then. With one lingering look at Dale who chewed happily on his toy, William limped to the end of the row.

Then he turned back. "My offer still holds, Lilly."

He walked away.

She didn't need to wonder which offer he meant. Divorce Tommy and marry him. Raise Dale together.

• • •

As winter developed into spring, Lilly continued to visit the library every week. She told herself it was for William's sake, so that he could see his son. The first few times, she went to the same deserted corner as their first visit and William would meet them there. Each time, he made sure to let her know his offer was good. One day, he even brought her a thin book explaining legal procedures for divorce-seekers.

"I can't take this home!" she whispered in a panic, pushing it back toward him.

He nodded toward one of the tables. "Have a seat. Read it here. I'll watch Dale."

He scooped the baby up and carried him over to the children's corner. He chose a book and gathered two nearby toddlers for story time. He sat on a low chair, Dale in his lap, and began to read the book aloud to all three children.

Lilly sat at the table and thumbed through the book, far more interested in the proceedings across the room.

After that day, Lilly worried less about hiding. When she visited the library, she'd spend time in the children's area until William came along. He was careful to engage with any other children present as well, but he'd inevitably pick Dale up and, if no other kids were there, read a book just to him.

One day Lilly used the opportunity to visit the ladies' room. When she returned, neither William nor Dale were in sight. Panic seared her heart immediately. He wouldn't. Would he? She searched the children's area and between rows of books. She headed for the counter, heart pounding. The employee at the counter was busy checking out a patron's book.

"Excuse me." Lilly tried to temper the alarm in her voice by clearing her throat. "Have you seen William Tidsbury?"

The young woman looked up with an annoyed expression, then pointed toward William's office. Lilly ran around the counter and through the door without waiting for permission. William sat at his desk with a giggling Dale on his lap. Together, they were thumping a rubber stamp onto some paper.

Lilly stopped short. "There you are."

They both looked up, and Dale immediately began to squawk, reaching out for Lilly.

She walked around the desk and took him, glaring at William. "Don't you ever scare me like that again."

"Sorry, Lilly. I was called to the telephone." He didn't sound all that sorry.

"Come on, Dale. We should be getting home."

William stood. "What were you thinking? That I would just take off with him?"

Lilly reached the door but turned around. Tears sprang up again. Were they from panic or relief?

"Close that." William nodded at the door.

She pushed the door shut. "I... I didn't know. After what you said about wanting him in your life, I... I thought you might have."

William shook his head slowly. "You really think so little of me, Lilly? That I would *kidnap* him?"

"I'm sorry. I just panicked. I don't know what to think sometimes."

William let out a sigh and studied her for a moment. "What kind of game are you playing? You're the one who brought him here, who keeps bringing him here. I love this kid, Lilly. And if you let me, I'll love you, too."

"I should never have come. It was wrong."

"Was it?"

"Nearly everything I've ever done in my life has been wrong. I can't seem to make good choices. I'm incapable of it. The only good thing I ever did was bring this boy into the world and I almost messed that up, too. Now I'm making more stupid—"

"What do you mean, you almost messed that up?"

Lilly wanted to bite her tongue, to take back the slip. She looked from the rubber stamp on William's desk to his telephone and back again, over and over, as though a plausible answer could be found there.

"Nothing." *Oh, it would be such a relief to finally tell someone.*

"Did you... think about ending the pregnancy?"

She couldn't meet William's eye, so she stared at the front of his shirt. "I... I didn't see any other way."

"Well, I'm glad you found one."

"I didn't. Dale did."

"What?" William looked at the baby, then back at Lilly with a confused expression. "What do you mean?"

Lilly's voice dropped to a whisper as she continued to stare at the floor. "I ended the pregnancy, William. I mean, I thought I did. Whatever was done... I don't know. But Dale survived."

A moment passed before William spoke again. "Oh, Lilly. Is he all right? He seems all right."

As if in answer to the question, Dale patted a pudgy hand on Lilly's tear-streaked face. She wiped them away with her sleeve and kissed the baby's head. "He's fine. We should go."

William moved around his desk and sat on the edge of it. "Look, Lilly. I'm sorry. Maybe I've taken too many liberties with him. But I'm convinced you and I could make a go of it. I care about you. You know that, right?"

She nodded, not trusting herself to speak.

"But I can't keep playing this game forever. You need to make a choice."

He was right. She needed to either break ties with him completely and devote herself to Tommy or start divorce proceedings. And the way things were going with Tommy, the decision didn't seem that difficult.

Except for one major hurdle.

"There's something you don't know. Something big." Her voice quivered.

William stared back, then glanced again at Dale. "You're not going to tell me he's not mine."

"No."

"Good, because I think half the town knows he's mine by now."

"He's yours. I'm talking about something that goes back much further. If I were to ever have a real relationship with you, well… I just couldn't… unless you knew."

"Knew what?"

"The whole story." Lilly had already confessed more than she thought she ever would. May as well admit to all of it and find out just how far William's care and compassion went.

A loud knock on the door behind her made Lilly jump. Dale started crying. The door opened, and the young woman who had been staffing the counter stuck her head in.

"Sorry to interrupt, Mr. Tidsbury, but we've got a line-up out here. Can you help me out?"

"Sure thing, Clarice."

Clarice left the door open and returned to her post. William followed her out, stopping in front of Lilly briefly. "We need to finish this conversation."

Lilly waited until William was busy with patrons, then slipped out and headed for home.

CHAPTER TWENTY-SEVEN

Diana

Dad's story is sounding more unsatisfying all the time, but I guess I shouldn't expect real life to wrap up in a neatly tied, happily-ever-after bow like the books I most enjoy.

Hearing about Lilly's confession brings Carly's proposition to the forefront as I navigate the remaining days of my conference. I desperately need to talk it over with someone—Becky, Dad, Shane, *some*body—but I don't want to betray Carly's trust. And once again, she isn't responding to my messages.

That doesn't stop me from talking to Shane nearly every night. He sounds like he is going through some stuff of his own.

"Can I pick you up at the airport Friday night?" Even his voice is different. Tentative. Unlike my normally confident, macho friend. "We need to talk. In person."

"That would be great." *Dare I say it?* "I miss you."

Shane pauses so long that I wish I could take it back. "Glad to hear it. I miss you, too."

• • •

My flight is delayed a half-hour, and by the time I land in Edmonton I'm antsy to see Shane and jittery with hunger. His smiling face is the best thing I've seen all week. We exchange a quick hug.

"You know," I say, "you could have waited for my text and picked me up outside."

"I know." He pulls my suitcase off the carousel. "Your last text said you were starving, so I thought we could eat something here."

"Really? Your parking permit's going to cost a fortune."

"Not worried about it. Follow me."

He pulls my roller bag to an Italian restaurant. "This okay?"

"You know it's my favorite." A waiter leads us to a table with plenty of room for luggage beneath it, and we both order lasagna. I text Becky to let her know I landed.

Shane's blue eyes rest on mine. "So... good trip?"

For the next hour, I fill Shane in on the conference and my visit with my family. Of course, he's keen to hear Dad's latest installment of his mother's story, and I am happy to share it. I long to tell him about Carly's big question, but it's not the time.

"Enough about me. How was *your* week?" I ask.

"*Two* weeks. You were gone two weeks."

"Technically, twelve days."

"Felt like a month. But it was enlightening, Di."

"Oh?" Am I ready to hear this?

"I should back up a bit. I haven't said anything, but... I've been seeing a counselor."

Oh–kay. Was not expecting that. "What kind of counselor?"

"A therapist. About my issues. My commitment issues."

I wait, nervous.

"You know my parents are divorced," he adds.

"When you were eight, right?"

He nods. "I didn't understand at that age that my mother had a mental illness. Among other things, she was a kleptomaniac."

This is new.

"I didn't understand any of it then. I didn't know she'd been bringing home stolen stuff or that she and Dad had been fighting about it. Then one day I was out with my mother. We were shopping for school supplies for me, to start Grade Three. I was excited. I picked out the trendy backpack I'd wanted forever." He chuckles softly, then his eyebrows come together. "We went down the list of pencils, crayons, and all that. I was too absorbed with my backpack to pay much attention. Mom kept adding items to the backpack. 'Here, son, put this on and let's see if it needs adjusting,' she said. She put the backpack on me and kept adding items to it. I could feel it getting heavier. When everything on the school list was in the bag, Mom added more stuff. I don't even know what all. Some makeup for herself. Hand lotion."

I don't like where this is going.

"I didn't realize my mother was gradually leading me to the store's back entrance instead of toward the checkout line. When I complained that the backpack was getting too heavy, she grabbed my sleeve and said, 'Come on.' She opened the exit door and pushed me out onto the sidewalk. 'Keep going,' she said, even after an alarm started going off. I tried to stop, but she got a firmer grip on my arm and kept forcing me along."

Shane stops for a deep breath and lets it out slowly. "A store security guard caught up to us. I felt the backpack jerk me backward. Some of the contents spilled to the ground. The hand lotion hit the pavement and the bottle split open. To this day, I can't stand the smell of Keegan's hand lotion."

"Oh, Shane." My heart suddenly aches for this eight-year-old boy I hadn't known. "I love that smell. Becky and I always found a bottle in our Christmas stockings. I still keep one in my bathroom."

"I know." An almost imperceptible shudder escapes him.

"Sorry. So what happened next?"

"Next thing I remember, we were in the manager's office where he accused us of shoplifting. The police came. I was returned to my dad."

"And... your mom?"

Shane swallows. "I haven't seen my mother since."

I moan, my fingers covering the bottom half of my face. I knew Shane's mom wasn't in his life, but I didn't realize it had been this long. Or this tragic. "What happened after that?"

"Dad told me years later that he gave her an ultimatum after that event: get help or get out. She chose to get out."

I press my lips together. "I'm so sorry. Do you know where she is?"

Shane shakes his head. "Last I knew—and that was years ago—she was on the streets. Dad remarried when I was fifteen. He's happy with Susan. He did the right thing." After a pause, he adds one more thing. "I went back to school that fall with the same plain blue backpack with the broken zipper I'd been using for three years."

I wait for a bit, but he seems to be finished. "So... this therapist is helping you work through it?"

"He's helping me see how I've let my mother's issues hold me back. That day in the store manager's office was the most humiliating of my life. I felt dirty, like I really was a thief. And I've always wondered if my mother's illness would be passed down to me."

"Have you ever stolen anything since then?"

He shook his head. "Never even been tempted. But then I worry that if I commit to a woman, she'll turn out to have some kind of compulsion like that and... I just can't go through that. I don't know how Dad managed to trust another woman. Michael—that's my counselor—says it's because I was only a little boy when it happened. Dad was an adult and able to sort it out in a healthier way, instead of projecting my mother's issues onto every other female."

"Is that what you've done?"

He shrugs one shoulder. "I don't know. Maybe. I know I've been afraid of relationships. And I don't like that about myself."

How can I say anything to that? My issues aren't too far off.

"But these past two weeks have opened my eyes, Diana. I've missed you more than I ever would have guessed. I love being friends. But... I want more. I need more."

I stare back. Shane is the warmest, kindest person I know. Losing his friendship would be more painful than anything I can imagine. But the thought of "more" makes me shaky. I just can't. Anyway, what would that look like after being friends for so long?

"What if I don't need more?" My words sound cruel and false to my own ears, but better to make a clean break if that's where this is going.

Shane must have been holding his breath because he lets out an elephant-sized sigh. "The ball is in your court. Michael convinced me that I needed to tell you how I feel. To honestly put it out there. Take the risk and see what happens. So... that's what I'm doing."

The last thing I want to do is hurt Shane. Or lose him. Why did he have to go and make this so hard? I send up a quick prayer for wisdom.

Truth.

One word, but it flashes through my mind like a neon sign. Shane has been honest with me, and I need to tell him the whole truth as gently and lovingly as I can.

"I won't lie to you, Shane. I missed you, too. I could hardly wait to see you."

He smiles, but when I don't continue he raises his eyebrows. "But...?"

"But... I'm not ready. I don't know if I ever will be. I don't want to lose you... or hurt you. Please believe me."

He looks away for a moment, then back at me. "I believe you. But now that I've pushed through this wall, I don't think I can go back to how things were."

He's right, even if I want him to be wrong. "Can you give me some time?"

His blue eyes close slowly, then open again. "Yes. I can give you some time."

• • •

We drive in silence. Guilt eats at me for leaving Shane hanging, but asking for some time is the best I can do. When my phone pings, I grab it.

It's Becky. *Hey. U home yet?*

Almost.

Got a surprise 4 u. Open ur laptop soon as u get home.

What is it?

Just do it.

I read her texts aloud to Shane.

"Oooh, I'm all a-tingle," he jokes. "Ask her if I can see what the surprise is too."

Shane wants to know if he can see it, I text.

Sure. Just go to ur email.

My house is a welcome sight, but the stuffiness hits us as soon as we walk in. Mouse goes nuts, meowing and rubbing up against my legs. Her food and water dishes are full, the litterbox recently cleaned. I'll have to bake the neighbors some cookies or something.

Shane goes around opening windows while I fish my laptop out of its bag and set it up on the kitchen table. When I open Becky's email, I find a link to an online chat service, and when I click on that I find myself staring into the faces of Becky and Dad.

They both smile and wave like idiots. "Surprise!"

"Hi, Princess!"

I recognize the painting of *The Grateful Poor* on the wall behind them. They are at Dad's dining table.

"Hey! This *is* a surprise," I say. "My father embracing technology? What is the world coming to?"

"I know, right?" Becky grins and kisses the top of Dad's head. "I showed Dad how to do a video chat and now he's hooked. Next step, a smartphone."

I scoot over so Shane can pull up a chair. "How did Becky talk you into this, Dad?"

"Hey, I'm not that bad. I figured out the email, didn't I? Maybe next, I'll do the Facebook. Hi, Shane. How are you?"

"I'm great, Dr. DeWitt. How are you?"

We chat for a few more minutes, then Becky announces she needs to get home. "You got this, Dad? When you're done, click here."

I chuckle when Dad leans in close to the screen, revealing a blurred image of his balding head. "Yep. I got it."

Becky says goodbye and seconds later I hear Dad's door close.

"Can you hear us okay, Dad?"

"Yeah, I can hear you. *And* I can see your lips moving. This is way better than the phone. Almost as good as being in the same room. You're never gonna get rid of me now, Princess."

"Well, that's good, because I don't want to. Ever." I give him my biggest smile.

"Sorry I kind of left you hanging there with your grandparents' story last weekend. I just got too tired."

"I know. Don't worry about it, Dad. We can't have you getting overtired again." Dad hasn't had any more issues since the blood clot emergency at my place.

"Did you get Shane up to speed?"

Shane answers for me. "She did. Lilly almost confessed everything to William but then she chickened out. I'm dying to know what happened after that."

"Got some time to hear it now?" Dad cocks one eyebrow. He is downright adorable.

My unpacked bags stand at the door. Shane and I look at each other and grin.

"No time like the present, Dad."

"Be sure to stop me if I've left confusing gaps or used some words wrong." Dad picks up his faithful yellow pad, adjusts his bifocals, and begins to read.

CHAPTER TWENTY-EIGHT

Lilly

1942–1943

When she returned home from the library, Lilly waited until supper was eaten and the baby settled for the night before she approached Tommy. "We need to talk."

He looked up from the newspaper he was reading. "About what?"

"I think it's time we confessed to William Tidsbury that we started the fire." There. She'd said it.

Tommy lifted the paper again and focused on it, saying nothing.

She tried again. "We can't keep living like this, Tommy. At least I can't. I'd rather clear the air. Tell the whole truth. He'll either forgive us or he won't, but at least we'll have done all we could to—"

Tommy slammed the paper to the floor and stood. "If it was so important to clear the air, why didn't you confess everything before you had an affair with the man, Lilly?"

She swallowed. His question was fair. "I know. I should have. *We* should have, a long time ago."

"No, we should *not* have." Tommy paced across the room. "Knowing the fire was deliberately set by us—by you—or by anyone, would only make it harder for William. But you! You go hop into bed with the man—"

"It wasn't like that!"

"—when one honest confession probably would have ended the relationship before it ever got to that point. Admit it. You didn't tell him because you were afraid it might end. You didn't want it to end." Tommy strode to the window. "Just admit it, Lil."

Lilly pressed her lips together. Tommy wasn't wrong. And he had every reason to be angry.

"I've been trying, Lilly. You and me, we're… like… I don't know. We're *you and me*, you know?" He turned to face her. "Tommy and Lilly, since we were kids. I'm trying to be a good dad to Dale, too. But every time I look at him, I remember what you did and who you did it with… and that only reminds me of what we did way back then."

Lilly stepped toward him. "All the more reason to tell him. To get it off our chests so we can move on."

"No! Absolutely not. If we have to carry this around on our chests for life, then so be it. It's what we deserve."

He didn't need to say the rest. She deserved to carry an even heavier load. "But this is not what William deserves."

Tommy glared at her. "Are you in love with him?"

The question startled Lilly. "What? William? No!"

"Because if you think I haven't heard what the wagging tongues are saying around town, you're wrong. I know you've been taking the baby to see him. Is that what this is about? You want the air cleared, convinced he'll forgive you and welcome you back into his arms? Don't be too sure, Lil."

In his anger, Tommy's voice had risen enough to wake Dale, who began to howl. Lilly tried to ignore it, but it only grew worse as Tommy raised his voice above it. "We had an agreement, Lilly. We said we'd never speak about it again, even to each other—"

"We were *children*!"

"You've already broken that promise by bringing it up." He pointed his finger at her, then thumped it on the table for emphasis. "Do *not* tell anyone else, do you hear me? No one."

Lilly went to pick up the crying baby. When she returned, Tommy was gone.

• • •

No more was said as the week progressed. Lilly stopped taking Dale to the library.

William is right. I need to choose, and the only right choice is to stay with my husband. I need to do something right for once in my life.

They may never have a strong marriage, but even Tommy agreed that they deserved each other. They'd make the best of it and raise their son as Dale DeWitt. He would never need to know his true lineage. If the day came when he asked about his father's military service and figured out that the dates didn't line up in his favor, well... they could deal with it then.

Tommy returned to his farm job in time for spring planting. With the increased income came an increased sense of security. And with something constructive to keep him busy, Tommy wasn't drinking or hanging around the apartment all day.

Lilly began to keep her eyes open for a house they could rent or possibly even buy. She imagined a place with a small, fenced yard for Dale to play safely and where she could grow vegetables and flowers like Aunty Margaret did.

The sooner we start acting like a normal family, the sooner people will forget what I've done.

Lilly even began to wonder about returning to church. Would she be shunned? The church people would no doubt make a hero out of Tommy for serving his country and returning wounded, only to increase his heroism by accepting another man's child as his own.

But could they rise above judging Lilly? Did it matter? She decided to broach the topic with Tommy that night, but he came home with a huge surprise. For starters, she wondered why he wasn't in his work clothes.

"I wasn't at work today." Tommy stood behind a kitchen chair and gripped the back of it with both hands. "Took the day off and went to the city for an appointment."

"An appointment?" Was he having more plastic surgery?

"With a lawyer." He pulled some papers out of a folder and laid them on the table before walking into the bedroom.

"What's this?" Lilly threw the tea towel she was holding over her shoulder and walked to the table to inspect the documents.

One glance at the letters emblazoned in large print across the top told her the story: PETITION FOR DISSOLUTION OF MARRIAGE. Lilly stared at the words, which grew fuzzy as she gripped the edge of the table to steady herself. She skimmed the page, trying to decipher the legal lingo. She could understand enough of it to know her husband had filed for divorce on the grounds of adultery.

Head swimming, she read through it a second time. On the bottom were dotted lines to be signed by her, by Tommy, and by two witnesses.

All the lines were blank.

Tommy came out of the bedroom carrying their only suitcase. "When you're ready to sign, let me know. I'll be at Mom and Dad's."

"Tommy, wait!" She ran to the door and stood in front of it. "I can't believe you did this without even discussing it."

"Well, this is what you want, isn't it?"

"No! I don't know. I thought we were doing all right. I haven't seen William since the night we talked—"

"Well, aren't you just the devoted little wife."

"Tommy—"

"Look. There's no reason we can't do this peaceably. I think we both know we got married too soon, under forced circumstances. We gave it a go. Now you've got another man's kid and I've got the face of a circus freak."

"Tommy, don't say that. You're—"

"William's unattached, Lilly. You may as well be with him. Let him raise his son."

She stared back at him, speechless.

"Think it over, Lil. It'll be easier to do if I'm not here. Now let me pass."

She stood aside. As she watched him leave, she was sure she heard an audible voice somewhere deep inside: *You are a miserable failure, Lilly DeWitt. Lilly Sampson. Who even knows what your real name is?*

• • •

Lilly couldn't bear to visit the cemetery anymore. When she felt too ashamed to confess her foolishness even to the dead, what reason was there to live? But then she'd see Dale asleep in his little bed, long lashes against his smooth cheeks. Wispy hair growing into wild curls. Joyful giggles when she played with him. Delight in his discovery of new foods. Splashing in the bath. She'd kiss his neck, his elbows, his toes, and feel like the most blessed person alive to have him in her life. He was worth living for. Fighting for.

She tucked the divorce papers into a drawer unsigned. Tommy had said to tell him when she was ready. Maybe that day would come, but it wasn't here yet.

• • •

One Sunday morning, she had just finished feeding Dale his breakfast and was cleaning his face when she heard someone coming up the stairs to the apartment. Tommy? No one ever came.

Whoever it was knocked. She tossed the washcloth toward the basin, leaving Dale in his high chair, and opened the door.

"Good morning, Lilly."

"William." Lilly ran a hand through her hair and wrapped her robe more tightly over her nightgown.

"Can I come in?"

She opened the door wider and William stepped inside. Before closing the door, she looked around outside to check whether anyone might have seen him.

"Don't worry. Everyone's in church." William removed his hat and went immediately to Dale.

"We're not."

"Almost everyone. Hi, little fella. Remember me?" William sat on a kitchen chair so he could be face to face with the baby.

"What are you doing here, William?"

"Came to see my son. And to finish a conversation."

Dale raised his arms toward Lilly. She lifted him from his high chair and carried him to the living room area. "There's a reason I haven't been back, William. I thought you'd figure out that I made my decision." She put Dale on a blanket on the floor with a ball and his monkey.

"And you were right. That *is* what I thought. So I kept my distance. Then I heard Tommy left you."

"He didn't—"

"Where is he then?" William looked around the apartment, sweeping his hand across. "Lilly, the whole town knows he's living with his parents. How long 'til you're divorced?"

"We're not—" Could she honestly finish that sentence? "I don't know."

"What are you waiting for?" William came over to where she knelt on the floor, took her hand, and pulled her gently to her feet. "Look at the facts, Lilly. You and I share a child. A child that I adore." He enveloped her in his arms. "And I've always adored you, too. I know I haven't shown it well. I know I'm not the greatest catch, and I haven't given you the respect you deserve. I'm sorry for all that, Lilly. But if you'll have me, I really believe we can make a go of things."

Lilly gazed into his eyes, convinced he was as sincere as could be. But he didn't know the whole truth. Nobody did, except Tommy.

"We had some lovely times together, didn't we? We enjoy the same things." He played with a strand of her hair, ran his fingers down one cheek.

Lilly's heart began to pound. Would he kiss her?

He leaned in so close that she felt his breath lightly on her cheek. Their lips nearly touched.

Instead he released her and pulled away. "Besides, I'm pretty sure I've figured out what your big secret is, and if you really feel you must get it off your chest before we can move forward, then I'm here to show you how accepting I can be."

He moved to the sofa and sat down.

Lilly sank into the armchair, stunned. How could he possibly know? Had he known all along? She couldn't seem to form any words, but William must have read the shock on her face.

He chuckled. "You're surprised?"

"Yes. I... how did you find out?"

"I'm quite sure the whole community knows. Anybody who knows you, I mean. Which is pretty much the whole community."

Lilly stared back at him. Could it really be that simple? William had frequently talked about how blessed he was to have a limp because he didn't have to worry about being drafted or expected to serve. She'd thought it was all bluster. Maybe he really did feel fortunate. Maybe he'd already forgiven her.

"But how can you just accept it like that?"

"It was a long time ago, Lilly."

She shook her head. All this time. This load of guilt and shame she and Tommy had carried could have been spared.

"Believe me, William, if I could go back and do just one thing over... just one thing, of all the stupid, *stupid* things I've done in my life... I never would have followed Tommy to your shed that night. I would do everything in my power to stop him. Everything! And if he'd insisted on carrying it through, I'd have followed him with buckets of water, I'd have made sure that fire was out. I'd have run and banged on your door to wake your family. I've felt so awful."

William's face had turned ashen.

"I need your forgiveness, William. If you and I are going to work, we need no secrets between us, and I need to hear you say you've forgiven me."

He stood to his feet, then quickly sat again as though afraid he might faint.

"William? Are you okay?"

"What are you talking about?" William's voice had taken a sinister tone.

Too late, Lilly realized her mistake. "I... I thought you said you knew."

"You're telling me *Tommy* set that fire? Tommy and *you?*" The gray of his face began to change to red, starting from his chin and working its way to his forehead. Under any other circumstances, Lilly might have found it comical. Now it struck her heart with terror.

"We only meant to burn down the shed, I swear! You and your dad were tearing it down the next day, remember?"

"I remember everything about that horrible night." William's voice had risen to an angry pitch and his eyes blazed directly at Lilly. "I remember everything about the next day and the day after that and every single day I lived through that hellish pain. Even when I want to forget, I can't."

"William, I'm sorry! I am so sorry."

"Now you're telling me it was *deliberate*?"

"No! No, it was only supposed to be the shed. Only the shed."

William stormed toward the door, then back to the table. "You—*you*... all this time! You have no idea how much I suffered. And not just physical pain, Lilly." He began to pace the room. "Do you know what it's like to go through high school not being able to dance with a girl, knowing you can't get a date because of your limp? Never going swimming with the guys because you can't bear to show your scars? Knowing everyone feels sorry for you? Everyone except those who think they can bully you around because of it."

The baby let loose a frightful wail and Lilly picked him up. Her own tears fell freely. "William, I'm—"

"I know. You're sorry. I don't know how you could stand to be anywhere near me knowing what you did, let alone..." He waved his hand toward Dale. "Let alone *this*! What kind of woman are you anyway? You think you can just toy with people's lives?"

Lilly pressed her lips together. He was right. She had no defense.

"I'll tell you what kind of woman you are. You're the kind who thinks only of herself, who wants what she wants when she wants it. You'd have made a terrible nurse. I doubt you'll ever be much of a mother."

Lilly let the painful words sear their way through her. They were nothing she hadn't already thought about herself.

"I want my son, Lilly."

"What? No!" Lilly hugged Dale to her chest so tightly that he began to fuss again. "I understand if you can't forgive me, but you can't have Dale."

"I don't need you to agree. I can go to court. He's my son. Once they know what you did, everyone will be on my side."

"No. William, please, I beg you! I'm his mother."

"His *single* mother. Who tried to end her son's life before it began. You think a judge won't side with me when he hears *that*?"

William picked up his hat and swept out of the apartment without another word.

Lilly stared at the door for a full two minutes. Then it hit her. What secret had William thought everyone knew?

CHAPTER TWENTY-NINE

AUGUST 1944

Surely this was a horrible nightmare from which Lilly would awaken any minute.

She and Tommy sat on one side of a large boardroom table. The same lawyer who'd supplied Tommy with divorce documents now sat between them, hoping to provide some guidance in a totally different matter that William and his lawyer—who both sat opposite them—were attempting to bring before the court. On the end sat a judge of the County Court of Manitoba, a round man with a grey horseshoe of hair.

Lilly had been in a fog ever since the notice to appear arrived, saying they were to be at the courthouse by ten in the morning. When she'd asked Tommy what the purpose of this meeting was, he'd called it a "nonsense meeting that William and his lawyer cooked up out of spite. Just make sure you call the judge 'my lord' and not 'your honor.' It's a federal matter."

At least there wasn't a roomful of observers—or worse yet, an actual trial with a real jury. She tried to understand the judge's words as she focused on his shiny head.

"The proceedings will involve a pretrial review of facts to determine whether there is sufficient merit to proceed with a trial to determine two issues. The court has received an application from Mr. William Tidsbury that includes both a compensation component and a fitness component." He shuffled some papers and adjusted his glasses. "This is highly unusual, and I need more details to determine whether this matter should even proceed."

The compensation part Lilly understood. William wanted recompence for his injuries from the fire. This was exactly why Tommy had never wanted William to know. But what was meant by a fitness hearing? Even the judge found that it was highly unusual.

Next, William's lawyer read a document which he said William intended to file at the police station. "Mr. Tidsbury will be requesting that the police lay criminal charges against Thomas and Lilly DeWitt."

So if no charges had been laid yet, what were they all doing here? Lilly's head hurt trying to sort it out, and she shifted her gaze to a man in the corner who typed away on a little machine unlike anything Lilly had seen.

William's lawyer kept reading the document. It explained how, sixteen years earlier, Thomas DeWitt and Lilly Sampson had conspired together to burn down the Tidsburys' garden shed. How the fire had spread, destroying the family's home and leaving eight-year-old William with permanent injuries and scars. How those injuries had cost him dearly.

Lilly couldn't bear to listen as the long report was read in detail, outlining the physical and mental anguish her actions had caused.

When the lawyer concluded, the judge spoke. "Just so I'm understanding this correctly, the applicant says he is intending to file with the police information that may lead to criminal charges against Mr. and Mrs. DeWitt from when they were eight years old, but he is saying he won't press for charges to be laid if he receives some sort of compensation for his injuries?"

"That's correct, my lord. But it's not money he asks."

"Well, if a crime has been committed, he should just report the matter to the police so they can decide if charges are to be laid. I can't get involved in what he intends to do." The judge turned to the other lawyer. "What have you to say?"

"My lord, the incident in question took place when both my clients were eight years old. If criminal charges were laid back then, or even if a civil lawsuit had been initiated at that time, their parents or legal guardians might possibly have been required to address the charges or pay compensation at the time. But it's been sixteen years. Life has moved on. I suggest this is a complete waste of the court's time, and quite frankly, of mine and my clients'."

"Yes, but my client only learned of it in the past year," the other lawyer argued. "Until the truth came out, everyone assumed the fire was accidental."

The judge considered the point. "All right. I'm curious. How *did* the truth come out?"

Lilly and Tommy's lawyer spoke again. "My client, Mrs. DeWitt, confessed to the plaintiff, my lord. She and Mr. DeWitt both have a great deal of remorse for their actions. Their lives have been wrought with suffering over this event as well."

The judge studied Lilly. "I realize your conduct as children is not a question to be decided by me, but I'm trying to understand what we're dealing with here. What made you decide to confess after so much time had gone by?"

Lilly's heart raced. "I—I had wanted to tell the truth for some time. To get it off my chest. I was hoping my husband would agree."

The judge turned to Tommy. "And you didn't want to confess because...?"

"Confessing did not seem to be in anyone's best interest." Tommy put the emphasis on the word anyone, and Lilly sensed his smoldering anger at her.

The judge looked at Lilly again. "But you decided to go ahead and confess?"

Lilly cleared her throat. "It... wasn't entirely intentional. William... Mr. Tidsbury... indicated to me that he already knew all about it. He told me he knew the secret I was keeping. So then... I started talking about the fire, and... well... it turned out he didn't know about that."

Her lawyer jumped in. "My lord, given that my clients were young children—"

The judge held up a finger to stop him. "Mr. Tidsbury. If you didn't know Mrs. DeWitt helped set that fire, what was it you thought you knew?"

"It was about her heritage, my lord. She was adopted by her aunt and uncle. Her birth mother was a... a woman of bad reputation... and nobody seems to know who her father is."

Lilly's lawyer frowned. "Objection. That's irrelevant, and his comment should not be entered into the record!"

"Perhaps you can explain why you think it's relevant, Mr. Tidsbury," said the judge.

William glanced at his lawyer. He hadn't looked at Lilly once since they'd entered the room. "Well... I was encouraging Lilly to follow through with her divorce, which her husband had already filed for. I had offered to marry her so we could raise our son together. She felt she couldn't commit to a relationship with me until I knew everything there was to know about her. Which I thought I did."

"Wait a minute, wait a minute. *Your* son? Together?" The judge waved his finger between Lilly and William.

"My lord." William's lawyer broke in. "While Mr. DeWitt was deployed overseas with the Canadian army, Mrs. DeWitt seduced my client—"

"Objection!"

"Overruled. I want to hear this."

"—and became pregnant as a result. Her husband returned before the child was born. The couple is now separated."

"Is this true?" The judge swung his attention back to Lilly's side of the table.

Tommy's lawyer spoke up again. "Mr. DeWitt was injured in a bombing in London and returned with severe burns to his face and neck, as you can see by his scars. Because of his injuries, he was honorably discharged and has suffered much. He, more than anyone, can empathize with the sufferings of Mr. Tidsbury. He and Mrs. DeWitt both deeply regret the mistakes of their childhood. I have no doubt that the guilt they each carry contributed to both the affair and the breakdown of their marriage. My lord, if Mr. Tidsbury reports this matter to the police, we will suggest that no criminal charges or proceedings against them be initiated, considering the long delay, their age at the time, and that they have paid their debt to society."

The judge let out a huff. "A magistrate will decide on that matter if Mr. Tidsbury files his complaint with the police, sir. Not the police. But quite frankly, I too am beginning to think this is a waste of the court's time." The judge turned back to William's side of the table. "Now I assume that the relationship between Mrs. DeWitt and Mr. Tidsbury came to an end when this information about the fire-setting was brought forward?"

"That's correct."

"So now we are back to this court's proceedings, and the question of whether Mr. Tidsbury's application is of sufficient merit to proceed to a trial. May I ask, then, if it's not a ruling for financial compensation that Mr. Tidsbury will be seeking from this court, what is he seeking?"

William's lawyer cleared his throat. "He seeks custody of his son, my lord."

CHAPTER THIRTY

Lilly froze. William was making good on his threat.

"Custody! So this is going to evolve into a child custody matter?" The judge made a note on a pad in front of him. "Based on *spite?*"

"My lord," Lilly's lawyer jumped in, "the boy will be three years old next month. He's been in his mother's care all his life—"

"—his *single* mother." Judgment dripped from William's lawyer.

"Objection!"

"Sustained," the judge said. "Need I remind you there is a war on? Millions of women are singlehandedly raising their children these days."

William's lawyer barely paused for a breath. "Sir, my client has a right to be involved in his son's life. Given what we know of Mrs. DeWitt's character—"

"Her character? You are calling into question Mrs. DeWitt's character, and her fitness to retain custody of the child, because she would be *single?*" The judge shook his head. "Even if this court were to award custody of the boy to Mr. Tidsbury, the child would still be in a single-parent home, is that correct?"

"No, sir," William replied.

Lilly looked up from her lap, where a stray thread had been keeping her hands occupied.

William replied. "I'm engaged to be married, my lord. Next month. My fiancée adores children. She is prepared to become Dale's stepmother."

What? Lilly bit her lip to keep from crying out. *Who?* How could any other woman love Dale the way she loved him?

"Does this child know you, or are you a stranger to him, Mr. Tidsbury?"

"He knows me a little, sir. I've enjoyed playing with him and reading to him on several occasions when his mother brought him to the library where I was the head librarian."

"Was?"

"I moved to Winnipeg after hearing Lilly's confession and realizing there was no future for us. That's where I met my fiancée."

"So your injuries have not prevented you from earning a living, Mr. Tidsbury?"

"No, my lord. But I miss my son terribly."

"Still." The judge continued. "You've not given me enough cause to proceed with setting up a trial to consider if this court should take a child away from the only mother he's known—whatever heinous misdeeds she may have committed as a child herself—unless you can provide me with some evidence that Mrs. DeWitt is not fit to be a mother, or that proceeding with a formal trial to determine that matter would be in the best interest of the child."

The room grew silent except for the tapping of the court reporter's little machine. Lilly found it hard to breathe. Surely the judge would dismiss the whole thing soon.

He continued. "Child custody, visitation rights, and so on will need to be determined by this court at another time *if* I decide a trial to determine the matter is warranted. But right now, my curiosity takes me back to whether criminal charges would be even remotely likely, if Mr. Tidsbury takes his complaint about the fire to the police. I need to ask Mr. DeWitt and Mrs. DeWitt both a question and I need you to answer separately, for yourself. Do you understand?"

Tommy and Lilly answered almost in unison. "Yes, my lord."

The judge turned to Tommy first. "When you were eight years old, setting fire to that shed in the Tidsburys' backyard, did you know that what you were doing was wrong?"

"Yes, my lord. I did. But I thought it would be only the shed. If I'd known what was going to happen, I would not have done it. I have regretted it every day of my life."

"Yet you told no one."

"No, my lord."

"And you made no attempt to make amends?"

Tommy hesitated before answering. Then a soft "No" escaped as he shook his head.

Their lawyer jumped in. "With due respect, my lord, Mr. DeWitt became a volunteer firefighter while still in high school and went on to gain his full-fledged certificate. He's helped put out many fires and no doubt saved lives and property in the process. He also served our country—voluntarily—until his injuries prevented him from continuing. I believe he may have been subconsciously trying to make amends."

"All right. Thank you." The judge turned to Lilly. "Mrs. DeWitt? Did you understand as an eight-year-old that what you were doing was wrong?"

Lilly nodded, fighting tears. "Yes, my lord."

"I don't want to know what you may or may not have done in the interest of making amends with Mr. Tidsbury. Under the law, a criminal court of justice might well find you and your husband both guilty of arson, given that you each knew what you were doing was wrong, and given the matter has only recently come to light. But it's also clear to me that you both regret your actions and have suffered guilt all these years. Is it enough? Some would argue it is." The judge folded his hands together on the table. "I think we can all agree you have not suffered as much as William Tidsbury has. Yet he asks only for custody of his son, based on him being better fit to parent the child than you, Mrs. DeWitt. While I allow that he should have rights to visitation, I am not a fan of breaking up a family. Nor do I have any desire to disrupt the life of a three-year-old boy unless it can be proven to me that it is in the best interest of the child to do so, or that the mother is unfit to such an extent that I should not let her retain custody of the child."

The judge removed his glasses and focused on William.

"I am sorry for all you have suffered, Mr. Tidsbury," he continued. "But unless there is still more evidence in this sordid, convoluted story, I can only see that the child should remain with his mother and that you be allowed to—"

"There *is* more information, my lord." William was staring directly at Lilly. "If Mrs. DeWitt were wise, she would tell the complete story herself rather than forcing you to drag it out of me."

Out of the corner of her eye, Lilly could see Tommy sitting up straight and looking in her direction.

Their lawyer leaned over to whisper. "What's this about?"

Lilly was not going to make the same mistake twice, giving out information that William might not intend.

She shook her head. "I have no idea what he's talking about."

The judge sighed. "Mr. Tidsdale, please stop wasting my time and give us this additional evidence you claim to know. And why was it not part of the initial report?"

His lawyer spoke for him. "Mr. Tidsbury wished to spare Mrs. DeWitt the added humiliation unless it became necessary, my lord."

"How admirable." The judge's tone was clearly sarcastic. "Well? I'm listening."

The man pulled another sheet of paper from his briefcase, then glanced at William. William nodded, and the lawyer began to read. "On her last visit to the library in June of 1942, in a conversation in Mr. Tidsbury's office, Mrs. DeWitt confessed to him that she had both sought and obtained an illegal abortion upon learning of her pregnancy with Mr. Tidsbury's baby."

Lilly heard Tommy inhale and felt herself go limp. How could William do this? She kept staring at the table.

"Mrs. DeWitt paid for the procedure, then returned to Summervale believing herself no longer pregnant. She told no one, not even the father of her child, William Tidsbury. When she later learned that the procedure had failed, it was too late in the pregnancy to try again." The lawyer looked up from his paper. "From her actions, Mrs. DeWitt has clearly demonstrated she never wanted this child and in fact went to great and illegal lengths to end his life. Therefore, my client believes the boy would be better off with him, his father, who would have fought to save the boy's life had he known Mrs. DeWitt's intent."

If only she could pass out. Or disappear.

Everything, Lilly's entire life, with all its shame, was laid bare like a laundry list for the eyes and ears of these six men. Her questionable birth. The father who'd abandoned her and the mother who had died giving birth to another child. The unexplainable attraction to flames that she and Tommy had shared as children and the destruction it had led to. The way their desperate secret had bonded them, leading to a teenage pregnancy and a rushed wedding. Perhaps that was the only thing that had not been mentioned today—the loss of her firstborn and the wedge that loss had driven between her and Tommy. His enlisting and leaving. Her affair with William. And now her attempt to terminate her pregnancy.

She rubbed her forehead with one hand.

I am a horrible, horrible person. An arsonist, an adulterer, a liar, a murderer. I deserve whatever I'm dealt. Still, she pleaded with God. *Please don't let them take Dale from me. Anything but that.*

The room grew quiet. Even the stenographer caught up and stopped. He looked at the judge, waiting for him to continue.

"This does cause me to see things differently." The judge shifted in his chair. "Is this information accurate, Mrs. DeWitt?"

Lilly couldn't look the judge in the eye. His condemnation fell on her as tangibly as if he'd covered her in black tar. She nodded slowly.

"You'll need to answer audibly, Mrs. DeWitt."

"Yes."

He sighed. "Are you aware, Mrs. DeWitt, that abortion is an indictable offense under the Offences Against the Persons Act of 1892 and those found guilty can face life imprisonment?"

Lilly's lawyer jumped in. "But my lord, the procedure failed. There are no charges to lay."

The judge raised both his hands, palms out. "As much as I would love to sweep this whole ugly story under the carpet, it behooves me to take into account the character—or lack thereof—demonstrated by Mrs. DeWitt. That she attempted to acquire an abortion, indeed believed she had achieved her aim and told no one, reveals that she not only wished this child dead but was willing to participate in illegal activity to make that a reality." He paused to scribble another note on his pad. "This brings into serious question your fitness to remain the parental custodian of the child. No one in this country owns a child, Mrs. DeWitt, as if the child were a piece of property to be disposed of." He looked at Lilly over the top of his glasses. "The courts will decide who is best fit to raise a child. Judges normally presume that it would be the mother, except when that is not in the child's best interest."

The judge looked down at the paper before him.

"Mr. Tidsbury." He sighed before going on. "You've provided persuasive evidence that Mrs. DeWitt may indeed be unfit to raise her son alone. I find sufficient evidence to warrant a trial to determine who should have custody of the child until he is of legal age. Counsel, would you please speak with the clerk and provide him with available times when a trial to determine the matter can be scheduled?"

Lilly didn't hear the rest. The room was spinning around her. The two lawyers were both talking at once, insisting on a declaration one way or the other. She wasn't sure who left and who stayed. She laid her head across her arms on the table and tried to slow her breathing.

When she raised her head, only Tommy and their lawyer remained. The lawyer was gathering up papers and stuffing them into his briefcase as he grilled Tommy.

"If she'd told me the whole story, I could have prepared better," the lawyer said. "Did you know about this attempted termination?"

"No." Tommy let out a huff. "I didn't even know about the pregnancy until I came home and saw her."

"Well. *You're* off the hook. Tidsbury may still get what he wants, but it won't affect you."

"Yeah." Tommy sighed and turned to Lilly. "You going to be all right?"

Lilly couldn't answer. She couldn't even shake her head. How could she ever be all right? She was losing everything—Tommy, William, *and* Dale. She may as well crawl into the grave that covered her dead mother and baby brother. Would they want her?

"I'm sorry things didn't go as you'd hoped, Mrs. DeWitt." The lawyer pulled more papers from his briefcase. "I don't know how much I could have helped you if you'd told me everything, but—" He sighed and turned back to Tommy. "Listen, as long as you're both in the city… I still don't have your signed divorce papers. Do you want to stop by my office?"

Lilly kept staring at the tabletop, as motionless as the furnishing itself.

Tommy spoke next. "I think she's had enough for today."

CHAPTER THIRTY-ONE

Diana

Shane is giving me space, like I asked.

I hate it.

The video chat with Dad floored us both, but we were too exhausted to hear any more or further discuss what Lilly experienced in that awful courtroom. Now half the week is gone and I haven't heard from him. I have a meeting with Carly and our worker at Big Brothers/Big Sisters for our annual check-in meeting. I still haven't given Carly an answer to the adoption question. Has she told our worker about any of this? Has she given up on me and gone ahead with the termination? I must be the worst big sister ever. Will she even still want me?

I desperately need to talk to Shane. But how dare I call him? After he poured out his heart, inviting me into a bold new relationship and my giving him the lame old "I need more time" line, how can I crawl back looking for emotional support?

But I can't make this decision alone. Which leads to an even bigger question: how can I ever raise a child alone? Work is nuts. I'm still exhausted from my trip, overwhelmed by Shane's feelings for me, and torn apart by Carly's situation and request.

I approach her apartment building, wondering if I should go inside and talk to her mom. But Carly is already outside, waiting. She hops into the car and I reach across to give her a hug.

"Hey. Long time no see."

She remains stiff. "Yeah. Welcome back."

"How are you?" I almost hate to ask.

"Okay."

"That's it? Just okay?"

"No. Not okay. Still don't know what to do. I know I don't want to terminate. I know I can't raise a kid. I know I can't give a baby away to strangers. So *you* figure out how I am."

I swallow. "Is your mom still pressuring you?"

"Some, yeah."

I pull into traffic and we ride in silence for a while. Carly flips on the radio, changes stations several times, listens through the last half of a rap song, then shuts it off.

With about a block left to drive, I glance over at her. "Have you told anyone at Big Sisters about it? Because if not, we're going to have to do that today."

"No. I thought you might have."

That might have been a good idea, but honestly I've been too busy. "Carly, I'm sorry I don't have an answer for you yet. I just—"

"No, I get it. It's a big decision."

Our worker, Charlene, welcomes us into her office and offers us something to drink. I have tea, Carly takes water.

When we're all seated, she begins with a smile. "So. Carly and Diana. Happy fifth anniversary! You guys should be so proud. Lots of matches don't last five years."

I chuckle. "Sounds like you're talking about a marriage."

Charlene opens a file folder on her desk. "How's everything going?"

I fix my gaze on Carly, willing her to cough up the important information. When she finally makes eye contact, I nod.

"Not that great." Her focus darts around the room. "I mean… it's been great with me and Diana." She waves her hand between us. "It's just… I got… well, I'm pregnant."

Charlene looks at me with raised eyebrows, then back at Carly. "You're sure?" Carly nods.

When she says no more, I jump in with answers to what I know will be the next questions. "We've done the tests. She's seen a doctor. Her mother knows."

"Have you decided what you're going to do, Carly?" Charlene's voice is gentle, if maybe a little impatient.

"I asked Diana if she would adopt my baby."

"Oh." Charlene sits back in her chair. Her eyes move back and forth between the two of us while her head, with its asymmetrical haircut, stays still. "This is... highly unusual."

I could easily convince myself I am having one of those dreams where you're looking for something over and over and can't find it.

When neither of us says anything more, Charlene continues. "What did you say to that, Diana?"

"I... um... well, it was unexpected. But I am considering it. I'm honored, of course. It's not a decision I can make lightly."

"I should think not. Carly, do you have another plan if Diana says no?"

"My mother thinks I should terminate."

I close my eyes. *God, how can you put me in this position?*

"Is that what you'll do then?" Charlene asks.

Carly remains quiet for the longest time. When she finally speaks, her voice cracks. "I don't think I could live with myself if I did that."

I won't be able to live with myself if she does that, either. Not when it's within my power to stop it.

"How far along are you?" Before Carly can answer, Charlene speaks again. "You know what? Don't answer that. Abortion is not illegal at any stage in Canada. Alberta has restrictions after twenty weeks. My job is not to sway you one way or the other. The two of you need to work out the adoption question and then go from there. Why don't we set up another appointment in a month and we'll call that our annual check-in meeting?" She closes the folder. "I'll need some advice from our director, but... I think the official match between you two will need to close if you go through with the adoption. And possibly even if you don't, all things considered. Continuing the relationship could be problematic. For obvious reasons."

I drop Carly off at home with a promise to give her an answer by the end of the week. "The pregnancy support center should be able to walk us through it, whether I adopt your baby or someone else does."

"I would want you to keep being my big sister, though."

"No one can stop us from being together, from being friends. Regardless what they tell us. I'm not going to abandon you, kiddo."

Carly opens her car door and puts one foot out.

"And Carly?" I say. "It's going to be okay."

She lets out a big sigh, nods, and closes the door.

I watch her go. How can I assure her that it's going to be okay? All the way home, I picture a child in a car seat behind me. How can I even afford it? I can't just quit my job and stay home. I'd need daycare. I try to imagine rearing a toddler, going to parent-teacher meetings, soccer games, talent shows. A high school graduation. I'll be in my mid-fifties by then!

I walk into the house and toss my keys on the kitchen table. The three Compassion kids I've been supporting for nearly a decade smile back at me from the fridge door. All three will soon age out of the program, and Compassion will be encouraging me to sponsor new children. Would the cost of sponsoring three children in an underdeveloped country cover the daycare costs for one Canadian child? I doubt it.

Mouse meows at me and I sit on the floor to pet her. "What am I supposed to do, Mousy? You want to share our space with a tiny human?"

I make tea and sit down with my Bible. Why do I read it only when desperate for something? Guidance. Encouragement. Hope. Maybe if I read it every day, I'd have stockpiled an entire storehouse of wisdom to draw on by now.

I open it. A verse I underlined years ago seems to hover just above the printed page:

> This day I call the heavens and the earth as witnesses against you
> that I have set before you life and death, blessings and curses.
> Now choose life, so that you and your children may live...[4]

My phone pings. *Shane.* My heart does that glad little leap as I open his text. *Had supper yet?* he asks.

No. Nothing 2 eat in this house.

I haven't been shopping since I got home from Winnipeg and have been living on canned soup and crackers.

On my way, he texts. *Figure out where u want 2 go. Got something to ask u.*

• • •

Forty minutes later, Shane and I are at our favorite mom and pop joint, Linda's Grill, feasting on burgers and sharing fries. I waste no time telling him what's going on with Carly, and he wastes no time offering his opinion.

"You realize you can't say no, right?"

I stare at him. "Maybe I should tell her to ask *you.*"

"If she did, I'd say yes." He takes a big bite of his burger.

"Shane. Please. You're just saying that because it's *not* you. Think about it a minute. You're as stuck in your ways as I am. I mean, I like my life the way it is, you know? In fact, my boss is hinting at a promotion that would have me traveling to conferences three or four times a year. Adopting a child would mean a huge shift in my routine. In my whole *life.* I'd have to find a bigger home, for starters. Can I even afford that?"

Shane swallows his food and takes a big gulp of his drink. "Okay. You're right, it's not a quick decision. But... what is your heart telling you?"

"Is that your way of asking if I've prayed about it? Because I have. Mostly asking God what on earth he's thinking. Can you see me, a mother? And a single mother at that?"

"Why would I not be able to see that? Diana, you've got what it takes to be a great mom. You can't let fear stop you from following the path God has for you."

Now that Shane is in therapy, he's all about grabbing life and rising above and all that. I'm not sure I like this new guy all that much.

I decide to change the subject. "Anyway. You said you wanted to ask me something."

"Yeah. My cousin's getting married this Saturday. Come with me?"

I can't believe my ears. "How long have you known me?"

"Uh... I don't know. Five years?"

"In all that time, have you ever known me to attend a wedding?"

"Uh..." Shane's eyes dart around the room as though he's on a quiz show with half a million dollars at stake if he gives the wrong answer.

"I don't *do* weddings, Shane. I'll send a card, I'll send money. But I do not attend weddings. Even when I'm invited, much less as somebody's plus-one." I toss my rumpled napkin on my plate and stand to leave. "Your answer is no. C'mon, take me home. I'm tired."

I head straight for the door without looking back. Shane's "What on earth—?" reaches my ears before the restaurant door closes behind me. Unfortunately, his car is locked so I have to stand there waiting for him like an idiot. Which takes a while because he still needs to pay for our food.

"Diana!" He charges to the car but doesn't unlock any doors. "How come I didn't know this about you?"

"That's what I'm wondering."

"Well, I've obviously hit a hot button. Care to explain?"

"Nope." I stare at the passenger-side door handle, waiting to hear a click.

Shane sighs. "Diana. I'm sorry. I had no idea. It was an innocent question. I really do have a wedding and I really do need a date. And frankly, I've always enjoyed weddings."

"Okay. Fine. You're forgiven. Can you unlock the door please?"

He pulls his keys out of his pocket but makes no attempt to push the button. "So... does that mean you'll be my date?"

"Absolutely not."

"Diana! You're being ridiculous."

"Open the door. Or should I walk home?"

He presses his lips together. "I'll open the door if you promise you'll tell me what this is about."

I turn around and head for the sidewalk. How long does it take to cover thirty blocks? At least I'll burn off some of the calories I just consumed.

"Diana, please. Wait!" Shane's footsteps quicken behind me. "All right, fine. You don't have to talk about it. I'll take you home. Just... come on."

My stubborn side really wants to keep walking, but I'm still wearing my heels from work. My feet will be dying by the time I reach home—if I even make it that far.

Reluctantly, I turn around. Shane's locks click and we both climb in. Neither of us speaks for the entire thirty blocks. Shane pulls into my driveway and kills the engine.

"Thanks for supper," I mumble. I know I'm acting immature, but seriously, why did this have to come up? Especially now.

Shane reaches out and touches my arm. "Diana, look at me."

His voice is so gentle and his eyes so kind, tears well up instantly.

Get a grip! I need to get out of the car, but he isn't done.

"Whatever this is about, it's clearly a big deal for you and I want to honor your wishes." He pulls his hand away. "I won't bring it up again, but... I really hope you'll talk to me about it. Or if not me, someone."

Great. He's going to push therapy on me.

"I care about you. I guess you know that already. I can't stand seeing you blocked from good things for bad reasons. I've been there and I'm finally finding freedom. I want that for you, too."

Then the clincher.

"I love you, Diana."

Dang it. I let out something between a sob and a gulp. Whatever it is, it's ugly.

"I can't do this, Shane. I promised myself when I left home and moved out here that I'd never talk about it. This was supposed to be my fresh start."

"It's okay. You don't have to."

But something holds me in the seat. Maybe I'll just tell him enough to leave me alone. Let him read between the lines. Lord knows, he figured out Carly's situation easily enough.

I take a deep breath and let it out. "Look, you know I was engaged once. Right?"

Shane stares back. "No."

"How has that not come up?"

He shrugs. "I don't know. Maybe one of us is skilled at avoiding certain topics."

"Ha-ha." I sound as sarcastic as I know how, even though it's hard to stay mad at him. "Ryan and I were high school sweethearts and kept dating through university. Nobody was surprised when we got engaged at Christmas before graduation. Set the date for June 21 so we'd always have lots of daylight on our anniversary. I was on cloud nine. Figured my life was all coming together."

"What happened?"

Then it poured out of me. The perfect wedding plans, the exquisite dress and exotic flowers, the string quartet. Dad walking me down the aisle.

"Ryan looked a little pale, but I figured it was just nerves. Dad handed me off, the pastor did his bit. We said our vows. Exchanged rings. My sister started singing. We moved to the registration table to sign the documents. I signed first, then handed the pen to the pastor, who handed it to Ryan."

I glance at Shane. The intensity in his eyes makes me look quickly away.

"He took the pen. His hand was shaking. Suddenly, he just dropped the pen on the table and said 'I can't do this. I'm sorry, I just can't do this.' He barely glanced at me before he ran off the platform and out through a side door. His bewildered best man didn't know what to do. Finally he took off after him, at the pastor's nudging."

"Oh, Di. How awful."

"Becky kept singing, unaware at first. That was the worst part, the way she kept going. The commotion in the room gradually registered, and she stumbled to an awkward stop in the middle of a line. Every second felt like an hour. The piano player tried to make it sound like a proper ending."

Shane takes my hand in his. "I am so sorry that happened to you."

I let out a jagged breath. How can it still hurt so much after ten years? "While the pastor tried to settle everyone down, Dad came to me and led me to a side room where I was at least away from all the eyes. He told me to try and relax, that he was sure Ryan just got cold feet and would come back."

Shane waits a bit. "I'm guessing he didn't?"

I shake my head. "I have not seen or heard from him since that day. Six months later, he married someone else."

To his credit, Shane says nothing. He just keeps holding my hand. But when I finally look up at him, I see a tear on his cheek and anger smoldering in his normally kind eyes. I know it isn't directed at me.

"Dad always tells me I'm better off without a man who would put me through that."

"Your dad's right."

"Anyway… now you know. Weddings are not my thing. Brings it all back and I can't control my emotions."

"That's understandable. But… how do you even know how you'll react if you haven't been to one since then?"

"Shane, I can't even watch a wedding in a movie without breaking out in hives. I squirm when I'm shown friends' wedding pictures. I've turned down three requests to serve as a bridesmaid and lost friends in the process." I wave my hand around. "I get anxious seeing bridal magazines at the checkout counter." Suddenly it all seems so petty. Childish. "You must think I'm pathetic."

"I could never think that, Di."

My phone chirps and I pull it out of my purse. A video call.

"It's Dad. I better—"

"Take it, yes. Of course."

Dad's face pops up on the little screen.

"Hi, Dad."

"Hey, Princess. Everything okay out there?"

"Uh… yeah… sure, fine."

"Looks like you're in your car. You better not be driving."

I glance over at Shane. "I'm in Shane's car, actually. Sitting in my driveway. Just got back from supper."

"Hi, Shane!"

Shane leans in. "Hi, Dr. DeWitt!"

"Well, I think I'll just stop responding to that 'Dr. DeWitt' nonsense and refuse to speak to that fella until he learns to call me Dale." Dad chuckles. "I won't keep you, Princess. Just wondering if this was a good time to chat, but I can see you're busy."

I look at Shane.

"I'll go," he mouths.

"You can stay if you want," I tell him.

For whatever reason, Shane is as invested in my family history as I am.

He stays. For the next hour, my angst surrounding weddings and my decision over Carly's baby fades into the background as Dad pulls out his yellow writing pad and shares more of Lilly's story.

CHAPTER THIRTY-TWO

Lilly

JANUARY 1945

L illy tried to find work in Summervale, but it was hopeless. Even when she'd finally been hired to work the sugar beet harvest in September, she had to quit after two days because the girl she hired to watch Dale found a better offer.

Mrs. Gordon at the grocery store informed her Tommy had moved to Winnipeg and found work in a warehouse. She'd not heard from any lawyers or from William since that day in court six months ago. The rumor mill said he was now married, and Lilly assumed he had dropped his pursuit of custody. But, like the proverbial wildfire, word had spread around Summervale about Tommy and Lilly lighting up that shed all those years before. His parents, along with Uncle Henry and Aunty Margaret, were all sharing in the shame.

When her landlord delivered the notice of eviction, Lilly couldn't blame anyone except herself. He had been kind, extending her stay there months beyond her last payment. But now he had a new tenant eager to move in. She couldn't blame him.

Desperate, she bundled up Dale and walked to Uncle Henry and Aunty Margaret's house prepared to humble herself and beg if necessary, for the sake of her son.

"Your uncle isn't here." Aunty Margaret's words were as sharp and cold as the icicles hanging above them. "He's clearing snow for the McKenzie funeral."

"Oh. I, um… need to talk to the two of you. I'll come back."

"If it's our help you're after, don't bother. Your uncle and I simply cannot contribute to the kind of lifestyle you've chosen for yourself, Lilly. Helping you now will only make it easier for you to keep making horrible choices." She pointed toward Dale with her chin. "Have you considered giving him up for adoption?"

Never. Lilly wanted to scream.

"You seem to be one of those people who can only learn things the hard way. Maybe things haven't gotten hard enough yet. We're doing you a favor."

She closed the door, leaving Lilly standing on the snowy sidewalk clutching Dale's hand, staring at the door until a soft click indicated it was now locked.

"We don't have to take her word for it," Lilly muttered as much to herself as to Dale. "Let's go find Uncle Henry. He'd never turn his back on us." She'd walk to the cemetery and catch Uncle Henry before he got home.

A commotion of men and vehicles captured Lilly's attention as she approached the cemetery. What was going on? They drove away far too quickly to be a funeral procession. She tried to rush Dale along, but by the time they reached the gate only one man remained. He was gathering up snow shovels near a freshly dug grave.

"Excuse me?" Lilly approached the short, slender man.

He pulled a cigarette from his mouth and dropped it to the ground. While he tamped it down with one foot, he studied Lilly without a word.

"I'm looking for my uncle, Henry Sampson. I was told he was here."

"Didn't you see all the ruckus?"

"Well, um, partly. What happened?"

The man took a deep breath and let it out. "Look, I hate to be the one to tell you this, but your uncle collapsed out here."

"Collapsed!"

"Prob'ly his heart. From the shoveling. Seems to get somebody every year. The other fellas are taking him straight to the hospital."

"Hospital?" Lilly froze.

"Well… one of them's headed for the hospital, the other will stop and pick up Margaret. I'd offer you a ride, but I'm walkin' myself. Somebody needs to stay behind and finish the work. Funeral here this afternoon."

Lilly scooped up Dale and started to run, but between his weight and the snow, she was exhausted in no time. They half-ran, half-walked the distance, Dale crying to go home. When they arrived at the hospital, completely bedraggled, an hour had passed.

Lilly hurried to the front desk and was relieved to recognize her former co-worker, a nurse named Jean.

"I was here when they brought him in and I know his wife is with him, but that's all I know, Lilly. Have a seat and I'll see what I can find out."

Lilly sat down in the waiting area and helped Dale drink some water out of a little pointed paper cup.

Jean returned with a somber face. "Lilly, I'm so sorry. Your uncle didn't make it."

• • •

Lilly closed her suitcase and hefted it to the door. She paused to look around the room, allowing good and bad memories to surface. Saying goodbye to this little apartment might have been easier if she had anywhere else to go. But Aunty Margaret's refusal to see her, her insistence that Lilly not attend the funeral, sent a message loud and clear. She had no option but to pack up her meager belongings and take her son to the city. At least there, people wouldn't know her whole story. With so many war widows around, she could easily pass for one.

She scraped together enough money for a train ticket and found a bench seat to share with Dale. Facing her sat a woman with a little girl. They smiled at each other but didn't speak. Lilly kept Dale entertained watching out the window and looking at his favorite book. The little girl across from them chattered away, trying to engage him, but he shied away. Finally, he settled down for a nap with his head on Lilly's lap.

When the little girl did the same, her mother smiled at Lilly again. "How old is your little fellow?"

"Turned three in September." Lilly stroked Dale's fine hair. "What about your little girl? Four or five?"

"She's three as well. Her birthday was in November."

Lilly gaped at the child. Had she heard correctly? "Really? She speaks exceptionally well."

The woman shrugged. "Does she?"

Dale hadn't spoken a word until he was two, and still didn't say much beyond "Mama" and "No." Lilly hadn't thought anything of it. She hadn't been around other children enough to make any observations.

"They say girls talk earlier than boys," the other mother offered.

"Yeah." No more was said, but Lilly studied the precious face of the little boy asleep on her lap. What if he was slow?

• • •

The cold blast of winter greeted her as she stepped down from the train. Inside the station, she paid for a locker and stashed her two suitcases inside. She would come back for them as soon as she found a place to stay.

Next, she bought a newspaper. Headlines declared that Canada had sent its first group of thirteen thousand draftees to war in Europe, but many of them had thrown their rifles overboard in protest. Lilly could relate. She was being sent into a war of her own, against her will.

She quickly turned to the classified ads and began circling rooms for rent and any possible job opportunities she could find.

Then she headed off down the sidewalk, tightly gripping Dale's hand. Her path led them past a familiar church. Lilly remembered stopping here four years earlier, after searching in vain for that charlatan doctor. She remembered the cleaning lady named Lilly and the kindness the woman had shown, her assurance that God saw her and cared. Maybe it wouldn't hurt to say a prayer now. If nothing else, maybe she could somehow pay tribute to Uncle Henry's memory even though she stifled her grief every time she thought of him.

Lilly led Dale up the stone steps, expecting to find the door locked. Instead it swung open when she pulled. They went inside, welcoming the warmth. She slid into the same pew, but this time she remained quiet and kept her eyes open. No one seemed to be around.

Dale fidgeted. Lilly gave him a cracker from her purse and let him run up and down the wooden pew while she tried to pray.

"God. Last time I was here, I was told that you see me. I hope you see me now. I know I've made a mess of things, but I beg for your mercy—if not for me, for Dale. I need to provide for my little boy. I need work and a place to stay. Please God."

When Dale tried to climb over the back of the pew, Lilly grabbed him up and left the sanctuary. As she crossed the foyer, a man with a clerical collar approached from a staircase leading down. He smiled at Dale.

"Oh, hello there, little fella." Then he looked at Lilly. "Can I help you?"

"No... I just stopped for a minute. To pray. I hope that's all right."

"Of course. Our door is always open."

Lilly pushed on the door, then stepped back. "I was just wondering... is there a... do you know a woman named Lilly? One of your congregants?"

The man's eyes narrowed. "I've only been pastor here for a couple of years—"

"She did some cleaning here, as a volunteer I think." When the man's face was still blank, Lilly ran her fingers along one side of her own. "Burn scars?"

"Oh! I know who you mean. Lilly Hoffman."

"I… didn't know her last name. I only met her once."

"Sadly, Lilly passed away about a year after I came. I didn't get to know her well, I'm ashamed to say. I don't think many did. The funeral was small."

Lilly nodded. "She was kind to me." She gripped Dale's hand and carried on her way.

By that evening, she'd found a boarding house where the landlady agreed to lower her price in exchange for some cleaning on Lilly's part. "Provided you can keep the kid quiet. I don't normally allow children, but you look like you could use a break. Let's call it a trial basis."

By the end of the week, Lilly had secured a night cleaning job at a department store simply by walking into the store and asking about the sign in the window.

Her new landlady agreed to watch Dale while Lilly was shown the procedures for the job. But when Lilly broached her about babysitting while Lilly went to work, the woman flat-out refused.

"I'll put him to bed before I leave for work." Lilly pleaded her case, prepared to pay more rent if the woman asked, but not wanting to offer. "And I'll be home again before he wakes."

"Absolutely not. You'll need to make other arrangements."

The pay would barely cover rent and food, and Lilly didn't know anyone she could ask to babysit even if she could afford to pay.

The first night, she took Dale along, being careful to arrive after the place had emptied out. She made a little bed for him in a storage closet and worked while he slept. She finished long before anyone arrived in the morning, then carried the still sleeping boy the eight blocks back to the boarding house.

During the day, she tried to rest and keep an eye on her growing boy at the same time.

The landlady began to complain. "If that kid has a father fightin' in the war, he's gonna want to turn around and go right back to the battlefront when he gets home and sees his rowdy offspring."

Fatigue began to catch up. One night, Lilly finished work completely exhausted. Her throat hurt. She didn't have the strength to carry the sleeping boy but couldn't bear to make him walk. She lay down beside Dale in the closet. She would just doze for a few minutes.

When the overhead light flicked on, she and Dale both awoke with a start. She blinked and squinted, trying to remember where she was. Dale started to cry.

"What's this?" The store manager towered over her.

Lilly scrambled to her feet. "I'm so sorry, sir, I—"

"Have you been *living* here?"

"No, sir. We have a room. We'll be on our way." Lilly gathered Dale's blanket and picked him up.

But the manager blocked the door. "You scared me half to death. How long has this been going on? Ever since you started?"

"I've never fallen asleep before, sir."

"I meant, have you been bringing your kid with you all this time?"

Lilly nodded. "I have no one to watch him. He just sleeps while I clean."

"Well, it's completely unacceptable. Not to mention deceitful."

"I'm sorry, sir. I'll try to—"

"You're fired." The man stepped back so Lilly could exit the closet. "Hand me your keys."

Blinking hard to stop the tears, she fished around in her purse until she found the ring of keys that had been issued to her. The manager accepted them from her hand. "You can collect anything still owed to you next payday. Otherwise, I don't want to see you here again."

Lilly walked home in a daze, half-dragging, half-carrying Dale.

• • •

When the amount owed her wasn't enough to cover rent, the landlady seemed happy to be rid of them. "And don't ask for a reference. I wouldn't wish your brat on anyone."

The woman's sharp words as she evicted them drove Lilly to do what she'd told herself she could never do. By bus, she went to the main branch of the city library and soon found herself standing before William Tidsbury.

"Lilly? Never thought I'd see *you* here." William came around to her side of the counter, then immediately crouched down to Dale's height. "Hi there, Dale. Remember me?"

Dale only buried his face in Lilly's coat.

"What brings you here?" William rose to his full height.

Lilly could hardly speak, but she had to. For Dale's sake. "I was expecting you to... I thought you were going to pursue custody. Why haven't you?"

William looked back and forth between her and Dale. "My lawyer advised against it."

"I see." Lilly felt weak and sank into a chair when William pointed to one. "Is that it?"

Lilly squeezed her eyes shut to stop the tears. "I can't do this, William. I can't... work and care for Dale. You were right. He needs two parents."

William didn't speak for a long time. "I thought maybe you and Tommy would work things out."

Lilly just shook her head. "You... said your wife was prepared to be Dale's stepmother. I came to see if that's still the case. If the two of you would consider taking him, maybe just during the week."

She could hardly believe she'd managed to say the words, but there they were.

William wrote his home address on a piece of paper and handed it to Lilly. "It's walking distance from here. Come by this evening but wait until after seven so I have a chance to speak with Helen."

Lilly waited in a nearby diner where she bought an order of toast and fed all of it to Dale. Perspiring and cold at the same time, she walked him to William's home, a midsized bungalow.

William opened the door before she could knock and welcomed them in. "This is my wife, Helen."

A woman of about twenty-five with long brown hair and kind eyes welcomed her warmly despite the awkwardness of the situation. "Hello, Lilly."

Once everyone was seated, Helen continued. "William explained things to me, and we've agreed to take Dale—with a couple of conditions. For starters, you should stay until Dale's in bed. It'll be easier for him to find you gone in the morning than to watch you leave tonight."

Lilly nodded. Helen was probably right. "And what else?"

"Best if we discuss it after he's in bed."

Lilly sat quietly on the couch while William and Helen played with Dale and read him books. At eight o'clock, all three of the adults tucked Dale into bed, then gathered again in the living room.

William wasted no time. "For the first month, you're not to visit. Give him time to adjust. After that, depending how things go, we'll consider weekly visits."

He'd even drawn up a contract for Lilly to sign.

Was this really best for Dale? She wanted to run to the bedroom, snatch her son, and leave. But where would she go? Lilly had never felt so utterly desperate or heartbroken. With shaking fingers, she signed William's contract. Before she left the house, she checked in on Dale one last time. He slept peacefully, his angelic face without a care in the world as he sucked his thumb and hugged his stuffed monkey.

She whispered in his ear. "I'm so sorry, my son. You're warm and safe. I love you so much. I'll come back for you when I can."

Too numb to shed tears, and her throat hurting worse by the hour, Lilly left behind one suitcase with Dale's clothes and toys. Then she made her way back to the church where she'd been told the door was always open.

It was locked.

She walked around to the back and discovered a small lean-to attached to the main building. When she tried that door, it opened to a small, unheated space. With no window to allow light in, Lilly held the door open until she could determine there was no entrance to the building from here. Life-sized Christmas nativity characters cut from wood took up the biggest portion of space. Behind that stood boxes of all sizes stacked to the ceiling. A wooden manger with some real hay offered her an ironic comfort.

Dragging her suitcase inside, Lilly put on all the clothing she could. She pulled the hay from the manger and laid it on the floor with one of her sweaters on top for a pillow. Last, she pushed some boxes up against the door for security. She lay down and covered herself with the last item in her suitcase: a gray woolen skirt. To keep her mind off the cold, she kept repeating the same prayer: *Thank you, God, that Dale is safe and warm.*

There, shivering and alone, Lilly spent the darkest night of her life.

CHAPTER THIRTY-THREE

Lilly awoke to incessant banging, rousing her from a dream in which she and Dale cuddled before a crackling fire and a mountain of warm fresh bread, dripping with butter and honey.

Someone was knocking on the door. "Hello? Who's in there? Can you open the door? Do you need help?"

Lilly tried to move. Her body was so stiff and cold, she could barely pull herself to a sitting position. The movement triggered a painful coughing spell that had her clutching her ribs. A sliver of daylight above the shed's door helped her orient herself. She crawled toward the door and tried to move boxes, but her hands were curled into tight fists inside her mittens and refused to open. She managed to shove one box a few inches by putting all her strength into it, then the room began to spin and she leaned back against the wall and coughed some more.

"Are you all right? Sounds like you might be sick. Can you open the door? I'm not going to hurt you, I promise. I want to help you."

"I can't," Lilly managed. Her voice was little more than a whisper. She tried again, but the second attempt was no better. Another coughing fit erupted, leaving her weaker still. At least it provided the volume she needed to be heard.

"I hear you!" the man shouted. "I'm going to remove the door and get you out, okay?"

• • •

The next thing Lilly knew, she was waking up in a bed. Where was Dale? Then she remembered. Safe with William.

The rails on the bed told her she was in a hospital room. How had she gotten here? She still felt cold despite the pile of warm blankets on top of her. An IV had been stuck into the back of her left hand. With her right, she reached up and felt a knitted cap covering her head. Daylight poured in through a window on one side. A curtain around her bed concealed the rest of the room. She coughed.

"Lilly? Are you awake?" A man's voice came from the other side of the curtain.

"Yes." More coughing.

The curtain moved a couple of inches and the man on the other side peeked around it. "Lilly?"

She recognized the pastor from the church. When she made eye contact, he moved the curtain some more and stepped around to her side.

"I'll find the nurse and tell her you're awake."

"Wait." Her voice was little more than a croak, but the man turned back. "How did you—?"

Her sentence was interrupted by another coughing fit.

"Lilly, I'm Pastor Gregg. I found you this morning when I arrived at the church. I saw your footprints in the snow, leading to the shed, but there were no prints leading away. I'm so sorry you didn't have a warm place to sleep last night. I remember when you stopped in a few weeks ago."

Lilly tried to recall the brief conversation they'd had. "How do you know my name?" she managed to whisper.

"I'm sorry, but I handed your purse over to the front desk and, together, we looked inside. The hospital needed to identify you, and we found your ration book. Your belongings are all safe here now. Your suitcase and all the clothes you were wearing." He glanced around the room, then at his wristwatch. "It's about ten o'clock, if you're wondering. I know I always want to know what time it is when I wake up."

He smiled warmly and Lilly tried to grasp everything he was saying. Her head hurt.

"Um… Lilly, when you came by the church that day, you had a little boy with you. Is he all right?"

Lilly nodded as tears welled up. "He's safe."

A nurse came around the corner. "Good morning. I see you're awake. Mrs. DeWitt, is that correct?"

Lilly nodded, still confused.

"Mrs. DeWitt, you're at St. Boniface Hospital, thanks to the pastor here."

St. Boniface? Oh, the irony.

Lilly wondered how many of the nuns, doctors, and nurses she'd trained with were still around. She didn't recognize this one, but she'd been gone four years.

"We're treating you for hypothermia," said the nurse. "That IV has a saline solution to help warm your blood, that's all. We're also watching you for pneumonia. The sooner we can get you up and moving, the better your chances of staving it off. Can you sit up? We'll bring you something hot to drink. Tea all right? Sorry I can't offer sugar."

The nurse kept up her banter as she helped Lilly into a seated position. The room spun for a few seconds, then came back into focus.

"Is there someone we can call for you?"

Lilly took in a shallow, shuddering breath. "No. There's no one."

The nurse looked at the pastor.

"No one at all?" he asked. Lilly shook her head. "You said your son was safe with someone. Do you want me to call—"

"No."

The pastor was writing on a little paper tablet, but he stopped abruptly to gaze into the far distance, like he was trying to remember something. "Would you happen to know a Thomas DeWitt?"

"That's my husband's name, but—"

"Does he work for Blumberg Textiles?" The man sounded excited.

Lilly was embarrassed to admit that she didn't know. "Do you know him?"

"He's been coming to my church. I'll track him down." The pastor disappeared around the curtain as an aide brought in a tray with hot tea and warm oatmeal.

Lilly wished the pastor had stuck around long enough for her to explain that his Thomas DeWitt could not possibly be her husband.

Tommy, in church? Not likely.

She should have mentioned the burn scars. That would have settled it right away.

Anyway, she wasn't sure she wanted Tommy or anyone else seeing her like this. She had to hurry and get out of here, then find a job and a place to live. Now she'd have a hospital bill on top of everything.

She finished eating, lay back, and felt herself drifting off.

• • •

The next time Lilly woke up, she felt much warmer. She studied the IV needle. Could she remove it and locate her clothes? The sooner she left, the smaller her bill would be, and the sooner she could look for work. Maybe she could find her way back to that church and get permission to sleep inside until she found a place. That pastor seemed nice enough.

She rose partway, then waited a bit before swinging her legs over one side of the bed and pushing herself to a full sitting position.

Immediately the room began to swim. Just as she feared hitting the floor, she felt arms around her, forcing her back into a prone position on the bed.

"Whoa! Not so fast, missy. You need to call a nurse before you try that."

Lilly looked up into a vaguely familiar round face with pink cheeks and wild blond curls under her nurse's cap.

"You're lucky I came around the corner when I did." The nurse reached around Lilly to adjust the pillows, then moved to the end of the bed. "Here, let's do this gradually. I'm going to crank your bed up." She bent over and began turning the handle. "Tell me if you start feeling dizzy and—wait a minute. Lilly?" She looked at the clipboard hanging from the end of Lilly's bed. "It *is* you!"

Lilly studied the friendly face, but the connection wasn't coming to her.

The nurse came back to Lilly's side. "Oh my goodness. Do you remember me?"

Lilly kept staring, trying to place her.

"It's me, Sheila! From nursing school?"

"Oh! Yes." Lilly couldn't recall the girl's last name, but Sheila had been the life of the party. "I'm surprised you remember me. I wasn't there long."

"You were so studious, and tops at everything. We were so sorry to see you leave."

How much did Sheila know? "I imagine there were a few rumors flying around."

Sheila shrugged. "I heard you got married."

That world seemed a lifetime away. So much had happened to Lilly since then, but she couldn't begin to share it with this girl even if she wanted to.

"Well, right now I really just need to get out of this bed and out of this hospital."

Sheila's eyes filled with compassion. "Oh, honey, I don't think that's a good idea. You're going to be weak for a while, and we need to keep an eye on you in case—"

"Yeah, I know. Pneumonia. Crank me up the rest of the way, will you?"

Sheila did. "How's that?"

Dizziness and another coughing fit nailed her, but she managed to croak out an answer. "That's good."

Sheila wheeled a table over with a supper tray Lilly hadn't noticed before. "Here. Get some food into you."

Lilly lifted the cover on a bowl of soup and began to eat as Sheila continued to hover.

"So tell me. Did you ever return to nursing school anywhere?"

Lilly shook her head. "No, but I did work in a hospital. At the front desk. I think I'm better suited to that."

"No kidding? Because if you're looking for work, there's a position opening here. How great would that be?" She didn't wait for a response. "When you finish eating, call me and we'll see how you do getting up for the bathroom. *With help*. Okay?"

By the time all of that was accomplished, weakness overwhelmed Lilly once more. She couldn't stop coughing, nor could she take a deep breath. A doctor listened to her lungs with his stethoscope and declared that he was putting her on penicillin. Sheila helped her back into bed, where she gladly lay back against the pillows.

Instead of leaving the room, Sheila pulled up a chair and sat beside Lilly. Was she *that* sick?

An older nurse walked in and raised her eyebrows. "Sheila, what are you still doing here? I thought you got off an hour ago." She popped a thermometer into Lilly's mouth and picked up her wrist to take her pulse.

"I thought I'd stay awhile. Keep an old friend company." Sheila winked at Lilly.

The older woman shrugged. "Suit yourself. Just make sure you get enough sleep between now and tomorrow's shift or Sister Rose won't let you hear the end of it."

After the other nurse left, Lilly turned to Sheila. "Why are you being so nice to me? Don't get me wrong, I appreciate it but…" Lilly paused to cough. "We were never really close or anything."

Sheila smiled and took Lilly's hand. "Something tells me you've been through a tough time. I thought maybe you could use a friend."

The compassion in her voice was all it took for tears to surface. Lilly turned her face away and tried to focus on the geometric pattern in the curtain fabric. Sheila wouldn't be so kind if she knew everything Lilly had done. "I don't deserve your kindness."

Sheila paused only a moment. "I'm sure you don't."

Lilly swung her head back toward Sheila so quickly that she had to wait a second until the nurse's face came into focus again.

Sheila chuckled. "Didn't expect that, did you?" She lifted her other hand so she could take Lilly's in both of hers. "Lilly, I don't deserve kindness and grace either. None of us does. In fact, when it comes to 'deserving'... well... here's the thing. I love Jesus. With all my heart. I love him because he has granted me so much grace and kindness when I didn't deserve it, I don't even know where to begin. And I want to be like him. He wants to extend his love and grace to you, Lilly. Through his followers. Like me. That's all. It has nothing to do with deserving, and everything to do with him. With who he is."

"I... remember you as... sort of a party girl."

Sheila's smile grew wide. "I like to think I still am. But I've learned that life is worth celebrating in the best possible way—with God. With the joy he brings."

Lilly studied Sheila's uniform. Had she become a nun? "You're not wearing a habit. Or a cross or anything."

Sheila laughed out loud. "I'm not even a Catholic, Lilly. Never was." She held up her left hand to show a slim gold band. "I got married last year. Bobby shipped out with the first batch of draftees last month."

"Oh. That must be so hard."

"Yes. I won't lie. But Jesus is right here with me, every minute, every day. I know He's with Bobby. He's with you, too. Do you have any idea how much he loves you?"

Lilly shook her head slightly. "I grew up going to church, but... it's too late for me. I've done too much, made too many bad decisions." Coughs punctuated her sentences.

"That's where you're wrong. He already knows everything. Past, present, future. He knows your very thoughts, Lilly. And he still loves you. That's why he died—for all of it. His grace never runs out."

"I'd like to believe that." Lilly pulled a hand away to wipe a tear from her cheek.

"I'm going to be praying for you."

Lilly heard someone clear their throat on the other side of a curtain. "Lilly? It's Pastor Gregg. Can I come in? I've got someone here who wants to see you."

"Y–yes."

Two men came around the curtain and Lilly thought her heart might stop. Beside a smiling pastor, with hat in hand, stood Tommy.

CHAPTER THIRTY-FOUR

Diana

Our conversation with Dad ends abruptly when Shane gets called out for an emergency. I go inside and spend the next half-hour telling Mouse about Grandma Lilly's life.

"I know she ended up with Tommy, because they raised Dad. Right?"

The cat meows her agreement.

I settle down on my couch and call Dad back. With or without Shane, I just need to hear more of the story.

Dad is glad to oblige, and we talk until long past his bedtime. He shares more of his mother's story and I share more of my indecision about Carly's baby.

"Play out each scenario in your mind and see which brings you peace," Dad counsels. "I'll be praying for you."

Before I fall asleep, I spend a solid hour on my carpet, asking God for his direction. I talk through the scenarios like Dad advised. What will become of my relationship with Carly if I refuse her and carry on with my life? I'm certainly not ready to let her go, but I see no way we could continue. Would she ever forgive me?

More importantly, what would become of the baby? Do I want to live with that?

But the scenario of adopting the baby doesn't bring me peace either. Sure, I could probably figure out how to look after a child's physical needs—keep them healthy and safe, as safe as anyone can be in this world. The overwhelming emotional needs of a child were another matter altogether. How could I begin to approach that when I'm a mess myself? I want to call Dad back and say, "Your advice isn't working!"

I flip open my Bible again, looking for words about peace. Instead, I find words about love. And fear. And how the two are incompatible. The line from 1 John 4 gets stuck on replay in my brain: *"There is no fear in love. But perfect love drives out fear…"*[5]

Am I going to allow fear to decide for me? I memorized enough scripture as a kid to remember the one that says God *"does not make us timid, but gives us power, love and self-discipline."*[6] Maybe I need to take his word at face value.

By morning, I know what I need to do.

The first step is talking to my boss. I go in early and find her in her office like I hoped. She responds cheerfully to my request for a few minutes of her time.

"Of course. Come on in, Diana. My door's always open, I hope you know that." She waves her hand toward a chair.

I grab a seat. "I want you to know I've made a decision about the new job offer."

"Okay." Her smile tells me she expects me to take it.

"I'm going to decline."

Her smile disappears. "What? But you're perfect for it! You've been working toward this for so long."

"I know, but… the timing is wrong."

"You know you don't have to decide yet, right? I don't officially need your answer for another week. Why don't you take some more time to think about it?"

I shake my head. "I don't need to. I appreciate the offer, but I really need to stay where I am. I will happily support whomever you hire."

• • •

With that out of the way, a sense of peace lets me know I am on the right path. Next step: tell Carly.

I text her, asking her to meet me at Linda's Grill for ice cream right after work because we have something to celebrate. I figure that will let her know my answer while still giving us the opportunity for a more intimate, in-person announcement. The more I think about it, the more excited I become. This is really going to happen! Unable to focus on work, I keep checking my phone for her reply.

When she finally replies to my text, it's nearly three in the afternoon: *Too late. At clinic with Mom.*

Panic rises in me so quickly that my thumbs fumble with the phone as I text her back. *Wait! Carly please? I'm on my way. Don't do anything yet.*

I grab my jacket and purse. I don't even know which clinic she is at.

I text again. *What's the address?*

As I stride past our receptionist's desk, eyes on my phone, I tell her that I have an emergency family situation.

Carly isn't answering. I crawl into the car, buckle up, and start the engine. Still no reply. I try calling but it goes straight to voicemail. *Think, think. Lord, please help me find her!*

When we visited the pregnancy support center, we noticed a women's clinic a few doors down. I'll start there.

Construction is blocking my usual path to the main thoroughfare I need. I pull up the GPS on my phone for the best possible route, then focus on breathing deeply and listening to the directions without driving at a speed that would only result in a delay.

Oh God, please don't let me be too late. Why would you guide me to this decision and then allow Carly to terminate her pregnancy? Did I hear you wrong? Was I just too slow to obey? Were you telling me all along and I let fear take over? Forgive me, God.

I find the clinic, but there are no available parking spots. What if it isn't even the right one? I'll be wasting time looking for parking.

God, what do I do?

As I drive past the building, I receive my answer. Carly's mother Tonya stands outside, leaning up against the building and smoking a cigarette.

Carly has to be inside. But surely her mother wouldn't step out for a smoke unless Carly is already in the procedure room. I must be too late. *Oh God, help me!*

I pull into a parking lot that claims to have spaces available, then proceed to drive around until I finally find one. Every second feels like an hour. I park, grab my purse and phone, then stumble right past the pay station without bothering to pay.

Oh Lord please don't let them tow my car. I don't have any time to lose.

Tonya is grinding out her cigarette on the sidewalk as I run up. She sees me before I can call her name.

"Why are you here?" Her squint tells me everything. I am not trusted.

"I need to see Carly." Something tells me to keep moving past Tonya and enter the building.

She grabs my arm. "Leave her alone. You're just going to talk her out of it."

"Tonya, please. Carly wants me to adopt her baby and I've decided to say yes. She needs to know."

I try pulling away, but she tightens her grip.

"She's made her decision. You have no right to interfere."

Something swells inside me, reminiscent of a mother grizzly rising to her full height. I yank my arm away and run the remaining five steps to the front door. I fling it open.

"Carly!" I shout before I even spot her. My eyes adjust from the bright outdoors and I scan the room. Carly is following a nurse around the corner. "Carly!"

She stops and turns. Spots me but doesn't move.

"Carly, I need to talk to you. Please." I hurry toward her, Tonya on my heels.

"You don't have to listen to her, Carly." Tonya passes me and goes to her daughter's side.

Carly grabs her mother's hand. Then she turns to the nurse. "I need a minute."

The nurse nods. "Take all the time you need."

I want to swoop the girl into my arms but dare not. "Carly, can we talk? There's a bench outside. You too, Tonya."

Carly glances at her mother.

Tonya shakes her head. "She'll only make this harder, Carly. Come on, I'll go with you as far as they'll allow."

Still holding Carly's hand, she heads in the direction the nurse had gone.

"Carly, wait." My heart is racing. "Please."

A receptionist steps over to me. "Ma'am, I'm going to have to ask you to leave."

"I've decided to adopt your baby!" I blurt at Carly's back.

Carly stops and slowly turns. "Wait, Mom." She lets out a deep sigh. "You're too late, Diana. I know you mean well, but I..." She presses her lips together.

"Can I just have five minutes? Please?" My eyes dart between Tonya and Carly.

"Ma'am, I'm not going to ask again. I can call security." The receptionist takes a step toward her desk.

"Wait." Carly lets go of her mother's hand and moves toward me. "Five minutes."

She strides past me without making eye contact and steps through the front door without holding it open. I run after her and hold the door open for Tonya.

Carly is already seated in the middle of the bench. She pats the bench with both hands. Tonya sits to her daughter's left and looks at her watch. I sit on Carly's right.

I proceed to tell them the story my father shared with me last night.

CHAPTER THIRTY-FIVE

Lilly

1944

"I'll see you tomorrow, Lilly." Sheila squeezed Lilly's hand. "Now that you've got company, I should go."

Tommy moved into the space Sheila had occupied and leaned toward her. "Lilly, I've been looking for you. Where's Dale?"

Lilly studied his face. Had he undergone more surgery? The scars were all still there, but she'd never seen such a lightness to Tommy. Not even before the war. "Dale is safe… with William and his wife."

Tommy's one remaining eyebrow shot up. "With William?"

The pastor cleared his throat. "I should probably go and let you two—"

"Please, stay for a bit." Tommy sounded urgent. "Can you?"

Pastor Gregg looked between Lilly and Tommy several times. "I suppose. Just for a bit. If it's all right with you, Lilly."

She nodded and the pastor took a chair off to the side.

Tommy reached one hand toward Lilly, then pulled it back. "I've been looking for you for the last month, Lil. I even went to Summervale and found someone else in our apartment. Nobody seemed to know where you went, not even Aunty Margaret. Tell me what's going on. How did you end up here?"

Between coughs, Lilly told Tommy her story. "I was out of options. Dale will be better off with two parents. I agreed to wait a month before going to see him. To give him time to adjust. I suppose that was just one more stupid decision, but

I didn't know what else to do. I was just so relieved to know he'd be warm and fed—" Tears blinded her.

"It's okay, Lil. You did what you felt you had to."

"Why were you looking for me?" More coughs.

Tommy took a deep breath and pulled Lilly's hand into his. "Because I... I have the best news ever, Lil."

Lilly glanced over at the pastor, then back to Tommy.

"Shortly after I moved here, I met a fellow at work—another soldier home early. Carl invited me to church with him and... well, between him and Pastor Gregg here... I finally understood that Jesus loves me. *Me!* God has forgiven me, Lil. For everything. I can't even describe what these past few months have been like. I'm finally free."

Lilly might have rolled her eyes were it not for Tommy's smile and glowing countenance. Clearly, something significant had happened to him.

"Carl's been visiting wounded guys and introduced me to some burn patients right here in this hospital. We've sort of got a group going, and—it's wonderful, Lil. They've helped me and, believe it or not, I've been able to help them, too."

Lilly stared up into this version of her husband she'd never seen, feeling more alone than ever. The one person in the world who knew her inside and out was a stranger.

"That's nice. I'm glad for you, Tommy."

"It's more than nice, Lil." Tommy wet his lips. "Don't you see? You can have this, too. That's why I've been trying to find you."

A coughing fit seized Lilly and she removed her hand from Tommy's to clutch her chest.

"I think we better let her rest, Tommy." Pastor Gregg stood. "Can I pray for you before we leave, Lilly?"

Lilly nodded through her coughs. What could it hurt?

He placed a hand on her shoulder. "Lord, thank you that you love Lilly so much. Please heal her. Bring complete restoration to her body, soul, and spirit. Please fill her with peace and help her to feel your presence. May she rest well, knowing her little boy is safe. I pray that you would bless him, too. In Jesus's name, Amen."

"Amen," Tommy echoed.

The pastor pulled a small Bible from his pocket. "And I just want to share a verse with you from God's word, too, Lilly. Maybe you can think on it while you rest." He flipped pages until he found what he was looking for. "'They looked unto him, and were lightened: and their faces were not ashamed.'[7] That's from Psalm 34. It means those who look to God can have radiant faces, Lilly. No shame. No condemnation."

The men said goodbye and left, but one word from the pastor's little pep talk wouldn't leave Lilly's head. *Radiant* was the exact word she would have used to describe Tommy, had she thought of it herself.

• • •

When Lilly was discharged from the hospital two days later, Pastor Gregg invited her to stay with him and his wife. By the end of the following week, she had been hired to work in the admissions office at the hospital—thanks to Sheila's recommendation. By the time she'd finished her first week on the job, she had moved into a boarding house near the hospital—again, with Sheila's help. This time, her landlords were an older married couple who played records and laughed a lot, filling their home with a much happier atmosphere.

Twice, Tommy stopped at her desk to say hello. Both times he had come to visit patients in the burn ward, and both times he exhibited that glow Lilly couldn't get used to. Though his newfound faith was not for her, his presence never failed to lift her spirits.

Dale was always on her mind, but the new challenges and people in her life helped her to pass the month away from him with less pain.

On the appointed day, she made her way back to William's house via the earliest bus. She wanted to make the most of her day off with her son. Her heart pounded as she stepped up the walk to the front door. How would Dale respond? She anticipated him running toward her, arms open wide for a warm embrace. She longed for it.

Helen answered the door. "Good morning, Lilly. William has already left for work, but I've got Dale ready to go."

She pulled the door open wide and Lilly stepped through.

Dale stood in the middle of the living room, completely absorbed in running a wooden toy truck up and down the coffee table. He wore a new outfit and his hair looked freshly washed and combed. He'd grown, too.

"Hi, Dale."

Lilly knelt and opened her arms to receive him. Dale turned in response. His big blue eyes focused on Lilly, then up at Helen and back at Lilly. Instead of moving toward her, he stepped backwards toward the kitchen. Two steps, then a third. His bottom lip quivered, and he began to cry.

"Oh, sweetie, don't' cry." Helen went to him and wrapped her arms around him. She then turned to Lilly. "He's just confused."

Dale squirmed away from Helen and stared at Lilly.

Surely her heart was breaking right in half, but Lilly had to be strong. "Hi, sweetheart. I came to visit you, Dale. Would you like to go on an outing with Mama?"

"Perhaps you should stay here until he warms up to you." Helen held out her hands to take Lilly's coat.

Though the weak beginning was far from what Lilly had hoped or planned, Dale came around. Lilly stayed at the house all morning, playing and reading storybooks. The next time Lilly opened her arms to him, Dale hugged her back. They ate lunch with Helen, then Lilly bundled him up in his winter clothes.

"William gets home around six, so he should be here when you come back." Helen began to gather toys. "We can talk more then."

Lilly took Dale back to her new home where they napped together on her narrow bed. When he woke up, she took him to the Hudson's Bay department store where they rode the escalators and elevators, looked at toys, and stopped at the soda fountain to share a milkshake. Though she'd only received one paycheck so far, she couldn't resist buying him a child-sized snow shovel when she saw how his eyes lit up at the sight of it. Back at the boarding house, they shoveled snow from the sidewalk and steps. In her landlady's kitchen, she made them scrambled eggs and toast for supper. Dale clutched his little shovel all the way back to the Tidsbury residence on the bus.

William and Helen were just finishing supper. Lilly tucked Dale into his bed and said goodnight, her heart lighter than it had been last time. Maybe this would work after all. Maybe it was the best possible solution. She'd still be involved in his life, but he'd have his own natural father to raise him and provide for him. Helen was a kind woman who would care for him well.

When she came out of Dale's bedroom, William stood looking out the living room window, hands clasped behind his back.

Helen carried in a tray from the kitchen. "Have a seat, Lilly. I've made tea."

William moved to the sofa and started the conversation by asking how the past month had gone for Lilly. Though she didn't give the details, she admitted to being hospitalized with pneumonia. He expressed concern for her health and relief when she talked about her quick recovery and her new job.

"I'm glad you're here, Lilly." Helen placed her teacup on the tray. "This month has been... well... more difficult than we expected."

"Oh?" Lilly clutched her cup and saucer with both hands.

William cleared his throat. "We care very much for Dale, Lilly. But... we thought we were getting a normal three-year-old. Why didn't you tell us about his... handicap?"

Lilly stared back. "What do you mean?"

"Well... you know. He's... slow."

"No he's not!" Lilly blurted it out faster than she could think.

Helen let out a long sigh. "We've taken him to a doctor, Lilly. He's not developing at a normal rate. For one thing, he should be talking a lot more by now."

They were wrong. They had to be. "That doesn't mean he's—"

"They checked his hearing." William cupped his hands over his own ears. "It seems normal... if a little selective."

Lilly shook her head. "I just had a perfectly lovely day with him. He's... he's fine. He'll start talking soon, he's probably just... well, he's had a lot to adjust to."

"There are other things, too." William leaned forward, resting his elbows on his knees. "He should know his colors by now. But if you ask him to pick out the red block, he's just as likely to choose a blue or yellow one. The doctor asked him to pick up a toy and drop it in a bucket, but it was as though he didn't even hear the second step. The doctor said he's mentally re—"

"No!" Lilly stood. She didn't have to listen to this. "He probably just wanted to play with the toy. He's a normal, lovable boy."

Helen reached out to touch her hand. "He is lovable, Lilly. No one is saying he isn't. He just... we think he's going to need more help than we can give him."

"So what are you saying?" Lilly threw the challenge at William.

He kept his voice calm and slow. "The doctor recommended an institution where he can be with other children like him."

What?

"Other children *like* him?" Lilly felt the room spinning again.

Not my Dale. No! It can't be true. How could this have happened? Then the most horrible thought of all: *What if this was a result of whatever was done to her by that charlatan?*

Lilly sat up straighter and raised her chin. "I want a second opinion."

William glanced at Helen.

"We did, too." Helen set her teacup on the coffee table. "The second doctor we took him to is a pediatrician. He gave us the same advice."

"Well, they're both wrong." Lilly stood and picked up her purse.

William spoke again. "Listen, Lilly, clearly this is all new to you. I didn't realize it would be. You need some time to digest it. We'll take good care of Dale for now. We'll talk more when you come back next week, okay? Don't worry, we won't do anything before then."

"Well, I should hope not!" Lilly would simply have to figure out a way to raise Dale herself. She had to ask. "Would you... would you consider helping provide for him if I take him back?"

William's eyes remained rivetted on Lilly. "I don't think you're taking him back is on the table, Lilly. That wouldn't be in Dale's best interest. If Helen and I can't provide what he needs, how on earth could you?"

Lilly tried to swallow the lump forming in her throat. "He's my son, I can—"

"Just take some time to think it over." William's patient tone came to an end. "I'm confident you'll come to the same conclusion and see why the doctors' advice makes good sense for Dale."

"Just don't take too much time," Helen added.

"Helen's right." William put his arm around his wife. "She's expecting a baby this summer."

CHAPTER THIRTY-SIX

Helen and William agreed to care for Dale for another month while Lilly figured out what she wanted to do. She would visit him weekly during that time, on her days off.

"They're wrong, Sheila," she told her friend over lunch the next day. Both women had brought a sandwich from home and now sat together in the basement staff room. "I know they're wrong. Dale might be a little behind his peers, but he's smart. If he ends up some place where they assume he's slow, will anyone bother trying to teach him? I can't let that happen, but what am I going to do? If I quit my job, I'll have no income. If I pay someone else to watch him while I work, who? And can I afford it? I'm barely managing now."

Sheila sighed. "I don't know, honey. Pray for wisdom, for starters. I'll pray for you too. And, if you like… I could come with you next time you visit. I'd love to meet Dale."

"Oh, would you? I'm sure he'll love you. And you'll see for yourself. He's not re—. Oh, I can't even say that horrid word."

Sheila swallowed her bite of food and looked thoughtfully at Lilly. "Have you talked to Tommy about it?"

Lilly shook her head. "I haven't seen him since last week." She paused, uncertain how much she wanted to share. "Um, Sheila… I told you that Tommy is not Dale's father, didn't I?" The early days of their friendship had been so clouded by Lilly's illness that she couldn't remember how much she had shared.

Sheila nodded. "You did. That's why you went to William. But... I've seen how Tommy stops to talk with you, how he looks for you when you're not at your desk. He still cares about you very much, Lilly. He might surprise you."

Shortly after Lilly returned to her desk, a melodic whistling wafted around the corner. Tommy approached with a smiling face and a spring in his step. Would she ever get used to this new version of him?

"I was hoping I'd find you here." He stopped and leaned with both hands on her desk. "I got big news."

"Oh?"

"I got on with the city fire department." The sparkle in his eyes almost erased his scars.

"Congratulations. When do you start?"

"Last night." Tommy chuckled. "I'll be on the late shift for the first six months to a year, but that's actually perfect. This way, I can spend more time with the guys here in the burn ward."

"Whoa! You need to sleep sometime."

"Oh, I will. I'm pretty happy about this, though." His enthusiasm was contagious.

"I can see that. Good for you, Tommy. I'm happy for you."

"Thanks. It's God's timing, I'm sure of that. Say, how did your day with Dale go?"

Lilly immediately felt tears welling up. She squeezed her eyes shut to make them stop.

"Uh-oh. Not so good?"

She pressed her lips together and shook her head, not daring to speak.

Compassion filled Tommy's eyes. "Anything I can do to help?"

She shook her head again. "I... can't talk about it right now."

Tommy drew his eyebrows together and leaned in. "Sounds serious."

"It is."

"Let me take you for supper so I can hear about it. You're off at five?"

Lilly nodded.

"I don't need to be at work until eleven tonight. I want to hear what's going on." He paused. "It'll be okay, Lilly."

• • •

Over burgers in the corner booth of a deserted little diner just two blocks from the hospital, Lilly told Tommy about William's assessment of Dale. "I know they're wrong. I had high hopes this was going to work out, but now they have a new baby coming. How interested will Helen be in raising Dale, especially if he needs extra help?"

Tommy looked at her without speaking for a long time. When he did talk, it wasn't about Dale at all.

"When I left you and Dale, I was a mess, Lil. I moved in with my parents, but I didn't work. I just grew more depressed. Hopeless. I drank every chance I got. Mom and Dad finally had enough and asked me to leave."

Lilly couldn't imagine it. Tommy's parents had been kinder to her than her own after she betrayed their son. "Oh, Tommy. I'm so sorry."

"Don't be. Their kicking me out forced me to hit rock bottom. I never would have come to the city, never would have met Carl or gone to Pastor Gregg's church. He wouldn't have had the opportunity to tell me about God's love and forgiveness."

"But... you always went to church. As a kid, I mean."

"Sure. But it was always about being good. Which I knew I was not. Maybe I'm being too hard on our childhood church, but somehow I was left with the impression that my only hope was for my good deeds to outweigh my bad."

Lilly nodded. Wasn't that accurate?

"I tried for a while, but... I knew I couldn't make that work. Pastor Gregg showed me that none of us can. If we could, we wouldn't need Jesus. He wouldn't have had to die for us. But he did. He paid the price for all of it, so I could be forgiven and set free. All of it, Lil. Think about that."

Lilly sighed. "Well, I can certainly see a change in you. I'm glad for you, Tommy."

"Now God has not only led me to this new job, doing what I've always wanted to do—but he's given me a ministry to other burn victims. Something I never dreamed of. I can see now how he's had his hand on me all my life." Tommy's eyes held such sparkle that Lilly felt herself being pulled into his passionate story. "He uses my stupid mistakes and the hard things that have happened to me and turns them around. Uses them for good. He can do the same for you, Lil. He wants to. He's offering freedom and peace and forgiveness, and... and good things. I don't know what they are, but they're for you."

Lilly chuckled at his enthusiasm. "Sorry, I don't mean to laugh. Everything you're saying is obviously genuine." She shook her head. "I'm just not sure what any of this has to do with Dale's situation right now, or what I'm supposed to do."

"That's just it. You don't need to. The first step is to trust God with *yourself*. Let him make a fresh start in *you*. Then see where he leads you."

Tears surfaced again at his words. A fresh start sounded too good to be true. "I want that," she whispered. "More than anything."

"Tell him." Tommy reached across the table and took Lilly's hands in his. "He's just waiting to hear from you."

She didn't pull away. With her entire face scrunched up, she prayed as honestly as she knew how. "God, I want you to do for me what you did for Tommy. I give you my messy life, for whatever it's worth. Please forgive me. Help me. Show me how to raise my son. If you really love us like Tommy says, I thank you for that."

She couldn't think of anything else to say.

"Amen." Tommy's eyes were bright as he grinned at her.

"That's it?"

"It's a wonderful start to what will be a wonderful relationship with Jesus. You'll see. You got a Bible?"

Lilly nodded. "Pastor Gregg gave me one."

"Good, because you'll want to be reading that." Tommy pulled one hand away and rubbed the scarred side of his face. "Want to hear what I think about Dale?"

"Of course."

"Have you forgotten how smart you are, Lil? You got top marks all through school. Constantly studying, loving to learn."

Lilly wondered where this was leading. Her school smarts hadn't gotten her very far in life.

"Nobody is more equipped to help Dale than you, Lilly. Nobody's as smart. Nobody loves him as much or knows him as well. Nobody else is going to have the determination and patience, whatever's required, to help him achieve all he can achieve—regardless what may or may not be wrong."

His words warmed her heart, but they didn't solve the problem. "That's kind of you to say. I just don't see how I could do all that and earn a living, too."

Tommy leaned back against the back of his seat. "What if you didn't have to?" He paused so long that Lilly began to think she hadn't heard him. "We're still married. The little house I'm renting has room for you and Dale. My new job will pay enough for us to get by."

Lilly could feel her heart pounding. Everything was happening so fast and she didn't know what to say.

"Things wouldn't be like before, Lil. If you want your own room… I would honor your wishes."

Lilly shook her head. "It's a generous gesture, Tommy. But nobody wants that kind of a marriage. I'm sure you don't. It wouldn't be fair to you."

"Lil, if I've learned anything these last few months, it's that I want you in my life. I *need* you in my life. And since you've been back in it—even a bit—I feel like a kid. I'm the smitten schoolboy I never was as an actual schoolboy. I didn't know how to love you or anyone then. But I love you, girl. Not just because of all we've been through together, but because… because you're my Lilly. I just love you. We can do this however you want, take as much time as you need… but I would dearly love to help you raise Dale. However I can."

CHAPTER THIRTY-SEVEN
Diana

"Wait a minute." Carly leans away from me and shakes her head in confusion. "Isn't your dad a *doctor?*"

"He sure is. And one of the brightest people I know."

Tonya has been listening intently, too, and chimes in now. "So Lilly was right? There was nothing wrong with him?"

"She was only partially right. Dad says that nowadays he would have been diagnosed with dyslexia. Maybe a few other things, too."

Carly's big brown eyes look even bigger and make me chuckle. "Wow. I know a couple of kids who have that. How on earth did he get all the way through med school?"

That had been my question, too. "Dad tells me his mother began teaching him fervently from the day she collected him from William Tidsbury."

"When did that happen?"

"The way Dad tells it, Lilly and Tommy went and picked him up together that same evening—*after* she threw her arms around his neck and agreed to a fresh start on the marriage. They both asked William's forgiveness for starting the fire, too."

"Did he forgive them?" Tonya's voice has lost its edge.

"No. Not until years later. But at his wife's urging, he surrendered my dad over to them immediately and never tried to interfere in his life. He showed up at Dad's graduation when he got his doctorate."

"Wow." Carly's head shakes slightly.

"And by the time Tommy punched into work that night, Lilly and Dad were moved into his house. Lilly quit her job so she could take care of him, and they never looked back."

"Does your dad remember living with William and his wife?"

"I asked him that, too. He said he'd always had a vague recollection of a different room in a different house, but he'd merely chalked it up to living somewhere else. His parents had always told him he had another father named William, but he said it was never a big deal somehow. When his mother finally told him the whole story, it all made sense."

Tonya looks thoughtful. "Lilly must have been quite the mother in the end."

"Dad told me that his mother devoted her life to making his the best it could be. He was in high school by the time he realized that other kids' mothers didn't spend hours after school hunched over them, helping them through their homework and making sure they understood what they were reading. She continued to help him all the way through college, and by med school he was in the top third in his class. Now he wishes that his mother had lived long enough to see his contributions to important, life-saving treatments and vaccines."

Carly is staring at her shoes. "I get why you're telling me all this."

I wait.

"Your dad wouldn't be here to do all those things if his mother's termination had succeeded."

I squeeze my lips together and nod. "I wouldn't be here, either. What a humbling thought."

Tonya lets out a long sigh and rubs Carly's shoulder gently. "You're changing your mind again, aren't you?"

Carly places a hand on her belly and nods slowly. "How do I know what this little one might do with their life?"

I want to tell her that really isn't the point, that a life is a life and every single one is valuable and sacred. But for now, I'm going with whatever works.

She looks up at me. "Well, Di. Looks like you're going to be a mom."

Suddenly, I feel like I've been holding my breath for two hours. The wave of relief shakes something loose inside, rendering my emotions completely out of control. "Yeah?"

She nods through her tears. "Yeah."

"Let the ugly crying commence." I throw my arms out wide and Carly falls into them.

With one hand, I wave Tonya into our circle. She has to be okay with this plan. Doesn't she? I guess she is, because she falls in as well, forming a sandwich with Carly in the middle.

Tonya is crying, too. "I wish I would've had someone like you in my life when it was me."

It's all I need to hear. Well, that and the voice I hear coming from behind me.

"Hey, what's all this?" Shane saunters toward us, grinning. "Got your text, but this doesn't look like any big emergency to me."

Carly wiggles free and gives Shane a hug. "It's not anymore."

Shane pretends to be bowled over by the hug. "Whoa-ho! What did I do to deserve this?"

"It's not what you've done, it's what you're going to do."

"Oh yeah? And what's that?"

Carly has a major eye twinkle going on. "You're going to marry Diana and help her raise this baby."

"*What?*" I whirl toward Shane, who lifts his palms up and shrugs.

It might have been my most awkward moment yet, but Tonya jumps in. "Carly, honey, we better go back inside and tell them you won't be doing the procedure after all."

Carly holds up her phone. "Can't I just call? I don't want to go back in there."

Her mother's head shakes slightly. "Come on." She glances from me to Shane over her shoulder as they walk away.

I turn to Shane, feeling the heat rise in my face. "I swear, I haven't said a word to her about our conversation."

"I believe you." He's still grinning. How can he be so nonchalant?

I sit on the bench again. "So then, who did? *You?*"

"Didn't have to." Shane takes the spot next to me. "She's not stupid, Di. She's hung out with us enough times to see what I've finally come to see. We belong together."

I want to believe him in the worst way.

"You know we wouldn't need to have a big shindig, right? I'd drive you down to the courthouse and marry you today if you'd agree to it."

I lean away. "Whoa. I thought you said I could take all the time I needed."

"I did. But things have changed."

"Oh?" Is he going to start pressuring me now? Because I'm not sure I can take it, on top of everything else.

"Yeah. You're going to be a mother. In a few short months. I'd love to have my bride to myself for a weekend, at least."

"Shane!"

Whenever I'd allowed myself to contemplate this scenario at all, I'd imagined adopting the baby first. Adjusting to him or her. And then—maybe—considering Shane's offer.

Lucky for me, Carly and Tonya come out of the clinic and I don't have to respond further.

Carly walks over for another hug. "Thanks for everything, Di."

"We'll need to work out some details." Tonya gives her daughter a stern look. "You know you're not going to have the say in this kid's life or—"

"I know, Mom. I know that. I trust Diana."

"We don't have to figure it all out today." I take Carly's hand. "The pregnancy center will have resources for us, people we can talk to who have done private adoptions that have gone well."

Shane nods. "I see a bright future for you, Carly. Graduation. College. The sky's the limit."

"Thanks." Carly looks suddenly shy. "And thanks for telling me your dad's story, Di. I'm going to hang onto it when the days get hard."

"Me, too," I say.

"We need to get home." Tonya looks up at me. "Thanks, Diana. I'm sorry for—well, I'm just sorry."

"I understand. You love your daughter."

She nods. "We'll be in touch."

Shane and I watch them walk away and turn to our own vehicles. "Where you parked?" I ask.

"Same lot as you."

"How'd you know where I parked?" Suddenly, I gasp and break into a run. "I never paid for my parking!"

Shane catches up and grabs my arm. "Relax. I saw your car with no sticker on the dash and put two and two together."

"You took care of it?" I stop and turn to face him. "You didn't have to do that for me, Shane."

"I'd do it again tomorrow and tomorrow after that if necessary—although this particular thing every day might start to get a little annoying." He reaches out and gently brushes a stray strand of hair from my face. "I'd love to take care of you for the rest of my life, Diana. I mean it."

What is wrong with me? This good, thoughtful, loving man cares for me and wants to spend his life with me. He's even willing to raise someone else's child with me. I must be out of my mind to say no to this.

"I'm wearing you down, aren't I?" He grins. "Do you need me to ask one more time? Because I will."

I let out a sigh and shake my head. "I don't know what I need. Some serious counseling, I think."

"Well then." Shane reaches into his jacket pocket and pulls out a business card. He holds it out to me. "We can solve that, too."

I look at the card. *Hope Restored Christian Counseling. CCPA Certification.* "You really think they can handle the likes of me?"

"Oh, I'm sure they've seen worse. Maybe."

I swat Shane's arm.

We reach my car. I unlock it and tuck the card into my purse. "All right. I'll see them once. If they don't manage to scare me off, I'll see them twice."

"Awesome. Hey, you didn't answer my question. Do you need me to ask you again?" Shane takes my hand and gets down on one knee.

"Shane! Don't be ridiculous. Get up." I look around. "We're in the middle of a parking lot."

"You need a bigger production? Because I can make that happen. I have access to fire trucks. Ladders, sirens, bells—"

I laugh. "No! I don't need a big production."

"Then will you marry me, Diana DeWitt? I love you. I even love your cat."

I can't stop laughing, but I pull him to his feet and into a tight embrace.

He hugs me back. "Is that a yes? No pressure, but is that a yes?"

I really want to say yes. I want to shout it and tell him I love him too, because I know I do. Instead I keep both hands on his broad shoulders and take a step back, letting the laughter die down.

"Let me get at least one counseling session under my belt, okay? I've got some work to do."

To his credit, Shane keeps smiling. "Fair enough."

He reaches around me and opens my door, then closes it after I climb in.

I roll down the window. "For the record? Please don't give up on me."

Shane leans in and gives me the softest kiss. It's far too short a kiss, but he pulls back and raises his hand in farewell. I back my car away, knowing I have an awful lot to think about. My life is going to be changing forever whether I marry Shane or not.

Despite my hangups, visions of myself in a long white dress surface all too quickly. The funny thing is, the image doesn't fill me with anxiety.

I pull out of the parking lot and glance in my rear-view mirror. As he walks toward his car, Shane executes an expert heel-click in the air.

CHAPTER THIRTY-EIGHT

Diana

Our wedding is a compromise, which our pastor tells us in premarital counseling is a great way to start practicing the art. Shane submits to the idea of just our family and closest friends. I submit to the white dress, the church, and lots of flowers. My therapist, Mindy, tells me that it's a fantastic step for me and wishes us well.

Dad rides out from Manitoba with Becky and her family. Becky serves as my maid of honor. She chooses a simple floral dress she figures she'll wear again. Shane's dad serves as his best man, and it warms my heart to see our two fathers hitting it off at the rehearsal dinner in our new backyard.

Shane moved out of his apartment and into an adorable three bedroom bilevel we bought together. I found a buyer for my place, and Mouse and I will move in with Shane after the honeymoon.

Carly refuses my invitation to be in our wedding party, claiming she is far too fat. She still looks cute in her red sundress, though. Shane and I both went with her to her ultrasound exam, but neither of us wanted to know the baby's gender yet. Carly was dying to know. We agreed to let her find out if she agreed to keep it a secret until our wedding day.

Dad is my rock. Does he know everything I'm feeling? Perhaps he's feeling it himself. While we stand in the church lobby waiting to walk in, he holds my free hand in one of his and places his other hand on my shoulder.

Without breaking eye contact, he prays a blessing straight out of the Bible. "My dear Diana. May the Lord bless you and keep you. May the Lord make his face shine upon you and be gracious unto you. May the Lord lift up his countenance upon you and give you peace. Amen."

"Amen," I whisper.

It seems God indeed answers. My nervous shaking ceases.

I link my arm through Dad's and we step through the doors. He walks me down the aisle for the second time, proud as punch. The sweet scent of lilies fills the air and the strains of Pachelbel's Canon accompany us.

At the front, my groom stands smiling. My Shane. He looks fantastic in his firefighter's dress uniform, but it's the smile on his face that melts my heart and fills me with joy and confidence. This man won't ditch me at the altar, or ever. I know it. I feel it in my bones.

Dad hands me off with a kiss on the cheek. He whispers in my ear, "Your mother would be so happy and proud. You've chosen well."

The pastor's words, the traditional vows, the ring exchange all waltz by like one of those schmaltzy video montages. But when Becky steps over to the piano to sing, she catches my eye and winks as if to say, *It's going to be okay*. I smile back.

Shane and I agreed to have Becky sing a favorite old hymn, "Be Thou My Vision." We both want God at the center of our marriage and home. We need him desperately. No other song seems more fitting.

Becky finishes and the piano continues to play. As we approach the register, my hand shakes so much that I fear my signature will look like that of someone in their nineties. To my surprise, the pastor picks up the pen but hands it to Shane instead of to me. The two of them exchange a look that speaks volumes, and in that moment, I know. Shane has arranged this ahead of time. He will sign first. If anyone's going to be jilted at this altar, it will be him.

He signs with a flourish, then presents the pen to me. The warmth in his smiling eyes gives me all the courage I need.

I sign.

Shane loops my hand through his arm again and holds on tight while our witnesses and the pastor sign the document. We are married. Shane is grinning like the proverbial cat. Does that make me the canary?

Our reception is held on the patio of Linda's Grill, reserved exclusively for us. Becky's toast to the bride is hilarious and filled with the crazy antics of our childhood. She warns Shane that I have been known to draw a never-to-be-crossed line down the middle of a shared bedroom.

As the laughter fades, her face grows serious. "Diana."

I can tell she's fighting a lump in her throat, which immediately causes one to form in mine.

"Mom would be so proud of you today." Becky smiles and dabs her cheek with a tissue. "*I'm* so proud of you today. I love you with all my heart. You're going to be a wonderful wife and mother because you're a wonderful human being. More importantly, you look to Jesus for your source of wisdom and strength. Don't stop. You're gonna do great."

Dad's speech is even more touching. "Shane, I'm pleased to welcome you to the family. I've been around you enough to know you're a terrific guy and that you love my daughter. You're getting a treasure, and I think you know that. Diana inherited some things from me and some from her mother. But the person I see in her most is my own mother, Lilly. Mom struggled with decision-making, but she had compassion and tenacity like no one I ever knew. If not for her, I wouldn't be here today, and I most certainly would not be a doctor. You've shown that same compassion, Diana, in becoming a big sister to our Carly here." Dad spreads his arm out in Carly's direction and she smiles back, swiping tears from her cheek. "And by welcoming her little one into your heart and life—both of you. I applaud you, I'm proud of you, and I know you'll do just fine."

That leads into Carly's big announcement, and I suddenly know why she insisted on being allowed to arrange for the wedding cake. Draped in solid white fondant and surrounded by real pansies, the gorgeous two-tiered cake greeted us when we arrived.

Carly rises from her seat but refuses to come to the front.

"Just cut the cake and you'll know the baby's gender." Her sparkling smile makes her whole face glow as she places both hands on her swollen tummy. "If it's pink inside, you'll know this is a girl. Blue, and it's a boy."

Everyone laughs and cheers as Shane and I make our way over to the side table where the cake has served as a beautiful focal point in the space. A ribbon-draped knife waits, and I pick it up. Shane places his hand over mine so we can cut through the cake together. Our photographer is going nuts, running her camera like a machine gun and going through entertaining antics to get shots from every possible angle.

We make one clean slice from top to bottom, and Shane and I look at each other. We can see the crumbs before everyone else. We make another cut, pull the slice out, and hold it up for all to see.

"It's a girl!" Almost in unison, the little group shouts and cheers. We place that first slice on a plate and Shane carries it over to Carly.

"Do we have a name?" Becky shouts.

Shane returns to my side and puts an arm around me. "We do." He waits for me to reveal it.

I look straight at Dad. "For a girl, we chose Lilly."

• • •

Later, as we say our goodbyes, I ask Dad something that has been on my mind ever since hearing the story of Lilly's affair and the failed termination.

"How did it make you feel when you found out, Dad?"

He presses his lips together and tilts his head to one side. "Grateful to be alive."

"That's it? You didn't need to forgive her?"

"I knew God already had. How could I do any less?"

I wipe away my tears and give Dad the tightest hug. "Thanks, Dad, for being here today, and for everything. I do have one more question, though. Did Lilly ever find out who her biological father was?"

Dad shakes his head. "She said it didn't matter. She eventually made peace with her Aunty Margaret. And she said God was the best Father anyone could ever ask for or imagine. That was all she needed to know, and I guess it's all I've ever really needed to know, too."

I take a deep breath and let out a long sigh. "Then it's enough for me, too."

IF YOU NEED SUPPORT

Facing an unexpected pregnancy can be confusing and overwhelming. If you need a caring, safe, respectful, and confidential environment to discuss all your options, a support center near you is waiting to help, whatever decision you make. To find one in your area, access the following resources.

- In Canada: Pregnancy Care Canada (https://pregnancycarecanada.ca/find-a-centre, 1-866-845-2151).

- In the United States: CareNet (https://resources.care-net.org/find-a-pregnancy-center, 703-554-8734).

- Anywhere: Heartbeat International (www.heartbeatinternational.org/worldwide-directory, 1-888-550-7577; their 24/7 helpline is 1-800-712-HELP).

ABOUT THE AUTHOR

Terrie Todd is a columnist, playwright, blogger, and author of one nonfiction book and six historical and split-time novels. Since 2010, she's written a weekly column for *The Graphic Leader*, and since 2021 she's been a monthly contributor to the *Heroes, Heroines, and History* blog.

In 2018, Terrie received the Janette Oke Award from Inscribe Christian Writers Fellowship. In addition to several other awards from The Word Guild, she was thrilled to receive the 2022 Debra Fieguth Social Justice Award for her novel, *Rose Among Thornes* and the 2022 Contemporary Fiction award for *The Last Piece*.

She lives with her husband Jon in Portage la Prairie, Manitoba, Canada where they raised their three children. They are grandparents to five boys. When she's not writing, Terrie can usually be found reading, cleaning, cooking, painting, planning, weeding, watering, or watching something. You can email her at terriejtodd@gmail.com.

To keep abreast of upcoming books and other shenanigans, sign up to receive Terrie's colorful, fun newsletter at www.terrietodd.blogspot.com.

ENDNOTES

[1] Psalm 121:1–2 (KJV).

[2] (NIV).

[3] "People," *Life Magazine.* April 14, 1941, 40.

[4] Deuteronomy 30:19 (NIV).

[5] 1 John 4:18 (NIV).

[6] 2 Timothy 1:7 (NIV).

[7] Psalm 34:5 (KJV).

OTHER TITLES BY TERRIE TODD

THE SILVER SUITCASE
A WORD AWARD WINNER

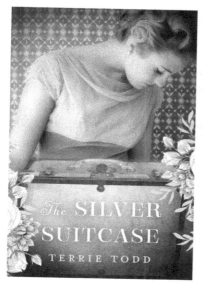

Cornelia Simpson's heart has been broken since the day her mother died five years ago. As a new tragedy provides reason to reject her parents' faith, a mysterious visitor appears in her hour of desperation. Alone and carrying a heavy secret, she makes a desperate choice that will haunt her for years to come. Cornelia pours out all in her diary.

Benita Watson is mourning several losses, including her grandmother Cornelia. On the brink of divorce, she discovers Cornelia's diary. Now the secrets of her grandmother's past lead Benita on a journey of healing, reunion, and faith.

MAGGIE'S WAR
A WORD AWARD WINNER

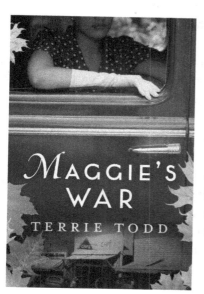

In 1942, telegrams always bring life-altering news in a war-hardened world—and the one Maggie Marshall receives is no different.

Charlotte Penfield, pregnant and exiled by her wealthy parents to work in Maggie's restaurant, runs away with romantic notions of a reunion with her baby's father.

When Maggie seeks the help of her childhood friend, Rev. Reuben Fennel, to find Charlotte, he's happy to aid her in the chase—though it may cost him his job and reputation.

Bleak Landing

In the dead-end town of Bleak Landing, Bridget O'Sullivan lives in a ramshackle house as the Great Depression rages. Routinely beaten by her father and bullied by schoolmate Victor Harrison, the fiery redhead succeeds in running away and making a new life. When her father dies and she returns to claim her inheritance, the only one who can vouch for her integrity is her old nemesis, Victor. But can he also prove he's a changed man worthy of her forgiveness?

Rose Among Thornes
Winner, 2022 Debra Fieguth Social Justice Award

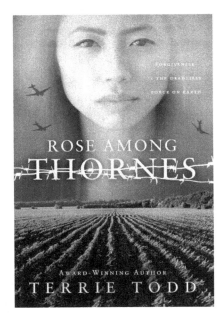

Forgiveness is the deadliest force on earth.

When forced by her government to leave her home in Vancouver and move to the Canadian prairies to work on the Thornes' sugar beet farm, Rose Onishi's dream of becoming a concert pianist fades to match the black dirt staining her callused hands.

When Rusty Thorne joins the Canadian Army, he never imagines becoming a Japanese prisoner of war. Only his rare letters from home sustain him—especially the brilliant notes from his mother's charming helper, which the girl signs simply as "Rose."

THE LAST PIECE
A WORD AWARD WINNER

When his father dies during the Great Depression, Ray Matthews is forced to drop out of art school to support his mother and sister as a jigsaw puzzle artist. Ray has only one painting he vows never to sell: the portrait of his beloved sweetheart. When pressured to break his oath, Ray sends the painting off with a promise and a prophecy. Through eight decades, the puzzle of the beautiful girl at the wishing well passes through four households, deeply affecting each. Part allegory, this story explores family relationships and self-sacrifice.

OUT OF MY MIND

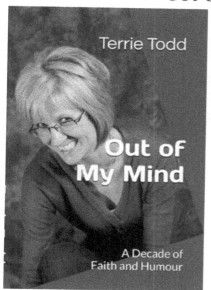

Since 2010, Terrie Todd has been writing a popular "Faith and Humor" column for The Graphic Leader in Portage la Prairie, Manitoba, Canada. This book celebrates a decade of wit and wisdom found in Terrie's hand-picked favorites.

CPSIA information can be obtained
at www.ICGtesting.com
Printed in the USA
LVHW050050210123
737605LV00002B/229